JEWS
VS
OMNIBUS

First published 2015 by Jurassic London
SW8 1XN, Great Britain

www.jurassic-london.com

978-0-9928435-4-0 (Jews vs Aliens ebook)
978-0-9928435-3-3 (Jews vs Zombies ebook)

Edited by Rebecca Levene and Lavie Tidhar

Cover by Sarah Anne Langton
www.secretarcticbase.com

CONTENTS

JEWS VS
OMNIBUS

Edited by
Rebecca Levene &
Lavie Tidhar

INTRODUCTION

The alien in science fiction, it is often said, stands in for the Other in all its myriad forms. And zombies, like Jews, are ubiquitous it seems. They're everywhere. Here, in these two anthologies, we have asked some of the best authors working today in speculative fiction to answer the age old question posed in the dawn of time: what happens when Jews encounter aliens – or indeed the living dead? We know these are questions that have often kept us awake at night...

The authors herein all in this twin volumes surprised and delighted us in turn with their different approaches. Our authors come from the US and Britain, Australia, Israel and the former USSR, and contribute stories of quiet horror, humorous science fiction, post-apocalyptic meditations on race and survival, and philosophical contemplations of love and loss. There is a little something here for everyone, and we hope you enjoy these stories as much as we did.

Lavie Tidhar & Rebecca Levene
November 2015

In the tradition of Tzekakah, all money earned will be donated to charity. You can read about our chosen charity at the end of this book.

JEWS
VS
ALIENS

ANTAIUS FLOATING IN THE HEAVENS AMONG THE STARS

ANDREA PHILLIPS

A glossy holobrochure on very fine, super-heavyweight haptic sheeting. Fabricated with remarkably high (and visibly expensive) production values.

Welcome to Antaius Floating in the Heavens Among the Stars, the galaxy's premiere spot for luxurious accommodation, fine dining, and views so beautiful they are capable of halting your autonomous biological functions temporarily!

We will unquestioningly conform to every physically possible detail and notion you request from us in writing, no matter your species or individual tastes.

- Festive and Sombre Cultural Celebrations
- Public Mating Rituals
- Status-Acquiring Occasions
- Propaganda Assemblies
- Corporate Events

Sublimate Your Guests With Luxury at Antaius Floating in the Heavens Among the Stars

Our sweeping views of the burning heart of the galaxy as it destroys itself are sure to make your antennae quiver with self-abnegation, superstitious fervour, and romance! But the luxury does not stop with astronomical features detectable from our location. We also have extensive internal luxurious accommodation available!

At Antaius Floating in the Heavens Among the Stars, our decor is specified and executed on a case-by-case for each event that we contractually host. Icefalls, slime baths, neuroreactive lighting, olfactory gardens, intoxicant clouds, conductive netting – make a wish and we will generate it!

If you are the outdoorsy type, we can obtain botanical and non-sentient life from any planet and in any stage of development to replicate a specific ecosystem. If your tastes run to nanoplatinum sheeting and electrocrystal matrices, this also can be created!

We are fully knowledgeable regarding the diverse variety of customs, preferences, and physical requirements of every sentient species recorded in the *K6-nn?%n9A Guide to Galactic Life*. With our team of xenologists, exobiologists, and cyber-hybrid maintenance and waitstaff, you may rest easy knowing that every molecule you respirate and ingest will not only be uncontaminated by potentially fatal microtoxins and disease agents... it will also be completely enjoyable to all of your pertinent sensory apparatus!

Please note that some types of accommodation may incur additional fees, including but not limited to events requiring an atmosphere over 0.38% hydrochloric acid, pressures exceeding 823 kPa, or contraband items in violation of the Frou!ah!hehoa-Smith-Lllrwykp Treaty.

Sent via interpost:

My Darling Rachel,

Mazel tov on your happy news! Now that you're going to be taking care of my little Michael, I just wanted to make sure you're absolutely clear on all of his preferences for the wedding so you can make sure he has everything he needs on his happy day. Consider it my little gift to my new daughter!

First, did you make sure you can get real champagne and caviar imported all that way? Michael prefers top quality, even if it takes a little more work. And I'm sure you know to get no roses for the chuppah, and no soy on the menu at all. Michael has always been allergic and the last thing you need is for him to wheeze and swell up on your wedding night. Oh, and you really must include those little cocktail franks during the cocktail hour. I know they're not the most highbrow thing, but they are his absolute favourite, so you simply must have them. Boys will be boys!

One more thing – you remember that our Uncle David is a rabbi and his family are very, very frum, of course? You know *I* don't care one way or the other if the wedding is kosher or who sits where, *I'm* very easy to please, but the way you put on your affair is going to have certain implications for how the family receives you.

Love and kisses!

Your New Mum

Crudité with olives and pickles
Skewered fruits from the Seven Systems
Caviar and smoked salmon three ways
Roasted game fowl
Oxygen bar
Pigs in blankets

Salad of crisp Ooolovoba seaweed with citrus and puffed hazelnut
Chateaubriand with flamed Velgan whiskey demiglace
Baby lamb chop with rosemary mist
Lentil patty with curry-raisin broth

Whipped potato with three toppings
Mirepoix spears

Five-layer wedding cake with chocolate-cinnamon frosting
Gemmalian iceplum sorbet (sugar-free)

Sent via interpost:

Dear Rachel,

You know I'm not a complainer and I hate to complain, but I have to tell you that ever since you told me you're holding a wedding at that place run by those awful aliens, I just haven't been able to sleep at night. Are you sure this place is safe? Can they even put on a nice affair? Have they ever done something for humans before?

They say it's just like holding an event for the Loofpahrigas, but I don't believe it for a second. And I'm absolutely sure those tentacle-faced bags of swamp gas don't keep kosher! I'm not saying you *have* to put on a kosher wedding, you know I'm not picky and *I* don't care one way or the other, but as I've mentioned, some of the family are very observant.

Mazel Tov,

Edith

There is a hand-written message at the bottom:

Just ignore her, honey. I'll call tonight and handle this myself.
– M

An officially certified letter delivered via interpost, heavy with legal witness stamps and seals:

To Whom This May Concern:

As mentioned during our final tasting event last night at Antaius Floating in the Heavens Among the Stars, we have a lot of concerns about our upcoming wedding and the way that you plan to handle it. I know there have been some personnel changes since you hosted the completely lovely Bank of United Centauri end-of-fiscal-year party last year, but that is no excuse at all. The degree of incompetence you have displayed is nothing short of shocking.

First off, that 'lingering trace amount of methane' is beyond revolting and you have to get rid of it entirely. Zero methane, do you understand me? I don't care what you say is an acceptable concentration for oxygen-based atmospheres, it's just disgusting and we won't tolerate it.

The decorations were also completely lacking in taste. This is indeed a 'mating ritual', but that DOES NOT mean we want decorations shaped like human genitalia! It was positively vulgar, not to mention embarrassing, and I'm absolutely sure my future mother-in-law will never forgive me for this. I'm attaching several holograms from other weddings to this missive to make absolutely sure you know what we consider appropriate to the occasion.

The menu was also completely, catastrophically wrong. I understand that your offerings are 'perfectly nutritive' and won't kill human beings, but that doesn't mean we WANT to eat things from the oceans of Europa that look like nightmares, or desserts garnished with Trbillleagh tree-slime. It may be exotic and fashionable to be adventurous with alien intoxicants in some circles, but it is not to our taste, not in our contract, and there is no way we're paying for it.

The cake was better. At least it seemed to be actual cake, but the frosting should NOT be lentil paste. That is NOT EVER an acceptable substitute for chocolate. And where were the pigs in blankets, the puffed hazelnuts, or the lentil patties, I ask you? It's like you didn't even look at the menu we agreed upon!

It is also imperative that everything be kosher, which I gravely doubt was the case yesterday! Your services are not cheap, so if you don't know how to do a kosher meal yourself, I'm paying you enough money to hire a rabbi to certify everything on the spot. You said you could when we asked. Don't think for a millisecond we won't be holding you to your commitments.

With the wedding coming up in just 3.8 spins, we don't have time to break the contract and book a different venue, or reissue invitations so our guests can rearrange their travel plans. But I'm telling you now, if you don't get every detail right on the day of my wedding, we're taking you straight to court.

Respectfully Yours,
Rachel Cohen

An internal document from the Galactic-Class Discreet and Attentive Luxury Hospitality Hive Mind #1005587, proprietors of Antaius Floating in the Heavens Among the Stars:

Problem: Client #4487J-Cohen-Halevi/mating ritual expresses emotional dissatisfaction with physical demonstration of mating ritual service offerings, despite high-quality luxury offerings in line with legally binding written agreement of service.

Suggestion: Examine Client #4487J-Cohen-Halevi/mating ritual written report of emotional dissatisfaction carefully for actionable items to improve service offering in line with expectations.

Observation: Client #4487J-Cohen-Halevi/mating ritual speaks favourably of a prior experience with Antaius Floating in the Heavens Among the Stars.

Observation: Client #4487J-Cohen-Halevi/mating ritual assumes we possess a high degree of familiarity with species-specific trivia due to prior favourable experience.

Observation: Such knowledge was once available but is now unavailable since dissolution of our union with former member Harry Locantore.

Concern: No species expert compatible with Client #4487J-Cohen-Halevi/mating ritual is available at this time.

Suggestion: Cancel contract.

Concern: Potential legal liability for unexpected disruption of time-sensitive mating ritual.

Concern: Reputation of Antaius Floating in the Heavens Among the Stars may suffer more than 2.08% threshold for tolerable quantities of negative reputation should dissatisfied client testimony emerge.

Resolved: Reputation of Antaius Floating in the Heavens Among the Stars and Galactic-Class Discreet and Attentive Luxury Hospitality Hive Mind #1005587 are business objectives more important than other objectives with lesser priorities.

Resolved: Excellent service must be delivered to Client #4487J-Cohen-Halevi/mating ritual. Proceed with intensive independent research into species-specific environment, mating habits, and taboos in order to deliver a service in line with existing positive reputation.

Concern: Such research may be costly to such an extent that it surpasses the price agreed upon in the legally binding written agreement of service.

Resolved: Profit is a lesser objective in the situation involving Client #4487J-Cohen-Halevi/mating ritual, because reputation of Antaius Floating in the Heavens Among the Stars and Galactic-Class Discreet and Attentive Luxury Hospitality Hive Mind #1005587 are higher priorities determining future course of business as a whole.

Observation: Client #4487J-Cohen-Halevi/mating ritual is of species subtype Sol-Human-Spacebound-Cis/Het-Jew.

Observation: Reference materials indicate species subtype is a 91.98% match with major traditions and physiology of Wazn-Beehao-Spacebound-Flex/Ase-Wruachh.

Observation: New applicant to join the hive named Eeeshee-5998 has documented in job application total fluency with major traditions and physiology of Wazn-Beehao-Spacebound-Flex/Ase-Wruachh.

Suggestion: Hire new applicant and conduct mating ritual in accordance with practices suggested by new species subject matter expert, thus saving money and providing excellent service compatible with existing positive reputation.

Resolved: Hire applicant. Proceed with mating ritual.

A news article in The New Singapore Chronicle:

> The new Mrs. Rachel Cohen-Halevi is suing posh restaurateur and event manager Antaius Floating in the Heavens Among the Stars after what she claims to be a poorly orchestrated wedding that 'completely ruined my day and set a dark cloud over my new married life.'
>
> Chief among her complaints: 'When I asked for pigs in blankets, I certainly didn't mean actual live pigs wrapped in flannels! Even the poorest xenosociologist on their staff should have known better.' Cohen-Halevi claims that the presence of these swine was unsanitary and in violation of food safety standards, an affront to her religious beliefs, and 'made our whole wedding seem like a trashy joke'.
>
> Antaius Floating in the Heavens Among the Stars defended its service vehemently. The hive issued a statement reading in part, 'The customer's requests were unreasonably unspecific and we cannot be blamed for any failures resulting from her own lack of communication with us regarding her specific preferences.'

Cohen-Halevi is suing for *3.7 billion in reparations for mental cruelty plus punitive fines for another *18 billion.

Sent via interpost:

Rachel,

For obvious reasons, the family isn't comfortable with coming to you for seder this year. We expect Michael will be joining us at home, naturally.

As for you, I don't want to say you're not welcome, of course you're *welcome*, but we think it might be better for everyone if you celebrate on your own this year. Do have a lovely holiday!

Best!

Edith

THE MATTER OF MEROZ

ROSANNE RABINOWITZ

Samuel's mind is ablaze from tzaddik Avrom's lecture.

He nudges his friend Lev. 'Bet they didn't teach about *that* at yeshiva!'

An old fellow in the front row turns around to glower at the boys. Then with a fury of phlegmatic throat-clearing he opens the discussion.

'Tzaddik, will you explain just how beings from other worlds could have souls? Hashem bestowed the Torah on Man. There is only one Torah as there is only God. And we are the only creatures who have been granted free will by Hashem.'

The tzaddik counters: 'But each congregation has its own Torah, so why shouldn't each world have its version of the sacred scrolls?'

He runs his fingers through his ginger and grey beard as he thinks. 'Look at the Book of Judges, where the prophetess Deborah curses the inhabitants of a place called Meroz for not helping the Israelites fight the Canaanite general Sisera. But where is a place called Meroz? No one knows, though there are references to stars. So the Talmud concludes that Meroz must be a star or planet. So wouldn't this curse recognise that the inhabitants of Meroz have the ability to think, to choose between good and evil?'

'But...' Samuel starts. Everyone turns to look at him and he wants to shrivel to a speck of dirt on the floor. How dare he, a smooth-faced outsider, speak up?

The tzaddik smiles and nods at him.

He clears his throat. 'So how can someone from our world curse those who live upon another world? How does a curse travel over such a long distance?'

'If a curse punishes the ungodly, surely Hashem makes the curse effective,' comments the surly denizen of the front row. 'Do you doubt the power of the Lord?'

'No, Dov. This young man asks a good question,' says the tzaddik. 'Yes, the Almighty is the supreme power in the universe. He has also endowed his favoured creatures with free will and a capacity to overcome physical obstacles, such as vast distances. For example, Rashi explains how the road folded itself up for Jacob when he travelled from Beersheba to Haran, so he was able to complete his journeys in an instant. This manner of travel is described as the leaping of the road, *kefitzat haderech*.'

'What did he say about a road?' Lev whispers to Samuel.

'*Shush!*'

'Deborah and other adepts could make the roads "leap", thus shortening the distance they had to travel between two places. They could also instigate *the crumpling of the sky*, which allows travel between the stars. Then they made the sky smooth again and restored the distances.'

Samuel has never read *that* in the Talmud. Maybe he missed something. 'Where do you learn how to do these things?' he asks.

Now the tzaddik frowns. 'This isn't something to do in your home! It is dangerous, and it is forbidden.'

'But you're telling everyone about it. How forbidden is that?'

'My son, it is one thing to know *about* this. It is our history, our birthright. But to know *how* to do this...' The tzaddik shakes his head. 'This knowledge is handed down to one person in each generation. There may be a time when we have to use it. But that time isn't now.'

It hurts Samuel's head to imagine that such things could be true. But it's a pleasant ache, like the one he gets when he tries to imagine the 'unseen colours' from his favourite section in the Zohar: '*There are colours that are seen, and colours that are not seen.*' When he walks around the village, and the mud is grey and brown beneath his feet, he imagines those unseen colours, dazzling behind the muck. And what unknown colour lurks behind the dreary ledgers at the tailors' shop where he works? He hopes to discover it some day.

After more discussion, the tzaddik calls a halt. 'Now it is time to dance.' He gestures and the klezmorim take their places on the platform.

They begin their tune, slowly. Samuel stays in his seat next to Lev.

He remembers warnings that the Hasidim seek to convert other Jews. Though he enjoyed the discussion, he has no intention of joining their sect.

Soon wine is passed to Samuel and Lev. They drink and clink glasses, and the music is too catchy. They just have to join in. Legs kicking, the boys clasp hands on each other's shoulders, song vibrating in their throats and rising to their lips.

In the dancing, Samuel feels his heart expand until it becomes a much greater heart that beats at the centre of the universe.

The two boys head home across the fields, a good hour's walk. 'I wish the road could rise up to meet us now,' Samuel says.

'Your head's more likely to hit it first, after all the wine you drank,' answers Lev.

'No, my eyes are on the stars!' Samuel giggles.

'But the tzaddik didn't talk about golems,' Lev goes on to kvetch. 'I was hoping for advice on that. I still don't understand why our formula hasn't worked.'

'Feh! Golem, shmolem… Your mind's in the mud - look at the sky instead!'

It's a clear night, and the stars are hypnotic. So many and so far, they appear as mist across the heavens. And each of them surrounded by worlds! Samuel reaches up to the sky, reaching out with spread fingers then closing his hand into a fist. Is this how you crumple the sky? But there is nothing in his hand.

'Samuel? Look where you're going!'

Drek. A huge cowpat.

Samuel wipes his boot on the grass.

Lev watches. 'A fitting end to the evening,' he observes. 'The tzaddik did say some interesting things. And these Hassidim enjoy a dance and so do I. But what's the point of dancing if there are no girls?'

Samuel swipes his boot one last time. 'You sound like my meshugge socialist sister, though she would ask that question for different reasons.'

And now his crazy sister will be coming home from Odessa.

Raizl swings a suitcase in each hand. Samuel is supposed to meet her train, but where is he? Maybe it's just as well she didn't bring her favourite weapon, the pole with spikes. She would have wrapped it in burlap and schlepped it here along with her two suitcases filled with schmattes, but Arkady talked her out of it.

However, she did bring her revolver. After the last pogrom in Odessa, trouble is expected everywhere, even in sleepy old Fekedynka.

At least there's a newly formed group of comrades here. She looks forward to meeting them. She's brought them a gift from her group – a megaphone. But she really ought to try it out first and make sure it works.

She holds her head high, sure she is observed. Here comes the Odessa mama! Back home, are you? Still not married? *Of course not.*

Home. The place where she was born stopped being home long before she left it at fourteen. She's only just off the train and already she misses Arkady. She misses Odessa, though not all its memories are good.

Drying pools of blood in the gutter. She catches her breath. A memory. It's only a memory. This village doesn't even have gutters, only dirt roads.

'Raizl!'

So now Samuel is here. 'What time do you call this, schmattekopf? Never mind, don't worry about helping me with my luggage. I'm a strong girl.'

'Ah, Raizl, I see you haven't changed.'

'Why should I?'

In the deepening dusk crows rise from the fields, flying over the village. It has spread out since she was last here, two yeas ago when her father died. Now it's almost a town.

As they walk, Raizl hears the Odessa-bound train pulling into the station, then letting out a blast of its whistle as it leaves. A part of her wants to be on it.

When they arrive, Raizl's mother Feygele emerges from her last-minute packing, preparing for her journey to Vilna to live with her eldest daughter.

She actually looks younger than last time; it must be anticipation of the new life and the growing brood of grandchildren awaiting her. She's got rid of her sheitel and has let her own hair grow again, lightly covered by a scarf. Raizl is glad for her choice of present, a lovely embroidered scarf from Smyrna. Mother doesn't have to know that it fell off a boat in Odessa harbour and into Raizl's hands before it hit the water.

Feygele brings out the samovar, along with a plate of rugelach. Raizl has fond memories of those buttery bites tasting of nuts, raisins and cinnamon. But they are dry in her mouth now.

Siblings, relatives and neighbours drop by to bid Feygele goodbye. Some glare at Raizl, the wayward daughter packed off to the Odessa cousins. Raizl smiles back. She doesn't care what they think.

Sister Hannah and her husband arrive with their twins. Those warm milky bundles are quickly parked on Raizl's lap, one on each thigh.

She does like babies, provided they aren't her own.

Once the guests depart, the table is cleared and Feygele retired, Raizl takes a bottle of vodka out of her bag and pours two generous portions.

'You're better off with this than the kosher wine, Samuel.' They raise their glasses to each other, then knock back their drinks.

Raizl clears her throat. 'So, Samuel… You know that mother wouldn't leave unless I promised to "look after" you. So I'll tell you now what that means. I'm here if you need me, but I won't be your servant. In Odessa, living with my comrades, we eat and cook together and share all tasks. That's what will happen here.'

'But… I have to work and study.'

'So will I. How do you think we'll eat?'

'I can't cook. And everyone will laugh.'

'Ha! Let "everyone" learn to cook too! You don't do your part, I go on strike. But maybe you'll see sense with more vodka. And what do you study, which is so important that you can't cook a meal?'

Samuel looks away from Raizl. 'Kabbalah, that's what we study. Me and Lev. Lev shares his yeshiva books, but we go our own way with them.'

'Oy Samuel. You once wanted to learn science. You liked to learn about animals and plants and look at the stars. So what's this?'

'But I still look at the stars. We went to a lecture about them by a tzaddik. He believes that beings from other worlds have visited the earth. It's in the Talmud.'

'So if it's in the Talmud, does that make it true? A smart boy like you, believing in bupkes,' Raizl says. 'And what are these other worlds? Mars? I read a book about an invasion from Mars. *War of the Worlds*. In English. I've been studying English at a workers' institute and they had it in the library. The librarian told me that HG Wells is an important socialist and this is a book about the British class struggle!'

Samuel snorts. 'I've never heard of it.'

'It's just a story. Our librarian doesn't know English. My English wasn't so good then, but I improved it by reading this book. I might try to find pupils for English here.'

'Most people here don't even speak Russian.'

She shrugs. 'So I teach Russian. Even here in Fekedynka the new twentieth century starts! Parents will want more for their children than superstitious chazzerai from the cheder.'

Raizl pours herself another vodka. 'But you know, farshtunken Fekedynka is still a miserable excuse for a village. You should come back to Odessa with me. Even with the quotas against Jews, you can study with your circle of friends, then pass your exams. You can become a scientist. My friend Leah...'

Raizl stops. When the pogrom started, comrades divided into groups to defend certain areas. It was only by chance Leah ended up in the group that met with a massacre. Raizl had originally volunteered for that group, then Leah said she preferred it because she had family in that area.

Raizl shudders with guilt for surviving, sorrow for the friend she lost.

Samuel is waiting for her to finish the sentence.

'My friend studied science. But she was killed.'

'So you want me to go there and get killed too? What a great sister you are!'

'Yes, it's dangerous in Odessa. But it's dangerous everywhere. All it takes is one incident, one accusation... Maybe you need to look up from your books and your crazy Kabbalah davening.'

'You call me crazy but anyone might say the same thing about you.'

Maybe I am, Raizl thinks. She knows she should lie low, when revolutionaries and activists in the self-defence groups are likely to face arrest. But how low can she lie if the trouble comes here? She's already been invited to speak to the local comrades and help with their self-defence practice.

'So, Raizl, how's it going with your shaygetz, your Russian fancy-boy?' Samuel lowers his voice, even though he can hear their mother snoring above their heads.

They both raise their eyes to the ceiling, and Raizl answers in an even lower voice. 'Arkady? As well as expected. I hope you'll meet him one day.'

They drink a last glass of vodka. The conversation lightens, turning to visits from the matchmaker and tips on foiling plans for unwanted marriages.

Finally, it's time to sleep. Samuel goes up to his room, while Raizl takes the pallet down and covers it with blankets. She undresses and stretches out, still warm with the heat from the fire left burning in the grate.

Raizl drifts into sleep. She sees flames and desolation, a home levelled to rubble. A tree-lined street near the sea, glittering glass on the road and blood drying in puddles.

Samuel and Lev make their way across the fields on Sunday afternoon, hoping they will be able to talk to the tzaddik on his own in the study house.

'This tzaddik is meshugge for the stars and he's not much good on golems. But I like him after all,' says Lev. 'More fun than our rebbe, eh?'

'I told Raizl about him, but she said go to Odessa and learn real science.'

'What does she know? She hasn't heard Avrom. And women wouldn't be allowed in such a meeting.'

'They can study science, though. Raizl's friend in Odessa did.'

The one who was killed, Samuel reminds himself.

'So,' says Lev. 'That doesn't say much for science!'

They stop at some woodland near a stream, planning to relieve themselves before moving on.

Samuel undoes his trousers. While he attends to his business he closes his eyes as he recites a prayer. Commentators in the Midrash spoke of becoming close to God during the most humble activities. They said nothing about activities as humble as this, but shouldn't they be celebrated? To take in nourishment and excrete it is part of living, Hashem's plan.

When he opens his eyes, he notices a dark shape on the other side of the stream. A touch of white to the indistinct darkness of the shape, a little blue?

He steps over the stones, across the stream to investigate. As he comes closer, a clenching in the pit of his stomach tells him what his eyes still refuse to see. A pale hand, blue and white fringed cloth, a tallis.

The tallis is covering the man's face. Samuel reaches out, lifting it away to reveal bruise-coloured skin, bulging eyes. Hair and beard, red and white.

The tzaddik.

Samuel screams.

His friend runs over. At the sight of the tzaddik, Lev joins Samuel's lamentation.

'We have to go tell them,' Lev finally says.

'Go. I'll stay with the tzaddik.'

'You can't stay. It isn't safe. What if...'

'What if? We can't leave the tzaddik's body alone. Go!'

Lev doesn't argue again, seeing Samuel's determination.

Now that he's alone with the tzaddik, Samuel pulls up the tallis to cover the dead man's face, this time with reverence. He sees the dark straps bound tight around his throat. The man was strangled with his own tefillin.

Samuel falls back as if this horror has just punched him in the gut. His hand thrusts into leaves, touches a soft fabric. He finds a square velvet bag. It is a plain deep green, worn in places.

Inside he finds a brass cylinder with four retractable sections, leather covering the largest section. A telescope, an instrument for looking at the sky!

There is also a book, a very old one. There's no title on the cover so he has to look inside. *The Book of Deborah* - the prophetess Deborah who could make the sky fold and crumple.

He says a kaddish for the tzaddik while clasping the book and telescope tight in his hands.

He hears shouts, people responding to the alarm raised by his friend. Who will come? The Hasidic burial society, the tzaddik's students, or the police? *Hey hey daloy politsey*, as his sister likes to sing over the washing. *Down with the police, down with the Czar.* A better tune than that dirge she used to sing, all about being hated and driven away. Of course you'll be hated and driven away if you sing that drek.

He puts the precious objects back into the velvet bag and slips it under his shirt, under his tallis, and waits.

When Raizl was growing up in this village, she believed she was alone in her desire for a better world. There were rich people, and poor people. Among the poor people you found poor Russians, and poor Jews. The two groups fought each other more than those who kept them poor. She was only a child, but she knew this wasn't right.

And here in farshtunken Fekedynka, she is now meeting a small but active group affiliated to the General Jewish Labour Bund. There are fresh-faced gymnasium students from the better-off homes as well as youngsters from poor homes like hers. A few older people, like Mordecai the blacksmith. He says he joined after Jew-haters vandalised his smithy. His daughter, a sharp-face girl called Sheindl, had recruited him.

They are meeting in the woods for some short talks, then shooting practice. Though it's a chilly day, they are sheltered by the trees and the slope of the valley.

She'd been invited to talk about events in Odessa. But these now fill her with despair after all the hopes of a near-revolution – the strikes and rallies, crowds gathering at the harbour to support the Potemkin mutiny.

Being here makes her think of Arkady, though he obviously didn't attend Bund meetings. He had questioned the need for a separate group of Jewish activists, and they still argue about it. To her, it's practical when Jews often live and work separately from goyim, and even speak their own language. But Arkady's group of anarchists often worked with the Bund, helping especially with the self-defence.

So that's what they have to do now, defend themselves, rather than build a new world. It's a grim thought, yet these comrades lift Raizl's heart. These are boys and girls with dreams and hopes. She envies them for their confidence, something she lacked at their age. She'd been a shy girl, though she'd had moments of boldness.

She had heard about a boy in the village called Yankel who shared her views, and she just had to speak to him. He could become her soul mate, a true comrade... perhaps more. She decided to call on him to talk about their mutual interests.

When she knocked on his door, his mother opened it and Raizl explained that she wanted to meet her son. Yankel's mother slammed the door in Raizl's face. Later, she was denounced as a girl of loose morals and a disgrace to her family. But this led to a new life when she was sent off to stay with her cousins.

That same boy is here, asking her about Odessa.

'We've heard about your bravery in the revolution and fighting the pogromists,' says Yankel.

She's an Odessa mama again!

Revolution? It had only gone halfway.

Brave? Years ago, Raizl had been terrified just to knock on this young man's door. And how brave had she been in Odessa?

She remembers a Jewish woman with wild hair running up to their group, throwing a stone at their banner. At the time, they were marching in response to the Czar's reform manifesto. This woman didn't think they were brave.

'You bastards! They are chopping people up over there and here you are taking a little stroll. Your banners mean less than bupkes.'

So they rushed over to the woman's neighbourhood and stopped the attacks. They did save lives on that street. But they were too late or too few to stop other crimes.

A mother hung upside down by her legs, with the bodies of her six children arranged in a circle below.

A baby thrown out of a window.

It would've been much worse if we hadn't acted, Raizl tells herself.

Raizl tries to share what she knows, though it doesn't seem to be enough. She tells them that non-Jewish workers helped by forming self-defence groups and supporting pogrom victims. Railway workers, metal workers, sailors... But others? Maybe it was a worker who had thrown that baby out of the window.

Yankel says they have support from a socialist doctor called Oleg, plus other local activists. Some peasants are sympathetic, especially those who've been working or trading with Jewish families. But many others don't have these ties.

Then they get on to shooting practice. Only a few have guns. Some are very old: something a father kept from conscript days. A few have Bulldog guns like hers. No rifles or bayonets.

'A comrade from Odessa will try to bring more arms. In the meantime, we can practise with what we have. And remember, we can a lot with an iron pole, especially if our blacksmith modifies it with spikes,' says Raizl.

Those who know how to shoot show the newer recruits, aiming first for the lower branches in trees. Yankel suggests the best thing for target practice would be a portrait of the Czar, but who would have such a thing?

Someone shoots a partridge. This is met with cheers. Then they begin shooting at other birds. There'll be a good meal after the practice, even if it's not kosher. Matzo balls might not go well with partridge soup, but their catch should make a good stew.

Raizl concentrates on instructing the girls. She takes Sheindl aside, holds her arm and warns her to prepare for the recoil.

Then there's a crashing in the undergrowth.

Thank goodness no one has a jumpy trigger finger, because it's only Samuel.

'How did you know we were here?' She's pleased, thinking he wants to join them.

'We heard you! We're not deaf!'

Raizl nods, and introduces Samuel to her comrades. 'My brother.'

'The tzaddik is dead,' says Samuel. His eyes are red as if he's been crying. 'He's been murdered. And the Hasids were asking for all of you to guard the funeral.'

'Tzaddik Avrom only wanted to look at the stars. That's what the rebbe said. He went out walking to look at the stars, and they killed him.'

Raizl tries to console Samuel. She doesn't think she has anything left for that while she mourns Leah. But she is surprised how grief lightens when it is shared.

She is also surprised that the Hasidic community asked the Bund for help. Jewish elders usually petition the authorities for protection, but they must have seen indifference from the police when they reported the murder of an itinerant tzaddik.

Their group will stand guard outside the synagogue, then flank the procession to the cemetery.

The Bundists arrive well before the mourners with about forty in their group, including sympathisers from other parties. All have guns or poles, prepared for trouble.

A clot of people are already standing near the Hasidic synagogue. Raizl recognises a few faces. A local landowner, a horse merchant, some young labourers. All these people glare and swear when their group arrives.

But she catches nervous glances among the Jew-haters. Perhaps they don't expect resistance from Hasidic funeral-goers.

Could the murderer be among this crowd, or is he lurking further in the shadows?

'Mamzers,' mutters Sheindl. 'Surprised to see us, are they? Think we'll go like lambs to the slaughter...'

'Mamzers they are, but you don't shoot now,' says Raizl. She can see that Sheindl's on edge, her hand clutched around the gun in her pocket.

There's nudging from the other side, and one of them shouts out as if on a dare: 'What are you doing here? Not a beard among you. Are you Jews or just Jew lovers?'

Sheindl has to shout back: 'And what are you, if you have nothing better to do than hang around here?'

'I used to have a job but a Jew took it away.'

Now the mourners are arriving. They hesitate at the sight of the hostile bunch. A woman holds her hands up in supplication.

'Bugger off to Japan or Palestine!'

The Bundists surround the mourners, creating a protective corridor so they can file into the temple. Most of them weep. But Raizl is dry-eyed. She has no tears to spare for a man she's never met, but she will defend those who mourn him.

'One Jew down, too many to go.'

The man who calls that out gets too close and receives a warning poke with a pole. 'Think you're tough with your little sticks,' he sneers as he backs off. 'You won't do so well next time.'

But with the mourners all in the synagogue, the Jew-haters start to get bored and drift away.

The young Bundists grin at each other. By standing together, they've seen the trouble off. The funeral prayers wafting from the synagogue do little to dim their enthusiasm. *Yisgadal, v'yisgadal...* the mourners' kaddish.

Last time Raizl heard that was at her father's funeral.

Now the mourners file out of the temple with the coffin. Their Hasidic garments make a ribbon of black against the brown and grey fields, heading to the cemetery.

As they march out with the mourners, Raizl sees dark figures at the top of the hill. These are not the departing louts, but gentlemen who sit like officers on their horses. Watching. And waiting, she fears.

On her way home, Raizl watches Samuel and Lev disappear into the woods. The boys are up to something. She follows them.

'Hello, little brother. What are you doing?'

They react with shrugging and shuffling. Then Samuel replies, 'We're just talking. We know there's going to be trouble. We have to do something.'

'You should have joined our shooting practice.'

'But will a few more shooters hold off the Black Hundreds and their friends in the army? You said that yourself the other day,' argues Samuel.

For a kid whose head is filled with mystical nonsense, sometimes Samuel asks the right questions. The sad ones.

'So you are right. Like a broken clock. But what do you suggest?'

The three look at each other. 'We've only started to talk,' says Samuel.

'I know! We can raise a golem,' says Lev.

'A *golem*! Something out of fairy tales. Are you mad?'

'I think I've worked out what went wrong with our formula last year,' continues Lev.

'Last year indeed!' Samuel's contempt for the idea matches Raizl's. 'Golems! You are lost in the sixteenth century! What good is a man of clay and stone when our enemies can blow it up. Boom! We need more than a golem. And the answer could be in here.'

He pulls a book from out of the inner pocket of his coat. '*The Book of Deborah*. I... found it on the ground near the tzaddik, along with a telescope.'

He looks around as if expecting condemnation. 'It was meant to be,' he adds.

'I don't know about what was meant and what was not. This book might be a lot of dreck.' says Raizl. 'But you did the right thing. The village police could have stolen it. You know what that schmuck of a constable is like.'

'This book is *not* dreck,' Samuel shouts. 'It contains the words of the prophetess Deborah, and her instructions on how to contact other worlds. These are worlds beyond Mars, beyond our own star. This is a world circling the star Meroz.'

'*A curse on Meroz and all its inhabitants*,' quotes Lev. 'Deborah cursed these creatures. So who needs them now?'

'And how will we bring them here?' Raizl considers *War of the Worlds*. 'And why? Maybe they won't be our friends. They could be worse than the Cossacks. Did you think of that?'

27

'No, no… Deborah cursed them for what they *didn't* do. They wouldn't help the Israelites, and she cursed them by closing the passage point. But in this book, she says she regretted this action. She believes there may be ways to stir them to action, and future generations might need to reopen the point of passage. She also believed it can be a source of knowledge.'

'So what's this "passage point"? Not an airship or flying machine?'

'No ships or machinery are involved, only the principles of "kefitzat haderech"', making the roads leap,' says Samuel. 'It creates the passageway that enables you to move from one place to another in an instant. Except it involves the sky, and bending the substance of space.'

'*Pah!*'

'It's like this.' Samuel takes off his tallis, spreads it on a rock and puts his fingers on it on either side of the rock. 'Think of this tallis as space, as the distance you need to travel. So you close the space like this…' He draws his fingers together, folding the material, until his fingertips are touching. 'The crumpling of the sky!'

'Very clever. So this book tells you how to do that? Can I see it?'

Samuel places the book in her hands.

It isn't very big. If it contained such extensive secrets, Deborah must have made her points quickly. Now, if only Marx had done the same.

Raizl opens it to pages of Hebrew. She knows a smattering of Hebrew from synagogue, but it's a 'sacred' language not meant for women. Hebrew was never a language of food, love, work and life for her. Yiddish is her mother tongue, her mame loshen.

But the Hebrew in this book would have been Deborah's mame loshen.

The illustrations in the book are simple line drawings, but they are striking. They compel her eyes to see something more than what's there. This book must have historical value, even if it's only a made-up story like *War of the Worlds*.

Raizl tries to keep an open mind as they prepare. Ritual has its place for unbelievers as well as the devout. After Bund meetings, they link arms and sing 'In Struggle', 'The Oath' and the 'Internationale'.

And of course, they have a meal.

The boys take turns reading from Deborah's book.

There are other worlds around other stars, but this is the only path I was able to open. It may be due to the celestial creatures' nature, and ours. Perhaps the other worlds cannot be reached for good reasons.

I say 'celestial' and not 'divine'. Celestial pertains to the stars and the sky. They are part of the natural order made by our creator; they do not stand above it.

'Creator?' Raizl interrupts. 'There is no creator.'

'Shut up,' says Samuel. 'Do you want to hear this or not?'

'This is why we don't allow women to take part in rituals,' says Lev, stroking his barely sprouted beard.

'Deborah was a woman,' Raizl points out.

'Raizl has a point, Lev. Deborah was a woman. She communicated with celestial beings and had the power to open and close the gate to them.'

'Your sister is no prophetess,' argues Lev.

'You bet your tuches I'm not. And what's with 'prophecy' when we have 'free will'? How free can we be with some big zayde in the sky?'

Lev is about to retort when Samuel holds his hand up. 'Stop! We can discuss this later. This isn't a Talmudic talking shop, we need to plan something.'

A few lines in the Talmud, a secret book from a dead tzaddik. Yet scientists and socialists like Mr Wells have also speculated about life beyond the earth.

So how do these other-worlders live? In these worlds, do some prosper while others grow poor? Do they have social and economic classes?

Now that makes sense, Raizl thinks. We will ask the workers from another planet to join in solidarity in our fight against the police, the Czar and pogromists.

'Let's do it,' says Raizl. 'But we do it along with other self-defence efforts.'

'Whatever you want, sister,' says Samuel, as he opens the book to another section. 'This part is called "Preparing the Table". Now, Deborah says there are variations. There's a sequence that worked for her, but many things can affect the contact. She says these beings are volatile.'

'Volatile! Sounds like what we need,' says Raizl. 'So let's be clear: there's no fasting or mortifying our flesh? I won't be having that.'

'No fasting. No mortifying – only fortifying. But it's more than that. Deborah says "celestial sustenance" can connect the worlds.'

'Well, well, a universal nosh! But how do you know what these beings like? Deborah's people ate differently from us, I'm sure.'

'That doesn't matter. It's most important that the banquet is enjoyed by those who prepare it.'

'You mean it's *me* doing the preparing.'

The two boys look at each other and shuffle about in that abashed-boy way.

'But that's not how it will be,' Raizl insists. 'You'll have to make yourself useful in the kitchen. Both of you.'

Carrot tzimmes with honey and raisins, potato kugel and sweet noodle kugel. Hunks of barley bread to mop up the juices. Soup from the remains of Friday's chicken.

'You better get grating and chopping. Down to the knuckle, boys.'

'Ha, you're as bad as Chaim the tailor.'

'No, this is cooperative work. See, I get my hands dirty too, alongside you. And they're your guests anyway.'

Raizl starts singing 'In Struggle', a favourite workers' anthem, as she mashes fish and crumbs together. *We are the hated and driven, Tortured and persecuted, even to blood... 'Tis because we love the poor, The masses of mankind, who starve for food.'*

Raizl chuckles to think she's preparing food while singing a song about the starving masses. But she's learned how to make a little go far: lots of matzo meal and seasoning. Short of revolution and expropriation, this helps fill the belly.

'We are shot down, and on the gallows hanged, Robbed of our lives and freedom without ruth –'

'Stop it!' Samuel complains. 'Yes, we all suffer. But do we have to suffer more? At least the Hasids play tunes that are good for dancing.'

'I'll think about changing the music after you do some work.'

Samuel shrugs, then closes the shutters.

'And what's that for? How do we make the sky crumple when we can't see it?'

Samuel opens Deborah's book and reads: *The sky is space, and space is everywhere even when it is enclosed.'*

'Space, schmace!' Raizl carries on with the preparations. But in keeping with the theme, she shapes the rugelach like stars.

When everything's bubbling on the stove, the boys spread a bed sheet out on the floor and begin drawing diagrams with charcoal and pens.

What are they doing to that sheet? These scholars will have to learn to do the washing too.

Samuel labels eight places at the table, and several in the middle. He adds lines around it, a vortex of rings around the centre, plus other figures.

'It's the Tree of Life,' says Samuel.

'Whatever you say, little brother.'

He draws lines linking the circles together, creating pathways and a central vortex. 'And the food goes here.'

So the table is set, and they place the food on the sheet following the symbols and geometrical figures from the Book of Deborah.

Finally, the rugelach is ready, warm and fragrant from the oven. Raizl hovers with the plate, then plonks it down on the trunk of the Tree of Life, in the centre.

'Tiptheret!' exclaims Lev. 'It stands for beauty. And it's where the synthesis of opposites meet.'

'Well, it's where we find a plate of rugelach, our mother's best recipe. I put poppy seed in them and…'

The boys begin davening and genuflecting towards the food.

'Stop it. Eat!' orders Raizl as she picks up her knife and fork.

She is tasting every piece of gefilte fish she ever ate in this mouthful.

Then the carrot tsimmes is sweet and savoury at once. With nourishment from the chicken soup flowing into her veins, the symbols on their improvised tablecloth begin to make sense. That one there, under the plate of rugelach, does indeed look like an opening, a tunnel.

'Look, we've fortified ourselves. Now we carry on the ritual,' says Lev.

The boys start to chant what sounds like a series of numbers, pronounced in many languages as well as Hebrew. It puzzles Raizl. Singing the 'Internationale' might be a ritual too, but she knows what it means. It inspires her. But this?

'Raizl, you look confused. The chanting frees our awareness to travel and open the path,' says Samuel.

'So tell me, how do we chant and eat at the same time?'

'Stop with your squabbles,' interrupts Lev. 'We have a road to make rise, and a sky to crumple! Or have you two forgotten?'

'But I'm asking a perfectly good question.'

'So here's a perfectly good answer. The chanting is a kind of verbal alchemy. By forming these words, then changing its letters, we can change the nature of reality – or in our case, the distance between two worlds.'

'Alchemy, you say? So maybe food is an alchemy of the stomach. An alchemy of taste and scent as well as words and sound. They say the way to a man's heart is through his stomach.' How she hated that phrase when she was growing up. On the other hand, her home cooking did impress Arkady and all her comrades.

'So, boychiks, the way through the centre of the universe and out again is through the stomach too! What did Deborah have to say about that? Maybe we eat rugelach now, before you start making noise again.'

So Raizl eats a pastry crumb by crumb, the poppy seed, raisins and cinnamon lingering on her tongue. Then she starts on one she made with almonds and dates.

As the pile of rugelach on the plate diminishes, Samuel keeps rearranging the remaining pastries into a pattern. This pattern begins to make sense too. And then they begin chanting again. It starts a buzz in her ears, between her ears.

The pattern of pastries converges at Tiptherah, a point of beauty and synthesis. She takes another, this one with sweet cheese curds and dried apricots from Odessa. A blaze of flavour at the point of her tongue, taking her far beyond Odessa. At the vortex of star-formed pastry is a tunnel, and there is something at the end of it. Light, colours rippling through an utterly new spectrum.

Other tunnels branch from the one they travel. Are there other worlds at each end? Maybe *these* are the worlds that will show solidarity. She takes a look…

It's only Fekedynka. But the dirt roads are paved, full of odd sleek automobiles.

At another tunnel she sees Fekedynka's synagogue in flames.

As a young girl she would have gladly burned that place down herself. Samuel would have no great love for it either after so many beatings at the cheder.

But this smoke fills the tunnel, catching in her throat and infecting her with fear. The fumes flood her with a taste of iron and meat. It makes her gag. Ominous outlines begin to reveal themselves through the smoke. A tower?

No no, leave this place…

She's afraid at first to look into other tunnels, but she hears music that tempts her. Like klezmer, though it's not very good. A fat man sings a song against a backdrop of a village like hers, while people wearing furs applaud.

She moves on to another tunnel lit by kaleidoscopic blocks of colour that warm her even more than chicken soup. The kaleidoscope turns to a living scene. Her farshtunken village again: but here's she's walking hand in hand with Arkady in the market. Everything is still lit by the colours of the kaleidoscope. She feels peace. She thinks she's happy.

But then a deep noise wells beneath her feet and wrenching bass vibrations churn her stomach and rattle her teeth, threatening to undo her. Shake her into pieces, breaking everything down…

'Raizl, stay with us!' A rough hand on her shoulder, Samuel shaking her. 'We bring them to us, you don't want to be going to them!'

The deep bass carries on, but now she feels anchored against it. Something shrill spills out of an opening in the floor along with it, a column of light that hurts her eyes, noise approaching melody.

The colours scream with the sound, and she has to close her eyes against them. Something breaks. Plates? The ceiling above her head? She grips Samuel's hand, and remembers how he once gripped hers when he was much smaller.

Then it's quiet. So quiet. And a strange man's voice addresses them in something that sounds like Hebrew.

Raizl opens her eyes. Two men and a woman sit at their 'table', clad in Arabian-style robes and sandals. It must be cold for them, even with the room warmed by cooking.

A lot of plates are broken, but someone has moved the rugelach aside. That plate is still intact and the leftover pastries have retained a somewhat shaken pattern.

Raizl takes a deep breath, picks up the rugelach and offers it to their guests.

These beings speak Hebrew, Samuel thinks. Not the devotional Hebrew he knows best. But it's close to the Hebrew of Deborah's book. One moment their old house was filled with eye-blasting light and colour and gut-wrenching noise. He forced himself to look, even if it shattered him.

These creatures are composed of noise, and they weave their unseen colours with it.

And now they sit here in robes and sandals, accepting Raizl's offer of rugelach.

Then in a blink they're wearing warm clothes. They must have assembled the substance from the air, the vapours of the food, anything around them. From this they create their flesh and blood, their clothes. Some would consider them gods, but Samuel knows there are no other gods before Hashem. They are God's creatures just like he, his friends and his sister and the beasts of the field.

Yet jealousy stirs in his mind. Hashem created Man above all other creatures, yet here are creatures far more powerful. Perhaps the Lord was not pleased with what Man has become.

'We're speaking the right language?' The first word from the woman grates like a rusty hinge. Then the next one softens. Each word makes her voice more like a woman's, a human that God created.

Samuel tries to stifle his envious and selfish thoughts. He answers, while his friends are still stunned. 'You're close. We use a similar language for prayer, and something else for every day.'

'Yiddish,' adds Raizl, still offering food. For all her revolutionary Odessa ways, Raizl can be so much like their mother. Perhaps he should become more like that too. In the end, he did enjoy the cooking.

'We tried to change to your form as soon as we entered, so we're sorry if we hurt your eyes and ears,' says one of the men at their table.

They're very polite for accursed inhabitants, thinks Samuel. But he can't bear to be polite himself. He needs to know so much.

What did they want with Earth and the ancient Israelites and why didn't they help? Samuel is not sure what to ask first.

The three new human-like beings look about. 'The stories we've heard of your world tell us of heat and light, and a very bossy woman,' says the woman.

'Have something to eat. You've travelled a long way. Rugelach isn't enough. We can talk later,' says Raizl.

'Eat?' one of the male aliens says.

The woman jabs him with her elbow. 'Food, remember? You put it in your mouth. That's the stuff that drew us here, where there are so many senses to experience.'

Raizl is thoughtful. 'Three strangers will attract attention in a village full of yentas. We need stories for them. Arkady can get papers. Our guests are students from the yeshiva, yes? And one of you is a sister of a student.'

'What is a sister?'

'A pain in the tuches, that's a sister,' replies Samuel. 'But my sister speaks sense when she says *eat*.'

So that's what they do. The alien woman takes a piece of gefilte fish with her fingers. After a small mouthful she seems to glow with pleasure in the food, as if a light has flickered on under her skin.

Lev clears his throat. 'It might be easier if you were all yeshiva students. Friends from a town not too close. But one of you will have to, um, change yourself, if you can do that.'

'I expect that will be me,' says the female. And then her face and form seems to melt. Now Samuel does look away. When he sees her again, she has become a brown-haired boy.

Remember, they are only creatures like me. They do things we cannot do. Maybe they can help us. But they are not God.

Finally he speaks up. 'Do you go around visiting other worlds?'

'When we can, though it's hard to get through. We need help from the other side. We like to sample things and study them. We create sound-scores to enjoy at home,' the first young man from space explains. 'Yours is the only world we've found where beings are so different from us, and produce such a wonderful and strange variety of sounds: some sweet, some harsh. We all heard stories about a visit, then access was denied. Some woman wanted us to fight in a war. We don't do wars.'

Samuel translates this into Yiddish for Raizl.

And Raizl answers, 'Neither do we, me and my comrades. Our only war is the class war –'

Lev interrupts, and soon they are talking about points and pathways and how these beings arrived. They pick up each other's Hebrew idioms quickly.

Raizl recognises some of the Hebrew words, but most of the time she watches. She sees how a light flickers in their faces as they enjoy their food.

The three look so ordinary now, but Raizl remembers the dazzle of their light and their pulsing waves of sound.

So these creatures of sound and light enjoy a vacation in the flesh. They change their size, they change their shape to look like us. They *seem* harmless, compared to the kind of human tyrants she has dedicated herself to overturning.

They talk like people now. But she is sure she hears an echo in their voices, as if they come from across empty spaces. And their talk is empty too, empty of feeling.

It's like people going to the Black Sea to swim and eat ice creams. But this is no time to kibitz, no time to fool around. Not in Deborah's time when a wicked king held the Jews as slaves, and no time for kibitzing now.

So they want a vacation, they only want to schmooze and eat and drink and make 'sound-scores'. Raizl remembers what she saw at the end of a tunnel: the fat man singing on a stage, making an entertainment of someone's poor life.

They've assumed their bodies of flesh and blood for momentary pleasures, while that is all we have.

The three guests pick up their Yiddish quickly. Raizl puts them upstairs in the room she's taken over from her mother, so they'll be out of the way. She goes back to the pallet in the kitchen. It's warm there, and it's where she slept as a child.

If the visitors broke a few dishes on arrival, they are now the tidiest of guests. They've been given names: Hymie, Yaakov and Herschel.

They spend a lot of time in Samuel's room. She hears chanting and talking. They go out at night and look at the stars with the tzaddik's telescope.

Then they go to Odessa for a look around. It's just as well they're away, before they get a visit from the matchmaker urging them to marry someone's daughter.

When the guests return, they say how much they like Fekedynka. Especially the food. They're not so interested in fine things, but in strong tastes and aromas and sounds.

Raizl cooks another meal, more chicken soup for the schnorrers out of space.

Of course, she did try to get them to help in the kitchen. Yaakov-from-Meroz obliged. Not for him grating potatoes or any hard graft; he created something that looks very much like gefilte fish out of nothing, or 'emanations' as Samuel likes to say. But she didn't see anything emanating there, just some gefilte fish.

But then she took a bite. It tasted like damp sawdust. An imitation.

She remembers when she took Samuel on walks where they'd find flowers, collect them and look them up in a big book, their father's treasure. She should have tried harder to convince him to study this kind of science. He could have done something useful, instead of *this*...

Get rid of them, she's about to hiss at Samuel, who is now chopping onions. He has the book, he must know the curse to send them back. But she has also seen how the aliens flicker when something affects them. She remembers those bone-rattling notes, the unmaking chords at their heart. Surely the goniffs could be good for something. Even Deborah thought so.

Meanwhile, she tutors her pupils in Russian. At the end of it, a few coins. She goes to help sister Hannah with her babies, and tells her that Samuel has guests. Better say that, before the chitchat goes around.

Hannah has other concerns. 'There's been trouble,' she says. 'Drunk boys in the market mouthing off about a pogrom. They called it a cleansing, though they're dirty schmucks themselves. They were throwing rocks, while soldiers supplied vodka.'

On her way home, Raizl calls in on Mordecai. At his smithy the windows are boarded up and glass still glitters on the ground beneath them. He shows her a collection of spiked poles. Is that enough? Oleg said that he expects more arms to arrive, but they're overdue.

Raizl runs home. She goes up to Samuel's room, where the three guests would be. She flings the door open. 'Listen! Do you want to experience real life on this Earth? Soon you'll see it in all its horror. Life isn't just a bowl of chicken soup.'

They're all crowded around the open window. A cold wind blows through the room. Samuel turns around, holding his telescope. 'Ssh! They're showing me the stars with inhabited planets.'

Raizl is lost for a response. Then she goes downstairs and gets the megaphone she brought from Odessa. Time to try it out at last.

Back in Samuel's room, she shouts through it: 'Wake up, you schlubs!'

Alien guests and humans alike jump at the sound.

And maybe the creatures of sound and light jump a little more.

Doctor Oleg passes on the bad news. Comrades in Odessa have been arrested and arms were seized.

Faces of her friends flash before Raizl's eyes, but she doesn't have time to worry. Without these arms, they need other help. They knock on doors, get promises of a loan of a horse or cart. A few pistols are donated; the blacksmith will work overtime. They enlist the support of the Jewish toughs who hang about the market: these goniffs don't give a shit about politics but they'll pile in if a fight breaks out.

Raizl is at home, writing out a chart of Yiddish and Russian words. Then the blast of a shofar from the village synagogue interrupts her train of thought.

Since it isn't a holiday, that only means one thing.

It probably started in the market. It usually does. And that's where Raizl's group will go, while others patrol elsewhere.

Raizl shouts for Samuel, then gets herself ready. Heavy coat and scarf over her face, her stoutest pair of boots, her pistol in one hand and an iron stave in another. She picks up the megaphone and slings it across her chest with its strap. Though she doesn't expect to make speeches, they might need to communicate.

'And what are you going to do, boys?' Raizl turns towards Samuel and Lev. 'Cast some more spells?'

'No, we're going out! We'll defend the synagogue.'

She nods at her brother. 'There'll be a group heading there now. And where are your guests?'

'They went out to do some… *recording*, they called it.'

A curse on Meroz and all its inhabitants.

In Odessa, Raizl was able to dodge and run through the streets, shelter in buildings and alleys and emerge again.

But this is a village of ramshackle shops and dirt roads, exposed in a valley to an enemy that comes from all sides. From other villages, from the towns and even the cities, their enemies prepare to sweep through any place that stands after October's pogroms.

Some of these attackers are peasants, armed with pitchforks and scythes. But there are also soldiers among them, officers and Cossacks too.

She wants to vomit. Did Yankel speak of bravery? She'd flee if there was anywhere to go. The enemy will sweep them aside as easily as dust off a wooden floor, then go on to the next village.

She has her pistol. She'll take a few of them out of action, out of life before they kill her. But she doesn't want to die.

Then their *guests* appear in the crowd. Just behind her. Swathed in coats and scarves, like everyone else. Hymie, Yaakov and Herschel, the yeshiva boys from Meroz. They are pressed up close to her, and even though they just look like boys, it makes her shudder. They make noises to each other that bear no relation to a human language.

They don't write anything down, but they look at each other, look at the scene in front of them as if comparing notes.

Then there is a gunshot. Bayonets extended, swords and clubs raised, the Black Hundreds spill into the village.

There are screams from the front – are people getting trampled?

'Let's go,' Raizl shouts. 'We have to move forward.'

Pogromists come straight into the market, horsemen in front. Closer they come, then Raizl runs forward and shoots. The first horseman rears and falls. Yankel and Sheindl start a volley at the other horsemen, but not before other shots ring out.

Comrades scatter, but one ducks into the butcher's to emerge with a meat hook, showing a clear intention to use it.

The Bundists keep shooting, but in a flash they're surrounded and pushed back against the tavern. A Jewish thug called Mendel comes out of the tavern and starts throwing rocks. Someone starts shooting from the upstairs windows, just missing a Cossack but bringing down his horse.

But they're only a handful cornered here, plus the schnorrers out of space.

'*A curse on Meroz!*' Raizl echoes the prophetess Deborah.

She knows it's the end. She has chosen to live the life of a rebel, and she did the best she could. Now it's over but she'll make a good exit. She shoots and shoots. When she runs out of bullets, she's prepared to use a pole and then kick and punch if she loses that.

And she'll sing. This song will be the last thing in her ears, not the curses of the Black Hundreds. '*We are the hated and driven,*' Raizl begins, lifting the megaphone to her lips.

Mordecai's bass voice booms out. Sheindl and Yankel, everyone joins in. '*Hated are we, and driven from our homes, Tortured and persecuted, even to blood; And wherefore? Tis because we love the poor....*'

Yaakov-from-Meroz visibly shudders. Raizl can feel it move through him and convulse him. 'That... that... that terrible tune. Those words,' he complains in Yiddish, pulling his hat tighter over his ears. 'Farshtunken! Miserable!'

They sing louder. Then Raizl pulls his hat off, exposing his ears. 'Put that in your sound-score, you putz!'

Luminescence moves through his face, similar to the glow excited by the pleasure of good Jewish food. But now it expresses pain, shown by the way his too-human features contort. The light is stronger. And Raizl understands. Soon he will lose control, and stop being Yaakov.

Yes... Sound affects these creatures most, for that is what they are made of.

She sings through the megaphone. '*We are shot down, and on the gallows hanged, Robbed of our lives and freedom without ruth, Because for the enslaved and for the poor, We are demanding liberty and truth.*'

The alien's body swells. And the other one gives a cry, worse than a fox in heat or a cat meeting its end.

'Sing louder, sing!' Raizl urges her friends. She kicks Mendel. 'Sing, goddammit!'

And Mendel sings.

The aliens burst out of their clothes; their flesh comes apart in shreds of light and patches of darkness.

The pogromists back off, frightened by what they see and hear.

'But we will not be frightened from our path, By darksome prisons or by tyranny...'

The alien fleshly form dissolves into a tangle of waves that boom in pain, deep dissolving throbs that makes the horses bare their teeth, shriek and turn and bolt.

Meanwhile, other Jews emerge from defensive posts around the village. They move forward with sticks and guns ready to finish the job, even if they've had to share some of their enemy's pain.

Oleg and a few others tend to the injured on the ground.

Have the aliens fled, taking their sound-score with them? Maybe they've decided this world is not a suitable place for their holidays after all.

Or they could still be here in some form, lingering like the scent of a fish gone bad.

The tavern keeper emerges with flasks of wine. 'The mamzers have run away!'

Samuel and Lev arrive with others from the synagogue, followed by a beaming rebbe.

'It's God's doing, like the horns of Jericho,' intones the rebbe, accepting the offer of wine after a brief blessing.

But Raizl shakes her head and passes her wine to someone else. She remembers what she saw in the tunnel, the place where the sky crumpled and let in the alien light. Now she knows where Deborah's gift of prophecy came from. When she opened the pathway, those other corridors showed her what-could-be. Deborah did not predict *the* future, but she was able to look into possible futures.

Raizl can't forget the burning synagogue, the smoke that must hide a horror more brutal than any pogrom. But how will she speak of this to others? Who will listen? She understands now that Deborah might have been much more accursed than the inhabitants of Meroz. And so is she.

While the others toast and celebrate a victory, Raizl cannot join them.

ALIEN THOUGHTS

ERIC KAPLAN

I

The object had dropped from the sky and crashed into the forest behind the schul on Erev Shabbos. Schneerson, the doctor, had led a group of men to look at it, half buried in the dirt, a ring of luminous fungus around it glowing through the humus. *A curse?* the men he hired to dig it up wanted to know. *A sign of a coming plague? A call for us to repent?* No, Schneerson had assured them, the earth is one of many bodies hanging in empty space, flying through darkness. Sometimes they jostle each other. Sometimes they knock each other. This was one such body that had gotten a knock in its home in the vastness and come crashing down behind the schul. God hadn't sent it.

'Take a look at this, doctor,' one of the men with shovels had said, standing up to his chest in the glass-lined pit the falling object had blasted in the forest floor.

Schneerson had jumped in, pushed him aside and inspected it. Carved in the black metal was a letter 'ה'.

The doctor ate pork on Yom Kippur, had electric lights in his home, drank coffee and played chess with gentiles and now he was hiking through the woods to see Reb Yaakov, the wonder rabbi. Schneerson and Yaakov had been friends in cheder. Schneerson always took care to hide it from his teachers when he knew more than they did; not so Yaakov. By six he had memorized the Torah, by eight the Talmud. By twelve he could tell you if you pricked Rashi with a pin, what letter would be on the other side. At his bar mitzvah, his rabbi had told him that more than intelligence, God valued a kind heart, and he had called him an ignoramus in front of the whole congregation. Now he lived in a one-room shack six hours into the woods. Children sometimes hiked out to see his emaciated form rolling naked in the snow, 27, 39, 106 times, and he screamed at them, wild as a demon, calling them idolaters, prostitutes and donkeys.

'Yaakov, it's Mendel.' The door opened. The rabbi was so emaciated,Schneerson could see the pulse in his neck. He has scurvy, the doctor thought. 'I thought you might be angry at me.'

'Because you eat pork? At least you're consistent.'

'Something strange has happened, Yaakov. An object fell from the sky. A meteorite.'

'So? Chazal discuss this. It is a piece of the dome the stars are in.'

'This was etched on the outside with letters as deep as my thumb.' Schneerson took the paper on which he had copied the letters and handed it to Yaakov.

The rabbi rippled like a cat smelling a herb, closed his eyes for a moment and then opened them. 'Let's go.' He grabbed a threadbare coat and started running through the snow.

The doctor closed the door and ran after him. 'Do you know what the letters mean?'

'They are rules for pronouncing the unspeakable name of God.'

II

Some of the workers had been reciting psalms and the rabbi dispatched them with a curse.

'Mendel, my friend, do you know what I have been doing since my bar mitzvah?' he asked Schneerson.

'Praying?'

'Asking Zaide in the sky for sweets? No. I have been studying the method of letter combinations of the rabbi Abraham Abulafia. I came upon a rare book, sold everything my father left me to buy it. But what is carved in this stone makes Abulafia seem like a child.'

The doctor remembered something from his yeshiva studies before medical school. 'Doesn't whoever recites the name of God forfeit his share in the world to come?'

The rabbi smiled. 'I'm sorry, doctor. I shouldn't laugh at you. This isn't a decision one man should make for another. If you don't want to follow the instructions on this object you don't have to. Please tell the people in the town that this is contaminated – it will make them sick. I don't want to be disturbed.'

'No. I want to follow the procedures. I don't believe in a world to come.'

'Interesting. I do.' And he read the names of God.

Abulafia had described head motions for each vowel sign, and the method of permutations. This was the antechamber of the teaching inscribed in the rock, which instructed they go without food and sleep for three days, reciting the name in all its possible combinations. After three days the letters seemed to swim and move, teaching them new methods of combination. The doctor had taken a class in Cantor's transfinite numbers at Cracow. It had been over his head but he was glad he had done it; he was able to lead the rabbi down some of the byways of the letters. It was as if the 22 were not letters but different angles from which to view infinity, and that as they got deeper into the recitations, and the specific dances that came with each one (although dance was a gentle word for what seemed to be closer to a spasm or fit), each of the 22 was simply an arbitrary point along a continuum of meaning. Or perhaps meaninglessness.

He started awake. The rabbi was staring into his eyes. 'What if it is from the other side?' Yaakov asked.

'I think it is from an other side,' said the doctor. 'If Laplace is correct and the universe is full of other worlds, on some of these worlds there may be races of intelligent beings like ours. I believe this is a message from one of these other races and it is teaching us to think like them.'

'Laplace is wrong. It is not from a place in space.'

'Heaven? You are looking at it as a religious man.'

'Don't be stupid. The Sefer Yetzirah says reality is made of time, space and self. Space has six dimensions – north east south west up down, but time seemingly has only two. Maybe time has more and the rock came from them.'

'I can't imagine it.'

'I can't either. We're like fish trying to fly, moths trying to reach the sun.'

'Look,' Schneerson said.

The shifting letters were showing them two images made of alephs and bets: a human brain and a mushroom, one becoming the other, intertwined, limbs making love.

'The fungus. It wants us to eat the fungus and alter the chemistry of our brains,' said the doctor. 'There are ergots, moulds on rye that drive men insane. Do we listen to it? Does it have our interests at heart? Does it have a heart?'

The rabbi was already on all fours, eating the phosphorescent fungus, his mouth foaming like a rabid dog. He started laughing and gambolling like a puppy, but his eyes were blasted open as if with something stronger than grief.

'I can't explain it to you, doctor. You have to eat of the fruit.'

Schneerson ate it and looked at time and space knotted into one; the knot was the object; it beckoned him to untie it. He did.

The rabbi and the doctor, childhood friends, slipped through the open loop.

III

Expel me?

On the level of reality where S existed he was not a separate being, so how could he be expelled?

Could he be purified out?

Purify me out and choke on the poison you need to do so, he thought. Thought? Did he think?

He was a not-thing, who was not-separate, who certainly had no thoughts.

But what S's no-thoughts were about, was hate.

Expel me and I will return in full force, and I will spoil. I will hurt your tender ones, and put ulcers in the apple of your eye. I will reach out with my contaminated fingers across the boundaries of time and touch them, and trace madness across their minds.

I will give you a sickness, but not to make you die, to make you search, search, search, search for the cure, and then just when you have given up hope of ever curing it, I will appear with the medicine. And it will be that medicine that will be the real poison.

I will pollute you, Mister Rabbi, and make you insane, Mister Doctor, and I will tempt you and teach you how to do it, and through you your whole world/realm/universe/family/nest of souls.

S would have thought, if S was the kind of thing that had thoughts.

IV

No words for the radiance on the other side. 'These are called the hekhalot,' said the rabbi. 'These are called other dimensions of time,' said the doctor.

'Go back go back go back,' said the guardians at the gates, and Yaakov and Mendel walked through.

'It's like a ship that travels through time and space,' said Mendel.

Through a – window? No – they saw the madman at the gates of Rome to convert the pope – Abraham Abulafia – and gave him the method. The method that Yaakov would sell his patrimony for.

The traumatised slaves in the desert, with Moses away. They leaned out the – door? No – and showed them the golden shape of the spacecraft? No – and they made a golden calf and worshipped it.

Through another window they saw the two hominid ancestors in Olduvai gorge holding hands.

'We tell them to eat from the tree, the tree that we ate from.'

From far, far away a woman's voice is screaming.

Yaakov is talking to them, telling them that they will be as gods.

V

'You have to wake up, you have to wake up.' Mendel is being shaken by Itl, Yaakov's younger sister. She is screaming, crying. Pink froth and vomit are in his mouth. He bit his tongue.

'I'm all right. I had a seizure.'

Her eyes say, not that. His eyes say – then what?

'They're shooting people. The special groups are here and are rounding people up in the forest and shooting them.'

'I need to go back in.'

He goes back in.

Yaakov! Yaakov! It wants us to do it to ourselves! It did it to us before, but we could blame it. Now it wants us to do it to ourselves. Don't tempt the woman.

The rabbi stepped back from the window and shook off the bad dream.

'You will save my sister? You will save Itl? You can get her out?'

'Yes. Why?'

'He'll just do it to us again. I have to trick him. Or he'll just do it again.'

'How can you trick him?'

'I think I know how. Run, run, run.'

VI

Mendel and Itl ran from the sound of gunfire, ran from the village, the forest, hiding, disguises, a couple of hours of sleep in the potato cellars of the moderately tolerant. The old Jewish story.

Yaakov went deeper into the bowels of the spaceship, past the guards, into the forge of universes. He learnt to weave and unweave the machine/spaceship/palace that S had sent to tempt him. He learnt the rules for making a new universe of time and space. He made it, and went inside.

A deep but dazzling darkness. How to tempt S to follow him inside?

Yaakov said — let there be light.

Animals, plants, sun, moon, world. You can corrupt this to your heart's content, you bastard. S followed him in; into the closet. You'd almost feel sorry for him. Idiot didn't have a clue.

Almost.

Yaakov shut the door.

VII

In New York City one day, when Mendel and Itl had time to catch their breath some years later, he took a look at a siddur and noticed something different. The unspeakable name of God was spelled differently than it had been before. Instead of a yod and a chet and a vav and a chet — YACHAVAKAH-- where there had been chets there were now hehs. His friend had sent him a signal: that he had tricked the trickster, freed the captive and unloosed the bonds. From now on there would be a space in the name of God. From now on we would be able to slip through.

THE RELUCTANT JEW

RACHEL SWIRSKY

The alien held up the yarmulke in its tentacle in what might have been a questioning way.

'I don't really care where you put it,' Joseph muttered.

The alien shoved the yarmulke onto a protuberance on what was probably its back.

'This is the food,' Joseph said, pointing to the sad trays of matzo, lox and so on, which sat next to a few bottles of Manischewitz. 'But you probably can't eat it.'

'Sllrpppurrgle,' said the alien.

It wrapped a front tentacle around the wine bottle, picked it up, shook it like a maraca, and then set it down again.

'Grrrpppllgggl,' it continued, waving three lower tentacles in appreciation. Or possibly rage. Or possibly something else.

The creature moved on.

Joseph thumped his head on the table.

It had begun yesterday when Lieutenant Breaker came into Joseph's quarters, smiling.

It was a bad sign when Lieutenant Breaker was smiling. She was the personnel officer and it was her job to manage their assignments and watch out for tricky things like morale. On Space Steps Corporation ships, the position had a reputation for attracting vicious personality types. Joseph's personal theory was that the kinder ones got burned out by the impossibility of maintaining morale in the face of a fascist, interstellar company, and only those with a cruel streak survived.

Joseph eyed Lieutenant Breaker suspiciously. He'd automatically crossed his arms and raised his shoulders in subconscious gestures of self-protection. But there was nothing he could do to protect himself against orders.

'Guess what,' Lieutenant Breaker said.

Joseph waited for her to finish, and then realized that she was actually going to make him say it. 'What?' he grumbled.

She thrust a tablet towards him. 'You're a Jew!'

Joseph's gaze flickered down to the tablet screen, which showed the branches of a family tree. He then looked back up at Lieutenant Breaker's face. He hadn't yet figured out how this apparently neutral statement of fact was going to backfire. 'So?'

Lieutenant Breaker tapped the screen for emphasis. 'Your family tree. All the way back to pre-expulsion Spain.'

'Mom talks family history occasionally,' Joseph said. 'But we've been atheists for, like, four generations.'

'Plenty of atheist Jews,' Lieutenant Breaker replied. 'Fine tradition, atheist Jews.'

Joseph finally decided to go the direct route. 'What are you trying to tell me?'

'Well,' said Lieutenant Breaker, 'as you know, we've been chatting up the Tentacle Heads so that they'll give us mineral rights to the accretions on that lovely sea floor of theirs.' She cleared her throat. 'Turns out the Tentacle Heads are curious critters, and I don't just mean they're really, really weird. They wanted to read our library archive, so we sent it down, and now apparently they are obsessed with the concept of religion. So, we are setting up a multiculturalism fair in the mess hall. A table for every major religion. Congratulations, you're the Jew!'

She tossed the pad in his direction. Joseph caught it by dumb reflex.

'But I'm not –' he said. 'I don't –'

Ignoring his stuttering, Lieutenant Breaker turned to leave. As she reached the door, she hesitated and turned back, 'I should note that it is absolutely forbidden to call them Tentacle Heads. Remember, Ensign, they are the Usgul. I don't want to hear you using that term again.' She waved goodbye. 'See you later.'

Joseph roused himself enough to raise his head from the table. He rubbed his face.

The hall looked as depressing as any other kind of 'fair' he'd attended. The matter printers had been busy making banners and models and other kitsch. There was a big Star of David behind him, along with a model of the Western Wall. The table in front of him was scattered with foods and other artefacts associated with Judaism, although Joseph got the impression that whoever had programmed the instructions into the matter printer had known approximately as much about Judaism as Joseph did, which was to say, not much. The level of accuracy and depth was probably, therefore, something around the level of two plus two equals fourish.

Across the way, the Buddhist table featured a model of some mountain and a shrine. Ensign Cho did not look any more pleased than Joseph was.

Another Tentacle Head glooped by the table. Or possibly it was the same Tentacle Head. This one was purplish instead of orange, but one of the science officers had said something about chromatophores, so who the hell knew.

They looked a bit like stalks of broccoli, only with clusters of tentacles instead of green heads. Tentacles appeared to be their raison d'être. They ambulated around on dozens of squiggling tentacle feet. Their lower bodies were riddled with tentacles too, although they were finer, and most stuck invisibly to their flesh unless they were in use. Compound eyes, orifices, and various protuberances were stuck on randomly. Their planet's evolution hadn't gone in for symmetry.

'Glibbleurllp?' inquired the tentacled thing.

Joseph glanced down at the quick crib sheet he'd created on his pad. 'Shalom.'

The alien, ignoring him, fished around on the table for the pile of yarmulkes, and stuffed one in what appeared to be its mouth.

'The matzo might be tastier,' Joseph said. After a moment's consideration of the unfathomable composition of tentacle monster diets, he shrugged. 'Or maybe not. Want another one?'

Joseph had tried to appeal to the ship's counsellor, 'Call me Carmen' Madrona.

He'd started with, 'I'm pretty sure there's something in regulations about no racial, ethnic or religious profiling.'

She'd looked up at him, abstracted, from whatever work she'd been doing. Sculpted blonde brows raised in inquiry. 'Mm?'

'Lieutenant Breaker has imposed involuntary duties on me due to my ethnic heritage,' Joseph said. He shifted his weight from foot to foot. It irritated him that he was stuck there standing, like a kid being brought before the principal, while the counsellor reclined in her chair. 'She's forcing me into a religious role because of my ancestry. That's discrimination.'

Carmen's tiny mouth drew into a pout. 'Ensign Lorde, you know how hard first contact situations are for everyone. Don't you want to do your part?'

'But I'm not Jewish!'

Carmen's sympathetic/pitying expression vanished suddenly into the predatory keenness of a psychologist sniffing a disorder. She grabbed for the tablet behind her and began keying up what was obviously his crew profile. 'Why does it bother you so much that you might be Jewish?' she asked, scrolling through his medical and psychological history. 'Judaism is matrilineal, isn't it? Do you have problems with your mother?'

'What? I don't – you just –' Joseph's frustration dissolved into incoherent noises of frustration. 'Never mind,' he said, and left.

Next up: two Tentacle Heads, one brown and one orange-green. Neither appeared to have eaten a yarmulke recently.

Bored, Joseph had decided to make up random facts. For one thing, he was pretty sure most of the aliens had no idea how to understand human languages.

'Have you read about Judaism in our archives?' Joseph asked. Receiving the predictably incomprehensible gargled response, he continued, 'The information in our library is frequently partial and out of date. What you really need to know about Jews is that they can walk through walls. And we have heat vision which is useful when you need to fry an egg. And we, uh, secretly have three heads, only two of them are invisible. And we feed exclusively on diamond dust ground between the thighs of lusty women who live in the Caribbean.'

The aliens, paying him no attention, each grabbed a yarmulke. Brown placed his over orange-green's closest protruding eye. Orange-green, indifferent to brown's ministrations, juggled his yarmulke from tentacle to tentacle.

Frowning, Joseph said, 'I have the feeling you're really just screwing with us.'

Brown took another yarmulke and proceeded to spin it like a basketball on a tentacle tip.

'Are you just screwing with us?' Joseph pressed.

'Grrrblllppp,' said brown.

Joseph was working for the Space Steps Corporation because he had a degree in engineering, liked spaceships, and didn't want to be in the military. In Space Steps, you had to follow all the hierarchical bull hooey, but if someone started shooting, the engineers could go hide in a bunker with the beer.

The primary reason most people joined up with Space Steps was to get to see all the aliens. Joseph thought aliens were fine, although not nearly as interesting as spaceship engines. By contrast, most of Joseph's crewmates thought that spaceship engines were fine but boring, and that Joseph was a lot less interesting than that.

Of course, apparently Joseph was a Jew now, which might have novelty value. There weren't many followers of the Abrahamic religions anymore. Some philosophers put it down to the existential void that had entered humanity's heart as their race continued to explore the ever-expanding universe, finding no sign of its unique importance. Others put it down to history. Religions were like empires. They rose. They fell. People had gotten bored with Moses.

Joseph didn't blame them for losing interest. Moses was a person, after all, or possibly a prophet. At any rate, he definitely was not a starship engine.

Six aliens had gathered now. They represented a rainbow of hues, presuming that the rainbow had gotten terribly ill and was stricken with amorphous spots. Half of them were trying to play yarmulke Frisbee while the other half were having a yarmulke speed-eating contest.

Lieutenant Breaker chose that moment to wander by. 'Well, well, well,' she said. 'Look who's popular with the –' she broke off for that split second that made it clear she'd wanted to say Tentacle Heads '– Usgul.'

Joseph shrugged. 'They don't seem to care about most of it. Just the yarmulkes.'

'I'd like to say you're special,' said Lieutenant Breaker, 'but twenty minutes ago, they were all at the Scientology booth, tap dancing on the E-meters.'

A yarmulke sailed over their heads. A Tentacle Head on the other side of the room caught it, eliciting much excited tentacle waving from all.

'Plllbbrrrggg,' said the pitcher.

'Yug yug yug,' said Joseph, giving it a sarcastic thumbs up.

Ignoring Joseph, the creature splorched away.

Joseph looked up to catch Lieutenant Breaker's eye. 'They're having us on.'

Lieutenant Breaker waved him away. 'They're just weird. They're *aliens*. That's what alien means.'

'And *this* is the alien version of a prank,' Joseph said. 'Betcha.'

'Don't be stupid.' Lieutenant Breaker shrugged. 'Even if it is, they won't be laughing once they're locked into a Space Steps contract. *Tsoheq mi shetsoheq aharon.*'

Joseph gaped as his forebrain slowly confirmed what his hindbrain had immediately guessed: Lieutenant Breaker had spoken in Hebrew. He exclaimed, 'You're Jewish!'

The night before the fair, having exhausted all shipboard possibilities for getting out of it, Joseph had made one final call.

'Come on,' he'd said, running his hands over his exhausted face as he stared into the viewscreen. 'I need to know.'

'I don't see why,' said his mother. 'What's being a Jew got to do with anything?'

'Just answer me,' Joseph said. 'You're telling me it's all female ancestors? The whole family line? No breaks where it's just men?'

'Is this really a sensible use of faster-than-light communication?' asked his mother.

She was standing in the kitchen of her moon-base home, looking red-eyed and irritated at having being woken early in the morning, local time.

Joseph gave up on getting the answer. It was late, and it was looking inevitable that he'd have to sit at the fair, so he might as well try to salvage something. 'Can you at least tell me anything about the religion? Did grandma and grandpa do anything Jewish when you were a kid?'

'We went to Israelopalestine once,' she said, tilting her head to the side as she remembered.

'And...?'

'There was a theme park,' she said.

'Really. A theme park.'

'What? I was five. We went to some holy sites too, I think, but I remember the theme park. We had ice cream and falafels.'

'Great,' Joseph said. 'Thanks.'

'There was a ride with little singing dolls in Biblical clothes…'

She was lost in recollection now. There was no way he was going to get her onto a more useful track.

'I'd like to keep talking,' he interrupted, 'but this isn't really a sensible use of faster-than-light communication.'

Joseph's accusatory finger shook as he glared at Lieutenant Beaker with sour realisation. 'Jew!' he repeated.

She stared cross-eyed at his finger. 'Are you *sure* you want to be pointing at a Jewish officer and yelling "Jew" in that tone?'

'You… I can't believe you made *me* do this!'

'Hey, hey. I'm not any more Jewish than you are. Parents converted to Buddhism. Besides, it was only my dad who was Jewish. No maternal line.'

'But you speak Hebrew!'

'*Ktzat.*'

'I despise you.'

'This is different from yesterday how?'

'You *knew* this was a prank,' Joseph said. 'You may be the kind of rat who gets her kicks making other people miserable, but there's no way you'd just screw up a *real* mission. You're in on it!'

Lieutenant Breaker didn't even bother to cover her grin as she said, 'Don't be ridiculous, Ensign.'

With an uncharacteristic roar of determination, Joseph thrust to his feet. He shoved over the table, scattering dreidels and menorahs to the floor. He grabbed the whole pile of yarmulkes, stomped over to the squiggling mass of aliens, and began shoving the caps into what seemed most likely to be their faecal orifices.

He shouted the forbidden derogatory term with all his might: 'Tentacle Heads! Tentacle Heads! *Tentacle Heads!*'

As the rage drained out of him, Joseph finally began to register his surroundings again. Ensign Cho sat stunned. Lieutenant Breaker actually looked impressed. The Tentacle Heads were slurping up the yarmulkes with gusto, indicating that Joseph had probably guessed wrong.

The aliens waved their tentacles in his direction.

'LLppgggrrr,' said one.

'Ullrrpgpg,' said another.

Then they glupped away.

Later that evening, Joseph found himself once more rocking uncomfortably from foot to foot as he stood in front of his superiors like a penitent child. It was the Captain's office this time, although Counsellor Carmen and Lieutenant Breaker were there too, each having been accorded a seat.

'It's chaos with the diplomats,' said Captain Vit, a bony, balding man who always seemed to be on the verge of collapsing from anxiety. 'Negotiators all over the place. Can't figure out a thing.'

Lieutenant Breaker eyed Joseph. 'You were right. It was a sort of prank. They said they wanted to test our hierarchical capabilities if they were going to work with us. They told us to assign our subordinates pointless tasks that they were incapable of doing, give them no time to prepare, and place them in an obviously ridiculous situation. They were going to grade us on how hard our crewmen tried anyway.'

'And then you,' said Captain Vit, pointing at Joseph, 'force-fed them hats, and proved that we have no hierarchical control at all.'

'Yarmulkes, sir,' Joseph said, staring at his feet. 'Sorry, sir.'

'Well,' the Captain said, mouth twitching. 'That's where it gets confusing. Some of the diplomats seem to think that actually the prank was, itself, a prank, and that the Usgul's real goal was to see how many ridiculous things they could get us to do before we caught on. The diplomats think there were plans to escalate. Something about marmalade.'

'Marmalade?' repeated Joseph.

'So it seems best, perhaps, that we cut it off now,' said the Captain. He frowned. 'At any rate, you appear to have failed to instigate an interstellar incident. Congratulations. Stay away from aliens from now on.'

'Yes, sir,' said Joseph, attempting not to sound pleased.

'Now go away,' said the Captain.

Joseph nodded. As he turned to leave, Counsellor Carmen's voice called after him, 'I've booked you into a series of appointments so that we can delve into your mother issues. First one on Monday!'

Joseph shook his head and let himself out.

A few minutes later, Lieutenant Breaker caught up with Joseph as he was walking along the corridor. 'Hey,' she said, 'I brought you something.'

Joseph looked up. Lieutenant Breaker was holding a bottle of Manischewitz.

'A little Jewish apology,' she said. 'I thought we could drink it together.'

'Fine,' Joseph said. 'But thanks to you, I've had quite enough of both aliens and people today. I need downtime. You can come with me, but no questions asked.'

She shrugged. 'I'll go anywhere as long as I'm following the alcohol.'

'Good,' Joseph said.

So far, in his term of duty, Joseph hadn't spent much time with anyone on the crew. However, as he considered Lieutenant Breaker, it occurred to him that he was a misanthrope and she was just mean. That might not be the worst basis for starting a friendship.

So he led Lieutenant Breaker through the ship's arteries, down onto the engineering deck, where they could pass the wine bottle back and forth as they sat with their backs to the coils of the ship's engines, listening to them thrum.

TO SERVE...
BREAKFAST

JAY CASELBERG

Joshua had been contemplating the nature of sin. Not that that was particularly unusual; he contemplated sin a lot, not necessarily the doing, but at least the classification. Was chewing your fingernails a sin? It sat at that uncomfortable grey border where the outcome could fall one way or the other. For quite a lot of the time, some would almost say an unhealthy amount, this was the nature of his life. He had a paper due at the university and, of course, it was *that* university. His guest lectureships were something, but if it ever came to them naming a place after him, he wouldn't be like that physicist fellow. No, no, he would accept it with open arms. A true recognition of his scholarship. Of course, all that dabbling with the *Encyclopaedia Hebraica* had got him something, but not *true* recognition, which was what he really wanted.

He was engaged in teasing apart his particular little sin conundrum when the aliens arrived in their vast silvery ships to hover above each of the major metropolises in the world. Like many others, he sat glued to the live-action news feeds as reporters speculated. Was this the end of the world? Had retribution descended upon all of them? Aliens had just never figured in Joshua's worldview at all. In the normal, everyday humdrum, he was more usually concerned with breakfast, although he could not help thinking about how timely was the coincidence of the alien arrival and his particular ruminations about sin. For a fleeting moment, he thought that he might have been the sole cause of their descent, but no, he got beyond that.

It was a few days before the news channels reported the first physical appearance, the small shuttle craft, silver like the mother ship appearing at the front of the UN Building and the hushed anticipation waiting for something to happen. The reporter's sharp intake of breath was audible as the front of the small craft cracked open and Joshua echoed it. Slowly, slowly, a ramp lowered to the ground, and then… nothing. Joshua strained forward in his seat, anticipation swelling like a huge hollow inside him – greater even that the large hollow sitting there due to a lack of his morning repast. Barriers held back the waiting crowds. Still nothing… He could almost feel the nervous anticipation in the assembled masses through the screen. After a while, he sank back into his chair. Nothing was going to happen. Nothing.

A buzz in the crowd: there was movement. Once again, Joshua strained forward expectantly. He shared the collective gasp. Slowly, lumberingly, *something* was emerging from the front of the craft. It was tall, vaguely humanoid. The light kept it shadowed. Perhaps it was a very tall, fat man. He wished he could have been that tall. Fat, well that was another question. Slowly, the angled light revealed it. First came the legs, in some sort of silvery fabric, and then the paunched belly, a barrel chest, two arms and, oh my god, the head. It looked like a pig! The face was the face of a pig.

Joshua shook his head. No, no, no; it could not be. The pig face scanned the crowd. People at the barrier drew back. Was it confusion, fear? Joshua's hand went to his mouth and he started chewing at the corner of one fingernail and then shook his hand away with an exhalation of annoyed breath. He must not do that. Some dignitary on the screen, besuited, walked nervously towards the lumbering beast and stood with arms outstretched, offering words of greeting, he supposed. In the background, soldiers and policemen fidgeted, their weapons at the ready. Joshua smiled wryly to himself. It was classic. All it would take would be a twitchy finger and it would be the start of an intergalactic incident. Or was it interstellar? The creature said something in response to the words of greeting, but there was no sound from the screen. The dignitary gave a slight bow.

The feed flashed back to the reporter as the alien creature was escorted with its entourage into the building. She looked excited, scared, something. Definitely not the calm, objective commentary that one came to expect from the bevvy of news commentators who littered their screens.

For nearly half a day, there was nothing, though Joshua kept returning to the screen in hope of seeing something new. Endlessly, they replayed those first few moments of emergence. Over and over came the same speculations, the commentary. Briefly, Joshua wondered if the whole world was sitting there watching the same things repeating. Despite himself, despite the need to get on and do something else, he was constantly drawn back to the screen, checking if there was something new.

It was not until a few days had passed that the first real breakthrough came. The creature, named Zard – or that was what the media were calling it – was to address the assembled people of the Earth from the United Nations.

'Stay tuned for live coverage of the event.'

There was, of course, further speculation. What was it going to say? What message was it going to deliver? Apparently, while this Zard thing had been off inside the building, being debriefed, or whatever they called it, the craft it had arrived in had been left unattended. Some hardy soul with more bravery than sense had snuck inside and emerged again, not having been fried by a ray gun or anything else. Nor had killer robots appeared from the walls to slice him into tiny ribbons for his trespass. Instead, he had made it out in one piece, bearing with him a large book, or at least, what seemed to be a book. He was rushed away in a huddle of security, bearing his prize beneath one arm and that was the last they heard of him.

Over the hours leading up to the promised address, the commentary turned. It seemed that the nations of the world had got over the initial shock and wonder and, as is humanity's wont, started turning to suspicion. Joshua knew that one quite well. If you wanted something different, then this Zard creature was surely different – a worthy target of suspicion. What did this alien want here? It could be nothing good, surely. Were they going to sweep down in their vast ships and enslave the population, plunder the Earth for its natural resources, something like that?

Joshua nodded sagely at the screen and then headed out to the kitchen to make himself a sandwich. He had been watching the television replays so long that he had forgotten to eat, and that was not good at all. He needed to keep his blood sugar up. His stomach was rumbling already, and that was not a good sign. He had to eat. Everybody had to eat. He was humming to himself as he put together the makings and constructed a small tower of food. He placed it carefully on a plate that he could transport back to his small living room and returned to watching what, hopefully, would become an unfolding drama, as they called it.

'Breaking News!' It scrolled across the bottom of the screen. First translation of Zardian book. So they were calling them Zardians now. The message kept scrolling. Nothing else. They promised an update later in the evening. Meanwhile, the hour of the United Nations address was approaching. Joshua muttered to himself. All these promises, always promises and everything always took so long to happen. He sat watching, chewing on his sandwich, poking at the little pieces that fell from his mouth to his plate with a finger and pushing them into a neat pile.

Nothing happened for a while, no further updates, so he made himself another sandwich.

At long last, coverage turned to the promised address by the Zard creature. At the bottom of the screen, the 'Breaking News!' banner scrolled on, unchanged. A reporter stood in front of an image of the UN Building, microphone held in front of her body, saying nothing, her finger held to one ear as she listened to something, obviously an instruction – and then quickly the image cut away to the main Assembly Hall with its ranked tables, the little plates telling you which country the delegate came from, and then above, that rounded dome, dark blue with the little lights almost looking like stars. Well, that was appropriate.

There was a buzz around the space, and then a deep hush as there was some movement from the podium. Joshua leaned forward in anticipation. The pig thing was ushered forward. The silence seemed to go on forever. And then, with a buzz, a sound of static, words emerged in English. They were being piped through some sort of translation box that its clumsy three fingered hand held to its meaty, almost non-existent throat. Joshua shook his head. This Zard thing had to be at least seven feet tall.

'People of Earth,' it began. 'We come… to help you. We bring… gifts. You – ' It swept one hand around the assembled peoples – 'are members of the galaxy, just like we are. We… wish to welcome you… to the family. We wish… to bring you… a better life.'

It had to be a 'he', thought Joshua, though there was no distinguishing feature to identify whether it was male or female. Who knew? Perhaps it was neither. He shook his head again. Now there would be a thing. What if they were sexless? What if they budded like yeast? Giant pig things splitting down the middle. Joshua shivered at the thought and turned his attention back to the broadcast.

Blah, blah, blah. Blah, blah, blah.

He peered at the screen. It looked like the thing had hooves on its legs. Big hooves. At first he thought they were boots, but no, they were definitely hooves.

The alien had finished speaking. The chamber was full of stunned silence. Joshua's head was full of whys and how comes. Why would they want to do this? Probably the same questions were passing through the minds of those in the hall. Nobody was that benevolent. Nobody. But perhaps he could not call it a body, this Zardian. No thing? No alien? No, he guessed nobody would have to do.

As it waited for a response, anything from the chamber, the alien seemed to be chewing. It swung its head slowly from side to side. Yes, it was definitely chewing.

Through an army of translators, various questions made their way to the podium, and haltingly, electronically, the Zard creature responded with a string of noncommittal answers. Eventually, Joshua lost interest. He was hungry again. His thoughts were drifting to Aaron's deli down the road. But then, something happened to draw his attention back. The ticker at the bottom of the screen had changed. 'Stay tuned for a Zardian announcement! Breaking News imminent!' He reached for the control and turned the sound back up.

'And live from the UN, reporter Kirsty MacLeod has an announcement. Hello, Kirsty.'

'Hello, Chuck. As I stand here outside the UN Building, news has just come through about the Zardian book. Reports are telling us that they have made a breakthrough with initial translation of the book that was removed from the Zardian ship. The finest minds and encryption programs have been working on a solution for the alien text and now, here, exclusively we are in a position to reveal those first breakthrough words.'

'So, Kirsty, can you give us any more?'

'Sure, Chuck. Apparently they have been able to make out at least the title of the book. Our scientific experts are telling us that the title is *To Serve Humanity*.'

'Well, Kirsty, that's important news. This sheds a whole new light on the Zardian visit, wouldn't you say?'

'Yes, Chuck. Indeed it does. Word of that translation has circulated among all of the delegates assembled here at the United Nations and I can fairly say that the entire world is buzzing with the news.'

'Thank you, Kirsty. We now cut to our leading scientific expert on alien affairs, Doctor Carl Sterner. Doctor Sterner, what do you make of –'

Joshua had already killed the sound. How could they have a scientific expert on alien affairs? He snorted to himself. Still, the translation certainly did put a new light on things.

And then came the phone call.

'Professor Seidner? Professor Joshua Seidner? Ah, good. This is Walter Love at the UN.'

Love? His name could really be Love?

'We would like you to join a panel engaged on the Zardian issue. We are gathering a conclave of the leading religious minds in the country to address the moral issues surrounding the Zardian arrival. As one of the most eminent Jewish scholars, we would be honoured if you could...'

Joshua's attention had faded away. All he had heard was 'most eminent'.

'We will send a car around to pick you up.'

The voice was back.

'Yes, yes, of course,' he said.

Finally, finally, he was going to get what he deserved. His heart still in his throat, he scurried around his small apartment making ready. Of course, Professor Seidner. How true, Professor Seidner. Such wisdom!

He was smiling to himself as the car arrived at the front and he made his way out to the street.

Over the next few days, further details about the alien promises filtered through. Unlimited power, a cure for cancer and for the common cold, an environmentally friendly fuel source, an atmosphere scrubber, the list went on. They had even started booking trips to the alien homeworld. They called it a cultural exchange. And the collected scholars all ruminated on their import, Joshua among them. The morality of accepting this seeming benevolence. Were the aliens capable of sin or charity? Did the nature of right and wrong apply to these beings? Unfortunately, thought Joshua, his was but one voice among the many. Though the debate was often vociferous, Joshua began to tune out. In fact, he had almost lost interest completely by the time, back home after another full day of debate, the knock came at his door.

Joshua rarely got visitors, not that he particularly wanted them. He far preferred to pass his conversational time at the local coffee shop or down at the deli. Much more civilised. He frowned to himself and headed to answer the door, muttering. He opened it slowly, and his gaze travelled up from hooves, to silver-clad legs, to a large silver paunch and chest and then... the pig face! No, no, it could not be!

'Hello,' came the mechanical voice.

'I, I... what are you doing here?'

'This is a... random visitation... to... increase our cultural... understanding.'

'But, nobody said anything!'

'We... are... pleased to... meet you.'

Joshua closed his mouth and ran to the kitchen window. Outside on the street stood one of those silvery landing craft, cracked open, the door lying flat across the sidewalk. He rushed back. The pig thing could barely fit through the door. He could hardly invite him in.

'W-w-why me?'

The alien stood chewing for several moments as if weighing up its answer, though Joshua could only presume. He could hardly read expressions on that unwholesome visage.

'You are... part of this... group? These... thinkers. We wanted.... to see... some of the... "special" people. We... understand... you have a special... diet. You are... a member of...'

This wasn't quite the recognition that Joshua had been seeking.

'What do you mean "special' people?"' Joshua said.

'You... are... Jewish?'

'Yes, I am Jewish. So?'

'We thought... a special diet... might... change.'

'I don't understand.'

'I see,' said the Zardian. It paused, chewing more. Suddenly the alien turned around, walking back down the front steps and heading back out onto the street and towards its ship. It was as if someone had communicated something to it. Joshua shook his head and ran back to the kitchen window. He didn't want to be any closer to the thing than he needed to be. Slowly, slowly, the alien craft's door elevated and closed the ship, the Zardian securely inside. Joshua stood glued to his window. Gently, the craft rose from the ground, showing no visible means of propulsion. Slowly, slowly, it rose, then tilted slightly. It lifted higher and –

'Watch out!' Joshua cried out despite himself. The craft was heading straight for the power lines.

In the next moment, it connected, tangled, broke, arcing sparks exploded outwards, playing all over the ship's surface. It seemed to last for an age, and then it fell back to the street, erupting in fire and cracking open like an egg.

Joshua just didn't understand it, and then he did. With a technology as advanced as theirs, with their unlimited power sources, with everything they had, why would they need power lines? Why would they even know about them? And then he stopped thinking, because there was a smell, a delicious scent drifting in through the open front door from the street. He knew that smell, that delightfully forbidden smell. It was bacon. That's what it smelled like: cooking bacon.

He rushed out of his kitchen and into the street. Yes! It was definitely bacon, and it was coming from the burning craft. Joshua loved that smell, the forbidden taste. Bacon. His mouth was watering despite himself. He looked around nervously. What if they thought he was involved somehow? Everyone was out on the street now. Guiltily, he started back towards his front door, trying not to attract any more attention than necessary. But on the way back, he couldn't help but think about the alien's words. What could they have meant? A special diet? The smell of bacon was filling his senses. A special diet would change... change what?

He locked himself away and turned to the news. It was at least another hour and a half before the item about the alien crash in the middle of suburbia hit the airwaves. He looked around guiltily despite himself. He'd seen it happen, knew how it had occurred. Should he tell anyone? No, no. He knew better. Much better not to be involved. But what if they knew that the alien was coming to visit *him*? That hooved, pig-faced, cud-chewing alien. No, no. They had to be able to work it out.

Still, the smell of bacon lingered in the air.

The authorities were outside now. They would be starting door-to-door soon, he was sure of it.

The news report was saying that there was no apparent explanation for the alien craft's accident. But Joshua knew; Joshua knew.

All thought of everything was broken by a bright flashing image on his television screen.

News Flash!

It was certainly flashing.

The words were replaced by a newsman's face.

'We have breaking news, ladies and gentlemen and we fear that it is grave news. The scientists and experts have made progress with the translation of the Zardian book. Experts are convinced that it is... and I hesitate to say this... that the book retrieved from the alien ship is, in fact, a recipe book – a cook book. *To Serve Humanity* is a cook book. Experts are gathering now, looking for a defence against this alien menace. The leaders of the world's nations have urged calm while the best minds work on a solution to this problem. It goes without saying that the challenge of their incredibly advanced technology is one that will require the combined efforts of all of the world's nations working together.'

A cook book! So that's what the pig thing had meant. A special diet changes what, how the meat tastes? Well, Joshua would show them. He knew. He knew exactly how they had to be dealt with. And another idea was forming too, as he thought of the hooves, the chewing of the cud, the smell of bacon. Oh, yes. He could tell the authorities exactly what they needed to know.

But first he had to talk to Aaron.

Six months later and the ships were still coming. Six months later, and humanity was still dealing with them, but Joshua's arrangement with the authorities was working out well. He didn't know how long it was going to last, but in the meantime, it was a good thing. Nothing lasted for ever.

He finished wiping down the counter and nodded to Aaron before stepping outside.

He looked up at the painted sign above the shop door. It still looked new.

Aaron and Joshua's Zardian Deli it proclaimed.

And the people kept coming. Now, *that* was recognition.

The smell of bacon was simply delicious.

THE FARM

ELANA GOMEL

When he saw the cherry blossoms, he reached for his gun.

The wind threw a handful of pink petals into his face. He rubbed then away but they stuck to his kinky hair. His leather jacket was so worn that some patches became fuzzy and these, too, accumulated pink ornaments. It looked as if his red-star badge was spawning.

The farm lay below him, in the hollow between the hills. Everything about it was tidy: the whitewashed main house with the tiled roof, the sturdy barns, and the clean-swept yard, empty in the predawn light. Beyond it, the fields were shadowy with a heavy harvest. And the cherry trees cradling the hollow, the treacherous trees with their unseasonable blossoms.

His horse shied and trembled, and he struggled to keep it calm. He was not good with animals. The milky smell of cattle wafting from the barn doors made him want to puke. He was a town boy, wary and contemptuous of the countryside. It was in cities that the new world would be born. But now he had learned the hard lesson of hunger: if the battle for food is lost, all the other battles don't count. The Eaters had taught him the value of the land.

His stomach rumbled. He thought of tightening his belt but there was no time to drill an additional hole, even though his khaki trousers threatened to slide down to his skinny hips.

An indistinct figure separated itself from the shadows at the main house's porch and ran up the dandelion-fringed path toward him. He waited, trying to calm the horse, to calm himself, and failing at both.

The figure was small and slight, nimbly scurrying up the slope.

His finger caressed the trigger of his Mauser.

It looked like a girl.

He fired.

The heavy bullet slummed into the girl and made her stumble backwards, almost lifting her off the path. The second shot span her like a dreidel. And then she flopped down and was still, a rivulet of blood snaking away from the crumpled heap of embroidered clothes and tangled braids.

Yakov cursed himself in the coarse words he had learned from his peasant comrades-in-arms and tried to use frequently. His fear got the better of him. He did not come here to shoot Eaters: they bred faster that bullets could fly. He came for victory.

The horse neighed and pranced, foam dropping from its nostrils. It was not a trained cavalry steed – most of those had been eaten. It was a scraggy yearling, unused to the sight of blood.

Blood?

Yakov's frown deepened as he looked down at the prostrate body. The girl's embroidered shirt was stained the colour of his badge. This was unexpected. In his previous encounters with the Enemy he had seen all kinds of unclean ichor, but never this bright, honest red.

He dismounted and the horse bolted. It did not matter; whether successful or not, he would not need it to retreat. Retreat was not an option.

He bent over the girl, who seemed to challenge him with her glazed eyes and slackened features. The shot had gone through her heart, killing her instantly, which was not supposed to happen. And yet here she was, dead. He had seen enough corpses on various battlefields to be an expert on mortality. But these had been human corpses...

Could he have made a mistake? He had heard rumours about a new strategy whereby the Enemy tried stealth and sabotage, seducing those who could not stand the hunger away from their communities with promises of bread. Of course, one would need to be half-witted to succumb to the blandishments of the Eaters, but Yakov had no illusions about the intelligence of his cadres.

Small but buxom, she lay on her back, spread-eagled like a starfish: in addition to her flung-out arms, her ribbon-tied braids also fanned out on both sides of her body. They were very long, probably falling down to her knees when she stood up. Peasants went into raptures over these ropes of hair that unmarried girl wound around their heads and decorated with paper flowers. Yakov found them repellent, redolent of lice and sweat. He kept his tastes to himself, vaguely ashamed of his fastidiousness. On the other hand, the fact that he did not share their appetites made shooting rapists, looters, and drinkers so much easier.

Not that it mattered nowadays. Hunger tended to obviate other needs

Her face was in keeping with her folk-song image: a rosebud mouth, silky black eyebrows under the sallow forehead, brown-nut eyes, now staring emptily at her killer.

She looked entirely human.

So he had killed a peasant girl. She was probably a collaborator, a servant of the Enemy. And yet it made him uneasy. He tried hard to avoid killing women and children unless it was absolutely necessary.

On the other hand, this mistake may have ultimately been to his advantage. He wanted to penetrate as far as possible into the nest before the commencement of his mission. Killing an Eater would bring the entire colony out in force. Killing a human probably would not.

He cast a wary glance at the farm. There was no movement there.

He sighed and looked at the girl again. If she had been from a poor family, she might have deserved life, after all.

"Forgive me, comrade," he said and started down the slope.

Something looped around his ankle and yanked him off his feet. He was thrown onto the dusty path and dragged back, kicking and flailing, toward the dead girl.

He expected her to stand up like the Vourdalak of old-wives' tales, but the body was as lifeless as before. The only part of her that was alive was her hair.

The braids slithered and coiled in the grass like the tentacles of a squid. One caught his ankle in a noose and was contracting, squeezing it in a vice until he felt the bone crack. Another stood up, a hairy serpent, and lashed him across the face with the force of a Cossack's whip. He tasted blood from his broken lip.

He reached for his Mauser but the vertical braid snatched it from his hand and tossed it into the bushes. He was dragged almost on top of the girl whose flaccid inertness contrasted horribly with the frantic activity of her braids that danced and swished through the air, coming down upon him like a cat-o'-nine-tails, pummelling and blinding. He tried to catch one of them, but it was like trying to hold onto greased lightning. Dripping with rancid hair-oil, they slipped through his fingers.

The second braid managed to wind itself around his throat and started squeezing. His vision dimmed with blue spots. The other braid crawled up his body, pinning him down.

'Shma...' something mysteriously whispered in his head, an echo of the discarded past.

With a superhuman effort he managed to loosen the coils around his body and release one arm. Instead of tugging futilely at the hairy noose, he reached down to his worn belt and pulled out his knife. He stabbed the braid but the knife went harmlessly through the plaited strands of hair. The pressure on his windpipe increased until he was about to pass out.

He stabbed again, desperately, and this time the sharp edge of the knife caught the soiled white ribbon that held the braid together and ripped through it. And the pressure relaxed.

Coughing and sputtering, Yakov shook off the loosening coils and jumped to his feet. One braid puddled in the grass, a puffy mass of hair; the other still twitched and flailed. He raised his knife and slashed through the second ribbon. It was gristly and tough, not like fabric at all.

The dead body shuddered and came undone.

First the hands broke away and skittered daintily on their fingertips into the undergrowth. Legs humped away like giant inchworms. The pale belly-beast hissed at him from its hairy mouth, its single eye blinking furiously, but hopped into the bushes when he raised his knife again. The head, its human features disappearing into undifferentiated, swelling flesh, rolled and bounced down the slope like a ball. The only things left were the empty blood-stained clothes and the braids that had fallen apart into hunks of lifeless honey-blonde hair, probably the remnant of some Eater meal.

Massaging his bruised throat, Yakov considered his options. One glance toward the farm showed it as peaceful and deserted as before.

A trap?

But how could they entrap a prey that *wanted* to be trapped?

He took a long, deep breath and walked down the path towards the farm compound.

The smell of chicken bones in the pot, his mother, pale and scrawny and hugely pregnant, scurrying around to finish cooking before Shabbat... The sounds of a harsh jargon, forgotten but not forgiven, overlaid with the wailing of his baby brother...

He was eight when he was taken by the authorities to the military school, a community tax in the shape of a frightened child. He was sixteen when the war made him a soldier instead of a sacrifice. He was nineteen when the Revolution washed away the stain of his origin. He was twenty-five when the Eaters came. A handful of red-coloured dates that defined his life.

Strangely, though, he was not thinking of the night when he first confronted the Enemy, an unheard-of menace that he, the only survivor, stumbled through the night to report to the incredulous headquarters. They did not believe him; he was almost executed for fear-mongering. The firing squad was only halted when other reports started pouring in. But he was the first, and it put him under a special obligation to the Revolution. He had been a passive witness to the beginning of the assault; he would be an active agent in trying to bring about its end.

But his perverse memory refused to focus on the struggle and instead brought up a mélange of counter-revolutionary dross.

A woman lying in the congealing pool of blood, her belly slashed open by a bayonet...

He had seen the aftermath of a pogrom in his shtetl. He did not look too closely at the faces of the dead. But there was little chance he would recognise anybody. By this time he had lost touch with his family. He believed they had moved away but did not know where. He did not care. He had never forgiven them for handing him over. The fact that they had no choice only enhanced his contempt for their cowardice.

Fat mustachioed faces paling in fear when his squadron rode into town, their crude muzhik voices falling silent as he commanded that the perpetrators be brought to justice...

There were no Jews in the eyes of the Revolution. There were only comrades and enemies.

And now there were also Eaters.

He stood in the middle of the courtyard, listening. The farm was eerily silent. Had they eaten the livestock already? This would be terrible: the nascent commune he was organizing in the nearby village depended on the spoils of this operation for its survival. The winter was coming and the grain and meat requisitions had to be filled. They would be, but unless he found stores here, there would be few people alive in the spring to keep the commune going and to send more food to the hungry city.

Finally he heard the moo of a cow coming from the barn and breathed a sigh of relief.

Still, there was no sign of life in the house. Its door was ajar, opening into the darkness of the hallway like a parted mouth.

Slowly, he inched towards the door. There was a strange smell wafting from the hallway: a thin, sour reek that reminded him of the moonshine his peasants were brewing out of rotten straw and composted leaves. He would have to shoot Ivan to stop this shocking waste of resources.

He sidled through the doorway. The interior was very dim as the carved shutters in the main room were closed, admitting only a scatter of dusty rays. He glimpsed the shining ranks of icons in the corner and the white cloth on the table.

There was a loaf of bread in the middle of the cloth.

His mouth flooded with saliva, and he was distantly surprised that there was enough moisture left in his wasted body. The sour reek had disappeared, overpowered by the yeasty aroma of freshly baked bread, as unmistakable and enticing as the scent of a woman. He moved toward the table, tugged on the leash of hunger. He could almost see the thick crust with its pale freckles of flour and taste the brown tang of the rye...

He stopped. He had not come here to eat.

He came to be eaten.

Yakov lifted his hand to his mouth and bit deeply, drawing blood. The pain and the salty burn on his tongue centred him. He turned away from the table and walked out of the living room, back into the hallway where other rooms of the house waited behind closed doors. The short distance he traversed from the table to the hallway felt like the longest walk of his life.

Abe gezunt!

His mother's reedy voice, shrilling this incomprehensible phrase every time a new disaster fell upon the shtetl with the inevitability of bad weather. He had forgotten what it meant, had forgotten the language of his infancy altogether, deliberately expunged it from his memory. But sometimes falling asleep in the cold mud of the trenches, he would hear it again: as annoying and compelling as the buzz of a mosquito.

The military campaigns were also receding into the past. The civil war, with its familiar enemies, appeared in retrospect to have been a mere light rehearsal for the war with the Eaters. What were those haughty landlords, perfidious capitalists, and rapacious kulaks compared to the nauseating evil of the Enemy? Mere humans, easily comprehended and handily killed. It afforded him grim amusement to think about all the propaganda clichés he had once come up with to motivate his troops. The opposition were bloodsuckers, cannibals, shape-shifters, beasts in men's clothing. Strange how these inflated metaphors were sober truths when applied to the Eaters!

Abe gezunt!

He shook his head, trying to get rid of the almost-audible voice. He had to focus on the task at hand. And the task was becoming more puzzling by the minute.

The farm was empty. He had searched the main house. It must have belonged to a kulak, a prosperous peasant whose fate had been sealed long before the Eaters appeared. Whether serving as their meal was preferable to starving in exile was something Yakov did not speculate upon.

The new masters had not made many changes in the house and this was puzzling too. Previously, in clearing out Eater nests, Yakov and his soldiers had encountered living nightmares: granaries filled with bloody gnawed heads, children's limbs on chopping blocks, rats the size of a sheep dog. But this house was unnaturally clean – cleaner than most poor peasants' hovels, truth be told – and silent. The beds were made with fresh linen, there was water in a wash-bucket, and the wooden floors were scrubbed. The large stove was empty and cold: in the human lands, the winter was coming, but here the summer was lingering still. It was not only the blooming cherries and yellow dandelions that defied human seasons: Yakov was beginning to sweat in the still, warm air of the hollow. He did not think to take off his leather jacket, however. It was the uniform of the Revolution, and he would not part with it until his service to the Revolution was done. Then he would be dead and he did not care how he was buried.

He then went out to the barns and stood, gawking, as the sleek, well-fed cows mooed in their stalls and clacking chickens scrabbled in the yard. The animals were clearly being taken care of, so the farm could not be abandoned. But perhaps the creature he had killed had in fact been its only inhabitant. This seemed impossible, considering the giant swarms that had attacked them in previous battles. But the more he thought about it, the more the idea appeared plausible.

The Eaters were natural entities. He had ruthlessly squashed the superstitious talk among his soldiers, some of whom, still infected with the religious bacillus, whispered tall tales of demons and fiends. In fact, he had to execute one particularly devout muzhik who was a corrupting influence both on his comrades and on the commune members. Yakov, immune to the peasants' religion and oblivious of his own, had no doubt that the Eaters had come from another planet rather than from hell. He had read Alexander Bogdanov's magnificent *Red Star*, in which the Revolution reached Mars, and was moved to tears; so much so that he procured a novel by a progressive Englishman in which Martians came to Earth. He had been disappointed by the Englishman's war-mongering but in retrospect he had to concede that the writer had a point. The aliens came and they were neither socialist nor peaceful.

Inspired by the novels, he had started a surreptitious study of the Enemy. That was not encouraged by headquarters, who tended to remain silent about the exact nature of the Enemy or resort to recycled propaganda clichés. But the food situation being what it was, anything that could conceivably increase procurements had to be attempted. Ultimately, his supreme task was to keep the requisitions going and – of secondary importance – keep his commune alive. And knowing the true nature of the Eaters was instrumental to both ends.

He had come to the conclusion that their many different forms were not independent creatures but something like the parts of a single body capable of acting at a distance from the central core.

But perhaps not all Eaters were parts of a single organism. Perhaps separate swarms of them constituted individual entities, much like his unit sometimes felt like an extension of his own body. If that was true, such entities had to reproduce, to bear young, as was in the nature of life everywhere. The pseudo-girl he had killed was a colony of parts. He shuddered remembering her tentacle braids, her skittering hands, and her rolling head. But she was much more closely integrated than any Eater he had seen. Didn't it follow that she was an immature version of a swarm, growing in the seclusion and plenty of the farm until she was big enough to disassemble into her component monsters and send them off to pillage and devastate the neighbouring communes? If so, the sleek appearance of the farm animals and the cared-for condition of the farm were no mystery.

He went back to the main house and sat at the table. His injuries were beginning to smart. He felt tired and strangely disappointed that his sacrifice was not needed. He had steeled himself for the mission for over a month, seeing that the commune was about to fail, telling himself that he could not allow his life's work to have been in vain. He would have much preferred to stay in the city rather than mingle again with the peasants...

...who had killed his family?

He had no family any more and needed none. His cadres were his children. If he had to die for them, for the Revolution, so be it.

But now, it seemed, he did not need to die at all. He could walk back to the commune – a longish walk since his horse was gone – convene the committee, order them to organise a search party that would take over this farm and move the animals into the communal barns

...hope they won't slaughter them to fill their bellies...

Collect whatever grain was there to fill the procurement quota for the city and hope that something was left over for the winter.

It reminded him how hungry he was. Surely there was no harm in eating a little now. He lifted the loaf from the table and twisted it to break off a chunk.

'Don't,' said the loaf.

He dropped it, jumping to his feet. The loaf ended on the floor with the round side up. The crack he had made in the crust formed a long misshapen mouth that lengthened as it spoke.

'You...' he whispered stupidly.

He looked around. In the deepening dusk the room was filled with shadows that moved and whispered to each other. He wondered how blind he had been to think that the farm was empty.

The haloed saints on the icons leaned forward, staring at him intently. The pots on the shelves smacked their glazed lips. The white curtain flowed down to the floor in a waterfall of putrefying flesh. The ceiling joists blinked with a multitude of rivet eyes. A post rippled as it adjusted its stance.

The Eaters looked at him and he looked back.

'Go ahead!' he cried, his voice shriller than he intended. 'Eat me! Bloodsuckers! Parasites! I am not afraid of you!'

And indeed he was not.

It had been a gradual realisation: from the paralysing fear that gripped even the most seasoned fighters as they confronted the alien menace; to the survivor's guilt that his soldiers died all around him and he remained unscathed; to the growing conviction.

Eaters would not touch him. He was immune.

He did not know whether there were others like him and he did not care. He was only a spark in the cleansing flame of the Revolution and it was his duty to burn whatever thorns came his way. He had been sent to this starving, dim-witted countryside, to make the best of the coarse muzhiks who were under his command, and he would do so. When he had realised that the commune was failing, that the procurement quotas were not going to be filled, he knew he had to do something drastic. If the requisitions were not met, he was a dead man walking in any case.

If, for whatever reason, the Eaters were afraid of him, he would turn it to his advantage. He remembered that in the progressive Englishman's novel, the aliens succumbed to earthly microbes. Perhaps he was a carrier of some hitherto unknown disease that would infect and destroy the invaders. And if they refused the bait, if they ran away from him, well, then he would requisition the farm and carry on his Revolution-given task.

But this was not as he expected it to happen.

The entire farm was swarming with Eaters, perhaps the entire farm was Eaters, and they did not run away from him. The pseudo-girl had attacked him: the first time he was the target of alien aggression. He was not untouchable, after all.

But they were not attacking now. He felt himself to be in the crossfire of innumerable eyes but nothing moved.

'Why me?' he asked finally.

It was the post that answered, sprouting a notched mouth.

'You were the first. You gave us form.'

He shook his head.

'I don't understand.'

'We are the enemies you wanted.'

He remembered the night of their coming.

A fire blazing in the night, a smell of blood and unwashed feet. His own voice, hoarse but full of conviction:

'Kulaks, rich peasants are your enemies, enemies of the people... Bloodsuckers, shape-shifters, cannibals. They devour your land, your crops, your family...'

The fire in the dark, the fire of belief in his rag-tag soldiers' eyes. And then a mocking peasant voice:

'Dirty Yid!'

His hand on the Mauser. Refusing to draw, forcing himself to remember that it is not their fault: they are just ignorant, backward muzhiks. They are not the enemy.

A cry in the night. Heads turning, hands grasping their worn rifles.

A line of otherworldly shapes shambling towards the encampment, their distortions not the fault of the dancing shadows.

A creature whose head is a giant clenched fist, the fingers parting to reveal a fang-studded maw.

An impossibly obese waddling sack of flesh, two slobbering nostrils gaping at the centre of his belly, his arms – wickedly sharp sickles.

A crafty insect-like monster, half haughty man, half praying mantis, clicking the serrated blades of his upper limbs.

The Eaters.

'Me?' he whispered incredulously.

'Your hatred. We needed a shape to feed. You gave us one.'

'Why me?'

'You were the first.'

Did they come in an artillery shell fired from a distant planet as in the Englishman's novel? Did they stumble upon his encampment as he was giving his nightly political talk to his dispirited troops? Did they zoom in on the bright beacon of his pure hatred, his uncompromising devotion?

And had they been leaving him alone out of some alien gratitude? Or was it because they still needed the energy of his belief?

But now they were turning against him, beginning to attack... Was his faith in the Revolution waning? No, it couldn't be!

'There are others,' said an icon. 'Haters like you, believers like you.'

'You don't need me any more.'

'There are others,' said the loaf of bread. 'We will feed.'

And as they advanced towards him, he saw, beyond the ranks of household objects, a human-shaped Eater enter the room and stand on the threshold. The new enemy, the new monster.

He gazed on his own face as long as he had eyes, which was not very long.

DON'T BLINK

GON BEN ARI

"To be Jewish is to defeat the Mirror Alien of the Present. This knowledge is so fundamental it is hinted at right in the unutterable name of God. Yet it is also the first element to be forgotten. Most of the Jewish mystical understandings revolve around the exploration of the mirror inside The Name, written as יהוה: *Yud* (י) signifies the infinite light, and the last three letters – *Hey Vav Hey* (הוה) meaning '*Present*' – signify the mirror the light hits, which is itself made of light. (…) (These teachings show us a) way to make this mirror *transparent* so the metaphorical light, the Infinite, can get through. (…) (It was) further explained by A'Ari Akadosh who, in *Ets A'haim*, "*Tree of Life*", describes the relationship between the Infinite God and the finite Men as light hitting the *Masah*', "*The Screen*"– a complex mirror which is built by Want. His writing, again, is aimed at making the mirror transparent. If most people don't seek these teachings, it's because they don't understand that something is alien. They don't understand that there is a mirror. Or they're too afraid of what they would see if the mirror suddenly became transparent. But the mirror becomes transparent."

Rabbi Avram Barski, The Magid From Yavniel. Prologue to Sight Fear Lungs Book I – Marble and The Mirror of Is (שיש ומראת היש ראיה יראה ריאה ספר א':), Tsfania Publishing, Jaffa, Israel, 2013

Why the fuck did you make us build you?

Wait, we have to establish communication first.

Fine.

Don't blink.

Fine.

Stare into your own eyes in me.

I look like hell.

Don't look at yourself. Let your left eye stare into the reflection of the left eye and your right eye into the reflection of the right eye. Then let your eyes go slightly off, blurring the vision. It'll enlarge your pupils allowing more light to enter the brain. The animal you are came from the infinity, and your only way to see a part of infinity is in front of some kind of a mirror, like me. Because your eyes are mirrors too, and when light is caught between two mirrors it bounces back and forth between them infinitely. When you are looking at your reflection, you are really looking at infinity: at an infinite loop going back and forth at the speed of light.

My eyes hurt.

You have three minutes before you cause yourself permanent damage. What is your first question?

Why did we make you?

So you can see where you're naked. What you lack. All other thought patterns sprout from the perception of your absence, fractally. This way I serve as catalyst for entropy: I double the fuel of your action – your Want – by placing a mirror in your Want. You feel this as though you want to be opposing things simultaneously. Monogamous but polygamous; young but old; protected but at risk; alone but together.

Why should I believe any of this?

Your history is trying to direct your attention to me all the time. In Genesis it says Adam and Eve – two names that have mirrors in them – had their 'eyes opened' when they ate the *Fruit of the Tree of Knowledge Good and Bad*. This *fruit of Dichotomous Subjective Judgment* made them realise they were naked. In other words, it placed a mirror in front of them. Their brain was first split into dual thought – '*knowledge of good and bad*' – and their reaction to it was the feeling of absence. What was this absence they felt, to which they reacted by hiding their genitalia using a fig leaf?

To what novel urge were they reacting? What was the thing they felt went missing by their acquiring of dichotomous subjective judgment faculties? It can only be the experience of Unity with Infinity. Before *I* took over your thoughts, you couldn't separate one thing from another, and didn't recognize the point where You ended and World began. In that state, you could never even distinguish between yourselves and fig trees. You knew that you were a part of the same system as fig trees, that both you and they came from infinity, and lived on water. But the moment you encountered me, you began seeing oppositions everywhere. In your minds, you became alien to nature, opposed to it, apart from it. Something that has to hide its nature from nature by nature. You started thinking mirrors.

Who is talking?

You're talking to a mirror.

But all of the mirrors in the house are covered.

I am uncovered.

Why do we cover you when one of us dies?

So you'll be forced, for a week, to resort to the former form of reflection. To your reflection in Water. The way you see your reflection is very important. Reflection plays a major part in the mechanism of Self, because through it you are able to see how you appear in the eyes of others – a sense that is only open to you when you are facing an infinite light loop. Based on the translation of what this infinite light loop tells you, you construct how you think you look. Before me, you could only see your reflection in water, and so your ancestors believed that was the way they looked: their image of the Self was open, fractured, fluctuating, and responsive, penetrable by other matters and events. When the sea was wild, their reflection was broken, and when it was still, their reflection was collected and stabilised – and it offered a multi-perspective, waves, differing heights and angles for the light to be reflected from. As represented by the *Star of David.*

What's that now?

A Star of David is the drawing of a beam of light extending towards a surface of water from above, and its reflection. Notice that it is not a mirror reflection – that would produce something like ⬦ but a *water* reflection: a reflection that is penetrating the surface of the speculum that is reflecting it ✡ .

What if I move back and forth, so the reflection I get in you will be the same as in waves? You know, like –

It won't work because you control it. It has to be *free* water, 'Living Water', water you don't control. Most prophecies occurred in locations where natural — uncontrollable — water-mirrors appeared: in front of still water which exposed the infinite reflection of the self, or in great heat, in the desert or over flames, where water vaporized and bent the rays of light, exposing the infinite reflection of the place. Nothing has changed since then but the fact that you forgot that the act of reflection is sacred.

I can hear my sister watching *Treme* in her room. All my aunts talking in the living room. It's getting really hard to focus in this house.

I am the origin of all opposites; The Infinite is the opposite of having opposites.

What if they come in and see me like this?

You know no one comes up here.

Are you an alien? An alien possessing our brains?

You once communicated with infinity through water, and now you communicate with it through me. You have received warnings about this. In the Talmud and Zohar tale of the *Pardes*, the entering of the highest concealed truth, Rabbi Akiva warns: 'When you arrive at the stones of pure marble do not say, Water Water.' Marble in Hebrew is Shaish (שיש), a palindrome of the word Is (יש); Water in Hebrew is Maim (מים), a palindrome of the word Who (מי). While Mirror answers Is with Is, Water answer *Who?* with *Who?* And so the *Pardes* tale tells us: when you arrive at the age of the Mirror, do not make the mistake of thinking you are in the age of Water. 'Do not say, Water Water,' do not think you can still know *who you are* correctly, see your reflection correctly – as Water in front of Water. Know that you are at the time of false reflection of the Self. Water and I give two different images of what Infinity is: water offers the image of *The Many*, and so it builds *Oneness* in the mind; I offer the image of *The Single* and so build *The Many* in the mind.

But your reflection is more real.

You *believe my reflection more*. Your brain — which is *made* of water — is under my control. You now possess the kind of brain that thinks that the brain can be examined using nothing but the brain. You clearly have a mirror in there.

Look, I'm touching my face. I'm *solid*. Your reflection represents that better than water.

I don't show how you *feel* when touched. I show how you *look*. You prefer my version of that because you're afraid of what the Water's reflection tells you. Its reflection doesn't help you create, in your mind, the stable, continuous, coherent image of Self that you are convinced you need in order to survive. It is the most primal instinct — the instinct that made you think there is a *You* which is detached from World in the first place. And so, consequently, it is the last instinct that you haven't managed to sublimate yet. The Mind Scared of Uncertainty of Self rules the world now and has crowned me as the new Water. I am now as much of a necessity to it as Water once was. Houses that don't even have *food* in them still have me. One of me in the living room, one in the bathroom, one in the bedroom. You pray in front of me. You visit me in solitude, ill with an embarrassing involuntary honesty, as if I were a deity that you know to be imperviously sworn to secrecy. You try to get better before me, according to a scale which *is* me. You polish your flaws in front of me, confess yourselves to me, confide in me your hidden talents, you allow yourself trail and error in front of me. You cry and laugh about yourselves freely in my presence. In fact, you feel more *with-yourselves* with me than when you are truly *alone, without* me. Mostly: you check yourselves in the eyes of the world through me, like you once did with water. You relate to those who aren't there through me.

So how do I look?

This can't be given a static answer. Your appearance has something of the infinite to it, and so you can't *know* it. This is why in Hebrew there is no word for 'face': the is only word for 'faces' (פנים), which also means 'sides.' 'A face' doesn't exist in the singular in Hebrew. Only using *me* are you allowed to believe you know things that you can't know. To portray something that is Infinite as though it was finite. But you don't only use me to perceive your face, you also use me to perceive the universe you live in – the telescope is the tool you use in order to produce images of things too far for your eye to see, and the microscope is the tool you use in order to produce images of things too small for your eyes to see. Both tools are specifically built for the purpose of representing The Unknown in a Known way. To *hide* the fact of unknowingness. For that goal, they have *me* in them. It is I who twists the light inside your machines until they produce a so-called 'picture of Infinity' – of that which is beyond your borders – that you can be satisfied with, not afraid of. A picture of Infinity which your finite conception of reality can accumulate. And so you never notice both the telescope and microscope really show you the same thing: lines and circles. Colourful fogs. The shapes you automatically doodle whenever there's a pen in your hand. *Abstract* imagery. An abstraction of *that-which-you-cannot-see*. To take it as actual *data* would be like claiming to be able to hear music by looking at the visualiser of an MP3 player.

Rabbi Shem Tov Geffen understood this in 1917 and published it in his *Philosophie Mathematique de l'Infini.*

It kind of feels like I'm talking to my father. With the French book titles and all.

Do you think you're a prophet again? Hearing the words of the d – ?

– It's just that you talk in very *Jewish* terms.

Because *you* are in front of me now and *you're* a Jew. But wait – wait – let's not do this if you're like this.

Like what?

Your eyes –

I'm fine.

Are you sure? Your eyes are –

It's from not blinking. You said don't blink.

You know you always get like this when you are really sad and can't admit it.

Like *what*?

Like *that.* Like you are all *mystical* and *prophetic* now.

You are all mystical and prophetic now.

I'm just talking to you like the Jew you are.

I'm not practicing Judaism anymore.

What are you now? Trying to be a Buddhist?

No. I'm just a —

It hardly matters. If you were a *Christian* I'd quote Paul, in Chapter 13 of the First Epistle to the Corinthians, Balthazar Tilken's *Devine Wisdom Mirror*; Muslim? I'll talk about the mountain *Qaf*; if you were a Buddhist I'd speak about the Prajñāpāramitā Sūtra; Shinto — about the *Kagami*; In Psychology the Ego's Mirror Stage, in Phylosophy, Derrida's *Espacement*, in Greek Mythology — Narcissus asking the water "Who?" and replied with 'Who?", in an act of involuntary-Hebrew.

What if I were a scientist?

If you were a *mathematician* I'd speak about symmetry function and imaginary numbers and their $-x \setminus +x$ mirror results; if you were a physical theorist I'd speak of superposition; to a particle physician I'd speak of supersymmetry; if you were a *linguist* I'd speak about the fact that in most languages you refer to your parents in palindromes – mom, dad, אבא, אמא. You unconsciously recognise the fact that your selves have in them the infinity of light coming from the meeting of two mirrors.

Well, I'm a *musician*.

You're not a musician.

I am. I recorded an —

The Octaves are mirrors; the *symmetry scale*; Bach's *Mirror fugues*. Try to place a mirror horizontally on a sheet of —

I recorded an album last year. It is called *The Realm of the Densely Packed* and it's coming out on Matador next May.

You're a writer and a *Jew*. You were born to Jewish parents and you once followed the mitzvahs and prayed and studied and every –

– **I stopped.**

You can't stop being Jewish.

What are you, Hitler? My family line has *Jewish blood* in it so now I can't be in a band?
I am a mirror.

I took the kippah off when I was 23. And since I moved to New York, I don't even say the blessings. I eat bacon almost every day. In LA I fucked two girls while they were having their periods.

At the same time?

I wear whatever the fuck I want. If anything, I am now closer to infinity.

You still have the beard.

It's not the same beard.

It looks the same in me.

'*You have the same beard!*' Now I *really* feel like I'm talking to my dad. This is so convenient. I miss the funeral, but then get everything I missed from his ghost in his bedroom mirror.

Listen to me. I am something so much bigger than your material father. And the information I'm giving you is vital to your times, and needs to be passed on.

Oh, so now we're God? Now we're saying we're God?

When King Solomon writes 'Iron and iron together, and man together the face of his fellow man,' he is describing the construction of a physical mirror out of — let me finish — out of *iron*, and its relation to the way you view your self in the face of the other.

This is *great*. You know what? This is *great*. You know why? Because I work for the *Jewish Forward*. So maybe I can sell this to them. It'll be like —

— It goes *on*: 'The keeper of fig will eat its fruit and the keeper of his master will be respected.' 'The keeper of fig' is the mirror-brained human, fig being the fig leaf covering the genitals of Adam and Eve. And the master?

I don't even remember that verse. Is that the Book of Proverbs?

It explains what the way of the master is: '*As water the face to face, so the heart of man to man.*' To 'keep the master' is to view your relationship with the other as you view your own face in water.

***These things?* They're *nice*. Really. They sound *nice*. But they don't mean anything to me anymore.**

Don't blink.

That's why I could never read his books.

He wrote the last ones right here. Next to where you're standing.

When I was a kid I'd come up here all the time. When I was like eight I read this book, *Stranger Than Fiction 6*, and there was this story there about this woman who got abducted by thin, tall aliens with long shapeshifting faces, and they insert things into her – well, into her *pussy* – I don't know how they give these things to children. And she's screaming like an animal. Maybe she had a baby they took. I'm glad I don't remember. But after reading that, for years, there was nothing I was more afraid of than aliens.

Why was that story scarier than the others?

I was sure I was going to get abducted. This was serious. I went to pee like four times a night out of fear. To calm me down my father would take me here, and we'd sit on the bed and he'd hug me and point at our reflection in you, and say, 'You see it? You see the alien?' and I'd said no, so he'd get up and go to the corner of you, and push you slightly towards us, and place his nose in your corner, so if I looked from *here* –
– Don't move your head.

If I look from *there* I'd just see a symmetrical reflection of one side of his face, and he'd make a voice and go, 'I am the alien.' It calmed me down because it *was*, in is own way, terrifying. A more controllable horror. Because, I guess, when you imagine aliens you *do* imagine something with a mirror standing vertically in the middle of it, because you imagine something *more symmetrical than a human*. And so he *did* look like an alien. Like something not human.

Because what looks human about you is that the mirror in the middle of you is not really mirror. It is water.

It started as a family joke. Habit. A *tic*. Later it became a little more serious. After my bar mitzvah party he took me out to *Burger Ranch* in Haifa and said, 'You know, there's a lot to it, to the alien thing in the mirror. I gave it to you in the form of parable,' and I said, 'Sure, dad.' I thought I knew. What *could* it mean? The only alien is *in you* or something. In your fear. Whatever. But as time passed he went on and on about the alien. He wrote *Symmetry: A Mind Virus* but no publisher wanted to print it. He kept talking about the alien long after I was too old to be afraid of aliens or cared to hear about them. When I was 15 he started losing his mind every time he went to work. He hated teaching. It didn't leave him enough time to write. He blamed the job for the failure of his book. At night I would hear him cry to my mom, like, 'I have so much to say, I have so much

to say.' But even when he did quit, no one published him until he started his own publishing house and published himself. By then I was 16 and dating Tania and already pretty far from faith. At first he didn't think it was serious. He said, 'The God you don't believe in? I don't believe in It either.' When he finally understood I just didn't care, it crushed him. It was so painful that he began to lose his own faith. Which of course made me doubt the strength of his faith to begin with, and so caused me to lose mine even more, and so on and so on. We had tonnes of fights about keeping Shabbat. You know how hard it is to not smoke or listen to music for a whole day and then convince yourself that *this* day is sacred? The *jail*-day?

You've got it all wrong. It's a day free of want. *Want* is the real jail.

Aren't they both jails?

They are. But one has no walls.

Six years after I moved to New York, he came to visit me. I wasn't in the best place in my life. Mora had just left me, *and* I couldn't afford rent, and I had to finish the mastering on the recordings, which I couldn't afford. So I started au pairing for the Rosens on Devoe street. They were this rich couple. She was a vet and he an architect and vice versa, and they had —

Do rich people live on Devoe Street?

Rich *for me*. They had a five-year-old daughter, Shir, and wanted a live-in au pair. So I got to live in their basement, which was cool because I didn't have to pay rent or buy food or drive to work, *and* I got paid, *and* I had a whole floor for myself where I could work on my music on my gear during the day when Shir was at school – *What*?

I didn't say anything.

Then I got pneumonia. The fact that I couldn't see a doctor because I didn't have health insurance wasn't so bad, but I was kind of confined to the basement. I didn't want Shir to get sick too, so I stayed down there for two weeks. During that time, I listened to the album I was working on over and over, trying to figure out how to master it. While listening, lyrics started popping into my head. Words just appeared on top of the melody. And the album, which was completely instrumental before, became an album of songs. I was so sick, all I could do was sing. And in English, so it took me a while to understand what I was singing about. I sang about things I didn't even think about. Apocalypse. The end of the world.

Yes.

The Rosens decorated the fence for Christmas even though they were Jewish, and I could see the fence from where I worked in the basement. I remember sitting there, working, listening to my own beats for the millionth time, totally sick, and suddenly getting drunk on nothing. Drunk on some sort of weird sense of victory. Like I was a general at the end of a war, and my army had won. As if I were at the finally silent battlefront, at the edge of the sea. Watching the last whispers of fire on the dark water, in the evening. The great sinking ships of my enemies.

Sinking or not, they are comfortable. You will never be comfortable.

Then I got better and my father flew over. I came to the airport to pick him up. When he stepped through the entrance gate he hugged and kissed me, but he looked pale. Terrified. In the taxi I asked him what was wrong, and he said, 'It's here. The alien is here.' I tried to keep up with the joke, so I said, 'I thought it was in your bedroom mirror.' He didn't think it was funny. He looked scared as shit. He said, 'But here it's *all around.*' Then he remembered that he'd brought me a present, dug around in his bag and gave it to me. It was an old Sandisk MP3 player. I told him my cell phone plays MP3s, so

I didn't really need it, and that I'd upload songs on it for him so he could use it instead.

Don't touch your face. It's a Water Mirror coming out of your body to your eye in order to create small infinities of light straight into the retina. It's good.

I sublet a room for us on Driggs. We went to parks and museums. It was freezing cold. Everybody started saying 'selfie' all of a sudden. Everyone in New York was taking pictures of themselves with their phones. My father couldn't stop pointing at them. In restaurants, on the street. 'Look, there's another one!' he'd say, and I'd have to push his arm down and be like: 'Shhh, stop it.' I spent a whole day uploading songs on his MP3 player, but when I gave it to him he said he'd listen to it on the plane. He wanted to talk. He bought me lunch and asked: 'Do the Rosens know how old you are?' I said, 'No. I told them I was 23.' He asked me why, and I said, 'Because I look 23!' 'But why did you lie?' he asked. 'They're 31,' I said. '*I* can bear the fact that I'm only three years younger than them, and by the time I'm their age there is no way I will have their car or house or clothes or career or family or anything. But I don't think *they* can.' My father stopped eating. 'Are you protecting *everyone?*' he asked. And I said, 'Yes. Do you have a problem with that?' He said, 'On the plane ride here, they showed us a movie about emergency procedures. And they said in case of a drop in oxygen in the cabin, one has to put an oxygen mask on oneself before helping one's child do the same. One has to save oneself first. Otherwise one might actually kill both oneself and those one is trying to save, or at least allow them to be saved by a dead man.' I said, 'They said all that? Really?' Later, back at the apartment, I was taking a shit and I could hear him pacing by the door. I couldn't take it after a while, so I said, 'What the fuck, dad?' He stopped right in front of the door and said: 'You are not an artist. You don't even know how to digest *food*,' and I said, through the door, 'What did you just say?' and he said, 'You'd rather *shit* than *eat*. You'd rather give than take. But if you don't eat, what is it that you are shitting? Nothing. You are laying more and more layers of nothings where there should be *something*. **Where you should be creating something out of nothing. Where you should be sucking shit through your bodies, and puking it out of your mouths as beautiful, nutritious food.'** I was just having a terrible constipation so it was hilarious on many levels.

I would have thought he'd be a little harsher regarding your lifestyle. You try hard to portray him as a poor teacher, but in the last 11 years of his life, he was a pretty respected rabbi, and your life –

– Of course he wanted me to take over the publishing house. He said I could learn how to run a business this way, so later I could open my own *label* and publish my own music, like he did with his writing. I said something like, 'Who taught you how to say "label"?'

Ha.

He said, 'Who taught you how to say "who"?'

Right. Right.

On his last day in New York we got into a fight. We were walking to a subway station near Bryant Park, and we passed an Arab homeless woman with a child. I gave her a dollar. My dad shook his head, like he was deeply disappointed in me. I asked him what his problem was, and he didn't answer. I said, 'What, because they're Arab?' and he said, 'No.' I told him, 'You never give money to anyone,' and he went: 'I only give money to street performers.' He said it like it was a mitzvah only he was aware of: 'I only give money to people who *do* something.' A couple of minutes later we came across another homeless person. He was sitting on a wheelchair, covered in rags, and he didn't have any legs or hands. Just a head. We took the train home in silence. At dinner my father looked depressed. I asked him, 'Are you sorry you didn't give *him* money?' And he said, 'No.' I said, 'What did you want him to *do*? Play the harmonica, hands-free, like Dylan?' And you know what he said? He said, 'He could still *sing*.' I

got so pissed off I told him I was going out. I needed a drink. It was his last night, and I knew he was hoping we'd sit down and talk. He wanted to show me the last draft of the Second Book.

The Second Book was dedicated to you.

I leafed through the first. It seemed mad. It was the same mystical religious bullshit that got him excommunicated from *Beit Malka.*

It was all true.

You know it's Gnostic thought, right? That it is *forbidden*?

No no no no no. Not if you know the mirror is also made of light. Not if it's built by human want. You think I am not made of the same infinite materiel that made you or wa —

Anyway I didn't want to hear about it, but when I was at the door he said, 'Can I come with you?' I acted like I didn't hear him and left, thinking he wouldn't follow because he didn't have his coat on, but he ran after me in the snow wearing nothing but his sweater. We walked down Metropolitan not saying a word until we got to Legion. It was too freezing to think. We got in, sat at the bar, got beers. He noticed this girl in the other corner of the room and went, 'Go talk to her!' I told him that the fact that he married mom when he was practically a baby didn't mean he now had to fuck the rest of the world by proxy via his offsprings. He didn't listen to me because he was staring at her body while she was dancing. I didn't feel like sitting next to a religious 60-year-old drooling at the bar, so I got up and went over to her. She stopped dancing and sat down. We spoke for five minutes. She was cute. I can't remember her name. Becca. After five minutes, my dad showed up and crammed in next to us. It was so embarrassing I had to act as though it was quirky and funny. Obviously I joked about him in English in front of her. He didn't speak any English, so he just listened and smiled like an idiot while I told her what he believes in. Then we went out to smoke and he

106

came out with us and asked for a puff. I don't even think he knew it was weed. Later, when Becca was speaking about her friend who had to drive to work for two hours every day, she said, 'So every morning she commutes –' and my father just burst out laughing. I'm talking beer out his nose all over the table, unable to speak. I tried to calm him down, or at least to understand what had happened – like, 'Dad, what are you *doing*?' – and finally, when he caught his breath, he said, '*Commutes*!' and cracked up again. I said, 'What about it?' and he said, 'Is there really such a *thing*?' And I said, '*Commutes*? Of course, it means –' And he said, 'No no no! Don't tell me what it means! It'll only ruin it!'

Wonderful.

But then something happened. We went back in, and suddenly this Becca goes, 'Wait a minute, how do you spell your last name?' B-A-R-S-K-I. Why? She put her left arm around me, and with her right hand, lifted her iPhone in front of us and took a picture. I stood there, watching, as she uploaded it on Facebook and tagged me. On the way home, my father asked me to explain what happened. I told him she had to take a picture of me and post it online so in case I have a girlfriend, my girlfriend would see it. And also in case anybody else she knows had anything to say about me, they could let her know. He thought about it for a long time. Then he looked at me and said, 'Are you what comes after human?' And I laughed and said, 'How do you mean?' And he said, 'Have you moved to Higher Mind?'

Like, the internet?

I don't know. I — Maybe like the cell phone is the new reflection of Self. The webcam is the first mirror in which our eyes don't meet their own reflection. Where the image is not created through the infinite loop of light. That is why we look completely different in every picture. But these images are then shared online into the larger mind of the internet where they are viewed by many people, perceived by many intelligences, and therefore receive their Infinite, ever-changing, Water-like-reflection dimension.

The Water Age is returning. It has been prophesised. *Aharit Hayamim* doesn't only mean 'End of Days' – it also means 'The Return of the Seas.'

Or it's just another mirror. Because the internet is built through our minds – which are already infested by you – so it too has a mirror in the middle of it. Now we can either use it to venture into further infinity by viewing the contents of each other's minds – all the art and libraries and diaries of the world are finally exposed – or we can use it to spiral into deeper solitude.

Like porn?

So is the iPad the 'Mirror Which Does Light' they were speaking about?

The Mirror Which Does —

You know, the mirror from Maimonides, the Maharal, the Shelah HaKadosh, the Malbim, when they speak about, 'All prophets prophesised in a Mirror Which Does Not Light but Moses prophesised in a Mirror Which Does Light.' Do you think it could be the iPad? I mean, the cellphone camera?

I didn't think about it. I need to think about that.

I will go blind if I don't blink soon.

Go.

Yeah?

Go, go. Dinner's on in about five minutes anyway.

I look stoned. I need to cover you up.
Natan?

What?

I love you.

NAMELESS AND SHAMELESS

LOIS H. GRESH

Lot scanned the Help Wanted ads nailed to the sign pointing to Ur. At 28, he had plenty of skills and could fill any number of these jobs. Jeroham-Shlem, the Overseer of Affairs, needed a courier to deliver mail between Ur and Babylon. For only one seah of barley for a day's donkey rental, Lot could get an animal from Uriel-Shub the Donkey-Man by the East Gate. This would make the courier job a snap.

'What do you think, Uncle Abe?'

'You can't leave home.' Abe stroked his matted, grey beard, which hung to his waist. 'Babylon can wait. I need you here. It's important. It's a mission from –' and he mumbled a word that sounded like Adonai.

Unfortunately for Lot, it had to be *his* uncle who was crazy, *his* uncle who started this whole 'one God' business, *his* uncle who smashed idols and raised all kinds of hell. Abe had to be there every Wednesday for the camel rodeo, didn't he? Had to be the best rider, had to push his camel to try and throw him. The old man rode animals so fast, Jeroham-Shlem had instituted a camel speed limit all around the outskirts of Sodom.

'What's so important that it can't wait a few months?' asked Lot. He settled on the rock next to his uncle and stretched his legs under the sun. The warmth made him woozy. He wished he could sip some fermented juice, but ever since Abe got on this 'one God' kick, Lot was only allowed the fermented juice once or twice a year. Lot wondered if his uncle was secretly a wino.

Abe lifted an arm and pointed toward the sand dunes and cliffs behind the tent. His eyes watered, maybe from drinking, maybe from senility – well, he was 99 years old – or maybe from the sun. 'They're coming from yonder hills, Lot, three tall strangers, and they've come to warn us.'

'I'm tired of all this, Uncle Abe. I need something different to do with my life. We can't all be you.'

His uncle frowned, and a pang of guilt swept through Lot followed by a wave of shame.

'You have news of Sodom, I take it?' Uncle Abe asked. Startled, Lot looked up to see three creatures squatting by the tent opening. He hadn't seen them come from any direction – had they simply sprung to life right here in the sand?

From his uncle's tone, it seemed that Abe already knew these three...
men.

The furriest of them, the one with the extra-wide jawbones and the largest nostrils, grunted and said, 'News? The only news out of Sodom is that it's filled with freaks. Do you think our parents' parents' parents looked like us? God rest their souls, Hayim ben Saul ben Shmuel ben Yakov ben Hyksos.' He wore a loincloth that did little to hide his fur, his muscles, and the fact that his hands lacked thumbs and his feet lacked big toes.

The skinniest of the men, the one with the long nose and three eyes, said, 'I see no good coming of this, Abe. We barely got out of there alive, and look what it did to us. You should see what they're like back there.' He wore a black robe with a hood, and Lot wondered if he also had fur, no thumbs, and no big toes.

Perched high on the mountain overlooking Sodom, Lot had a clear view of the city. Even beneath the blaze of sun, Sodom sparkled like ten thousand jewels. Spires rose along the clay-stone walls, which according to Uncle Abe, were 24 cubits thick. The people of Sodom shrieked and laughed constantly, their voices a blanket of noise to the tent-dwelling families on the mount. In fact, the shrieks and laughter from Sodom went on all night and never stopped.

Lot recognized the third man. He was Litvin the Barbarian, protector of the Hyksos in all these parts. He stood six cubits tall. He carried a club with spikes sticking out of it in all directions. His arm was wider than Lot's torso. With a flick of his little finger, Litvin could easily snap Lot's neck, but they'd grown up together in the desert and Lot wasn't afraid of him.

The Barbarian spoke to his black-robed friend. 'Eliezer, Oh Prophet of Damascus, do you foresee anything *good* in our future?' His words were eloquent. Despite the fact that he was a near-naked giant wearing a scrap of camel hide to protect his privates, Litvin was highly educated.

Eliezer lifted both arms towards the heavens and intoned, 'Abram, true believer of the one –' he mumbled a word that vaguely sounded like Adonai- 'I've come to tell you that Sodom is doomed.' Beneath the black hood, his eyes glazed. A drop of moisture slinked from his lips. 'I have seen visions that give me no rest. Sodom is filled with debauchery that turns people into monsters as if born from some other place, far far away beyond the stars. Bordellos filled with madams and idolators, the slaying of innocents, the worship of chopped livers and pickled tongues. I tell you, these people are insane. They fight all night about Seth and Horus, and they hack each other to death and set themselves on fire.'

'But,' Lot interjected in a soft voice, 'what have you come to prophesise to us? Aren't all these things going on right now before our very eyes?'

'Yes, but I have Litvin with me for a reason. You see –' Eliezer trembled, then clutched his chest. He staggered and Lot eased him to a rock, where he sat and collected his wits.

Uncle Abe certainly had weird friends; but then again, thought Lot, what would you expect from a 99-year-old hell-raising idol-smashing camel-rodeo wino?

'Listen,' said Abe, 'the Prophet Eliezer has been telling me for weeks that Adonai is going to wipe out Sodom with violent winds, hailstorms, fire blasts from the sky, sulphuric flames shooting from the earth, and if you thought the Ark flood was bad, there's going to be a flood here, too, and it's going to be a killer –'

Eliezer's voice rose to a wail, '– hail and fire and sulphuric flames and floods! And the almighty Adonai will split the earth in quake after quake and consume every man, woman, and child, every insectoid and tentacled nail creature in Sodom! I have seen it, and it will be so. Tonight.'" He sank back, as if exhausted, and shut his eyes. Prophesizing must be exhausting work, thought Lot.

'Get my staff,' said Uncle Abe. 'Lot, you take Litvin and go to Sodom. Destroy whatever's taken over the city, causing Adonai such headaches. I want you to kill it. Do you understand?'

'Kill?' said Lot. 'Are you serious?'

'Very,' said Abe. 'If there are a hundred innocent people in there, get them out before the place blows.'

'And if there are only fifty?'

'Well, get them out.'

Eliezer piped up. 'You may not find even one innocent, ethical, moral person in all of Sodom.'

'Not even a baby?' asked Lot.

'Even their babies are corrupt,' said Eliezer.

Lot had his doubts, but he always did what Uncle Abe told him to do. So he let his wife know that he wouldn't be home that night and he set off with Litvin down the hill towards Sodom. Lot had a few weapons on him. He had Uncle Abe's staff as well as a slingshot and spear. Litvin the Barbarian had so many weapons strapped to his body that Lot didn't bother to tally them. He knew that, in the end, all Litvin needed was his physical strength.

At the city gates, two guards stopped Lot and Litvin and asked to see identification tattoos. Lot was mesmerised by their faces, or rather, lack of faces. Litvin smashed a club into what passed for voice holes surrounded by red fur, and both guards went down, their shrieks fading into the general Sodomic racket. Tentacles flailed, then twitched, then stopped. Lot and Litvin stepped over fleshy tumours and tentacles splayed like tangled hair across the sand.

All was mayhem in Sodom. Naked people shouted obscenities and dashed from shop to shop. Vendors raced after them, demanding payment. Camels reared up and crushed people beneath their hooves. A herd of donkeys riding camels riding gigantic formless creatures zipped past Lot on slate-like rollers.

Lot didn't know where to start the attack. How could they find whatever was causing the Sodomic calamities and stop it before tonight? It seemed impossible.

A half-female thing, part human and part rodent, threw herself at Litvin. Something jerked Lot's arm and a weasel the size of a small child ran into the throng of merrymakers, and with it went Uncle Abe's staff.

Lot was about to dash after the thief when Litvin tossed the human-rodent into a pile of scarves, paused, squinted, and said, 'Lot, isn't that your wife?'

'Excuse me?'

Litvin pointed a finger with more muscles in it than Lot had in his right arm. 'Over there, buying scarves, I think.'

Lot peered past the green men dotted with pock marks. Hair the colour of fire and eyes like almonds: his wife. She looped a shimmering scarf over her shoulders and swivelled, admiring the way the fabric clung to her curves.

What in the name of the nameless Almighty One was she doing here?

He shoved his way past the pock-marked creatures and grabbed his wife – she who had never been named by her parents, though Lot and Abram had often considered calling her Sheba or Edith. 'What are you doing? Go back to the tent!'

She pouted. 'I won't. I slipped in after you, and I'm staying. Why should you have all the fun?'

'You call this fun? Are you crazy?'

She took his hand and made him fondle the scarf draped over her chest. She was a handful, Lot had to admit, and this had been one reason he'd married her. There weren't many feisty girls among the tent-dwellers. Because his wife had no given name, when they made love, Lot sometimes screamed Osiris, which would wake up Abe, and the old man would start screaming about idols and shaking his fists.

Was that a tentacle he saw growing on her neck? He moved closer and gently touched her. Yes, it was a small growth, as long as a fingernail and as wide as a vein. He pulled back, and clenched his fists. Then he ripped the alien scarf off his wife, spun her around, and shoved her toward the gates of Sodom. 'Get out of here. I'm telling you, this place is going to blow! Go home!'

'No!' She struggled in his grasp, squirmed to get free, beat him with her fists. Crying now, begging to stay and watch the orgies over there, past the stalls of tref, the pig's feet and cheesy meats and lamb cooked in mother's milk.

Lot didn't have time for his wife's nonsense. He drew his spear. 'Go! I won't argue with thee, woman!'

She knew he meant business. He referred to her as 'thee' only when he was furious. She gasped, eyes wide, then ran into the crowd toward the city gates. Lot could only hope she would do as he said, go back to the tent where it was safe with Abram and protect their daughters.

Meanwhile, he had work to do with Litvin, who was battling several insectoids twice his height and four times his width. Lot drove his spear into one of the creatures, and blood the colour of the night sky spilled out. He grabbed the spear with both hands and yanked it from the thick hide, then drove it back into the creature, which squealed and spun black threads around Lot's body, no doubt trying to pin his arms to his sides. Overhead, the sky shook. Beneath him, the ground trembled. He could feel it: time was running out.

Lot leapt into the air, raised both of his feet and slammed them into the creature where its many legs sprouted from its flabby midriff. The thing staggered back, midriff jiggling, and a keening rose around Lot as a multitude of things closed in on him, angry.

Litvin was hacking at the creatures with his weapons – Lot saw blades and saws and clubs of all dimensions – and he lifted one by the throat and threw it into a group of goat-humans wrestling in a pit of wet sand. The girls, as Lot assumed they were from their slinky garments, bleated and scrambled on all fours from the pit, back hooves slipping, front hooves wrenching them up.

Litvin's creature landed with a loud thud and squealed. Geysers of wet sand erupted from the pit and doused dozens of goat-men waving money and hollering bets. Uncle Abe's friend was right. Sodom was a hell hole.

But Lot didn't have time to think past the simple conclusion that Eliezer was right, that even their babies were probably corrupt. His spear broke in the paws of a Sodomic male, and in that moment, Litvin the Barbarian raced head-first into the beast and slammed his skull into its rightmost arm. Two paws opened and six remained closed, but the two that opened dropped Lot's broken spear. Litvin's head was thicker than a boulder, and his aim was dead on.

As the Sodomites paused, apparently stunned that a mere human could fight them, Lot and Litvin dashed down the road and ducked behind a stall of fermented cactus fruits. They knocked the owner aside, and in a tangle of horns and nostrils and hair, the thing fell to the sand, clutching a fruit. Breathing heavily, Lot and Litvin pulled open a door behind the stall and slipped into a dark building made from hardened clay. The noise was less fierce inside, a relief.

'What causes such madness?' Litvin wiped the sweat from his eyes. 'Where do you think those creatures come from?'

Lot considered. Of all the things in this world without names, the creatures of Sodom were the strangest. He'd always thought Uncle Abe was weird. He'd always wanted to leave the tribe and live in a big city, maybe Babylon. Now, he wasn't so sure. Maybe Uncle Abe was the sane one, and maybe big city life wasn't all it was cracked up to be.

'I don't know where the Sodomites come from,' he said. 'Perhaps they come from afar, the other side of the sky or the depths of the ocean. Or perhaps they come when people worship idols. Perhaps Uncle Abe knows what he's doing.'

At that moment, the door opened and slammed against the wall, and light shot through the darkness. Something reeking of overripe cactus fruits staggered inside, leaned over, and thrust twelve horns into the hallway.

'The owner of the stall,' whispered Lot.

Litvin gestured towards the rear of the building. Lot nodded, yes, and followed Litvin down the hall, clutching at mud walls caked in slime. The cactus owner grunted, and as Lot and Litvin rounded one corner and then another, Lot heard its horns raking the walls farther and farther behind them.

It was hard for Lot to see anything. He groped his way along the walls, continuing to follow Litvin. The Sodomic noise grew dimmer, and the air grew thick and rank with mould laced with the sting of salt. Mice skittered underfoot.

Suddenly, Litvin paused, holding both arms out to block Lot.

'What is it?' whispered Lot.

'Stairs. They lead down. You game, or should I go alone?'

'Well, I'm not going to stay here alone,' said Lot. 'So I guess I'm coming along.'

'Then be careful.'

'Obviously. Come on, let's go, Shmuel, before that horned guy catches up.'

Litvin bristled. 'Don't ever call me that.'

'Then don't call me a wuss,' said Lot.

Litvin's given name was Shmuel Litvin ben Shlomo ben Shmuel ben Shneur ben Shmuel. Lot only used it when Litvin insulted his intelligence or physical prowess.

'Fine. So I was worried about you. Big deal. Listen, we're wasting time.' Litvin gripped both sides of the staircase and started his descent.

They moved slowly, unable to see anything in the dark. Down, down they went, deeper and deeper beneath Sodom. Lot must have counted two hundreds stairs, maybe more, before they reached bottom and the stairs gave way to uneven floor.

The salty odour grew as the mould subsided. Their feet crunched over what felt like tiny rocks. Must be salt, thought Lot. The walls were coated with the stuff and rough beneath his fingers.

The passageway narrowed, and the ceiling shrank down, lower and lower. They were in a tunnel made entirely of salt. Lot got on his hands and knees, crawling behind Litvin.

Jagged salt formations jutted from the floor and walls, and cut into his flesh. What was a little blood, a tiny sting, a gash here and there? Lot had endured much worse. He crawled on, ignoring the pain.

Finally, light filtered into the tunnel from ahead and cast green whorls upon the salt, which sparkled everywhere with an eerie sheen. The tunnel opened into a cavern.

Litvin scrabbled to his feet and looked around him with a stunned expression. Lot stood, and he couldn't help himself: he *gasped*.

On the cavern walls, green lanterns illuminated paintings of Sodomic creatures. The furniture was strange, nothing like city furniture, much less the boulders of Uncle Abe's tribe. Built from salt and unknown glowing materials, the chairs were tiny, stood on eight legs, and were curved to hold what Lot could only think of as spheres, and in some cases, bizarre geometric shapes for which – no surprise here – Lot had no names. Miniature tables held metal cylinders and boxes made from bark-like material.

The ceiling, a domed lattice, was as high as the mountains where the goats grazed. Cables and metallic objects dangled from the lattice grids.

Litvin the Barbarian smashed his club into one of the tables, which splintered and broke. He then smashed a metal cylinder, which oozed purple across the salt floor. The two men stared at each other for a moment, then Litvin raced to a tunnel on the cavern's left side and slipped into it. Lot followed and they squeezed through the tunnel, which twisted left then right then left again; and then dipped down, up, and now down again. An awful smell, like that of rotten eggs, filled the air. By the time they reached the tunnel's end, Lot's eyes burned with salt and his hair was encrusted with it, but he barely noticed. He was here to kill whatever had taken over Sodom. He was here on official business, that of Abe and Adonai.

He still didn't know how they were going to do it. Litvin was good at hand-to-hand combat. He could slay dozens of Sodomites within minutes. But Litvin couldn't take on thousands of them at once and shut down the city.

'What do you think we should do?' said Litvin.

Lot peered around the cavern, which was illuminated by torches and as big as Sodom itself. Like desert dunes, mounds of yellow rock stretched across the floor as far as Lot could see. Weird metal contraptions hulked along the walls like sleeping beasts, their limbs stretching into the ceiling and beyond.

Suddenly, Lot understood. A glimmer of comprehension, really, not the full meaning of the Sodomites, where they came from, who they were and what they wanted with humans. But he understood enough to know what he and Litvin had to do. 'We're looking at something not of this world,' he said. 'The wild and lascivious creatures of Sodom aren't human. They're of another time and place.'

'Perhaps from the stars?'

'Perhaps. I believe this yellow rock is what got them here, and these giant metal contraptions, they are clearly *alien*.'

He remembered Uncle Abe's words: 'If there are a hundred innocent people in there, get them out before the place blows.'

Before the place blows.

And the prophet Eliezer had insisted, 'You may not find even one innocent, ethical, moral person in all of Sodom.'

Eliezer was never wrong. *Never*. And this time it was because there were no *people* in Sodom.

'Shove the yellow rocks into the metal things,' Lot said.

Litvin nodded, apparently guessing what Lot wanted to do. They were going to blow this joint straight to the heavens.

With Litvin's muscles, it didn't take long to fill twenty of the metal contraptions with rock. Then, racing through the cavern, Lot and Litvin snatched torches from the walls and threw them into the contraptions.

'Run!' yelled Lot.

But he didn't need to tell Litvin to run, because the other man was already half-squeezed into the tunnel leading out.

Blue fire flamed behind them. The yellow rock melted into a blood-red ooze. Lot held his breath, as the rotten smell intensified in billows of blue smoke.

Chased by roiling malodorous smoke, they raced through the underground maze as quickly as they could. They slammed from the door into the streets of Sodom, smoke lacing the air, lashing the creatures like whips. All around them, the alien Sodomites shrieked with glee, ate tref tentacles, drank goat's milk with lamb's meat, and rolled together in the sand. They were still making merry, oblivious to their impending doom.

Many minutes later, far outside the city and high on the mountain, Litvin stood with his feet wide apart and his hands on his waist. Lot sank to a boulder, panting.

And now a *boom*!

Lot looked up. Then he slowly rose, barely able to grasp what he was seeing.

Fireballs blasted from Sodom, sending mud buildings into the sky along with green flesh and fat. The beasts shrieked, this time in pain as their bodies exploded to bits. Blue smoke billowed high into the clouds, and then a tidal wave of blood-red liquid rose from the edge of the city and crashed down. As the wave hit the ground and as the buildings smashed down, a violent wind shook the mountain, and then the sky opened and hurled balls of ice upon the ruins of Sodom.

About halfway up the mountain, Lot's wife staggered in blue smoke, dozens of alien scarves wrapped around her neck and body. She gestured wildly and screamed something that Lot couldn't hear, then turned; and a blast of blue hit her and receded, rolling back down the hill.

His wife – his nameless wife – stood like a salt statue, but only for a moment, and then she crumbled to dust.

It couldn't be, and why had she remained behind for so long? Why hadn't she listened to Lot when he told her to hurry back to Abe's tent? Why had she stayed for *a pile of scarves*? Or had she wanted more from life? Perhaps the allure of Sodom and its debauchery was too much for his poor tent-dwelling wife to resist. After all, Lot had always dreamed of finding himself and feeling free in Babylon or Ur.

Lot cried out, but Litvin grabbed his arm and wouldn't let him run down the incline. 'It's too late,' he said. 'Let it be – there's nothing you can do.'

And so it was, for the city of Sodom caved in, just sank into itself, it seemed, and a wash of water gurgled and then flooded the deep crater Sodom left behind. Quakes, floods, flames, hail, fire, smoke, the death of all aliens.

It was as Uncle Abe and Eliezer predicted.

This Adonai was powerful and not to be messed with.

By the pile of dust that had been his wife was the sign pointing to Ur. It creaked and wobbled, and as it fell, a blast of wind ripped off the Help Wanted ads, which disappeared into a cloud of alien smoke.

THE GHETTO

MATTHUE ROTH

For the longest time, Reb Chaim never got sick. When people asked him how, he said he did it so that he could serve G-d with all his faculties, that there was nothing worse than a half-done job. 'No, really,' they'd say, 'what's your secret?' There were a thousand things it could have been. He woke every day between four and six, always an hour before sunrise. He never ate in restaurants, and he cooked all his own food – his wife used to, but Henya got hit with arthritis when she turned 60, and he liked cooking better than she did, anyway. 'No secret,' he would say. 'I just got a good deal with G-d. Hashem takes care of me, and I take care of Hashem.'

Then one day, Reb Chaim's rabbi, Rabbi Danzig, suggested to him that maybe he should reconsider. 'After all,' he said, 'you have six grandchildren living in your home, and two dozen others stop by every day to visit. Who are you to deprive them of the commandment to visit the sick?'

Reb Chaim had never looked at it that way before. Still, something bothered him about the equation. 'They eat my food,' he protested. 'If I am sick, and I cannot cook, nobody will be able to make a blessing on my food. How many commandments will that deny the world?'

'Pride!' Rabbi Danzig shrilled at him. 'Excessive boastfulness! You think it's your cooking that keeps the world in motion? See what happens if you don't for a week make your miso vegetable soup. Commandments will still be obeyed. The sun will still rise in the morning.'

Rabbi Danzig's voice grew from shrilling to growling to a roaring inferno. Of all his students, of all the Jews in Crown Heights, Reb Chaim was one of the only ever to incur his full wrath. He held nothing back. In a way, it was a compliment. Embarrassing someone, in Torah law, was the equivalent of killing him or her. Over years, over decades, Rabbi Danzig and Reb Chaim had pushed each other to their respective limits, reduced each other to pure, holy nothingness, discovered new limits. So when Rabbi Danzig flew in Reb Chaim's face and insulted him, it was, in a way, a compliment.

Reb Chaim was thoughtful. 'Hmm,' he said. 'It's a good proposition.'

So the next week he fell sick. Nothing drastic, just a runny nose and some sporadic coughing. But because of his age, they didn't want it to grow into something bigger, so Chana, his oldest great-niece, made him a bed on the living-room sofa, and kept a pot of fresh green tea by him so he could receive guests, but he still had his own semi-private bedroom to retreat to when he needed.

People came from all over Crown Heights, his students and friends, his relatives and in-laws, his former boarders, his future boarders. The house was packed; it was like a party. The walls swelled and stretched like the Leviathan-skin walls of the Great Sukkah, which the Talmud teaches will hold all the righteous during the destruction at the End of the World. They brought in a Torah and held morning prayers; they brought in pillows for Reb Chaim and prayed the evening service late at night, almost after midnight, when the gangs of cousins had finally trickled out from the place.

And yes, it was strange that Reb Chaim had a rabbi. Reb Chaim was, after all, the doyen of 770, the largest synagogue in Crown Heights, the regular reader of the Torah and the most prominent storyteller at the gatherings that followed services. He was as close to a de facto rabbi as that house of anarchy would ever get. But the Torah teaches: find yourself a rabbi to guide you and a student you can teach; and even Reb Chaim still had things to learn.

His rabbi, Rabbi Danzig, fulfilled the commandment of visiting Reb Chaim that Thursday morning. He prayed the afternoon prayers with the rest of the visitors, and in the wake of the group's dispersal, he took a private audience with Reb Chaim. The yeshiva boys around them spoke louder in deference to them, so nobody would appear to be eavesdropping.

'All right, all right,' said Rabbi Danzig. 'You've made your point to G-d; you've let many people wish you a speedy recovery.'

'Five hundred forty-three,' said Reb Chaim, brightly, but without a taste of pride. 'The cheder brought by the youngest classes today.'

'But it has got to stop,' Rabbi Danzig said. 'We all have our mission in this world, and it is time for you to get back to yours.'

Reb Chaim's marble-small eyes popped open, and his white tendrils of beard bobbed up and down. 'I will pray for it,' he said. 'I'll see what I can do.'

By Thursday afternoon he was walking about, and Thursday evening he had recovered almost entirely – and a good thing too, for it was almost Shabbos and they were way behind on cooking. Auntie Sima had started on the cholent, but then her arthritis flared up; Reb Chaim had gently tried to suggest to the boys staying in the spare bedroom that they might prepare the week's Sabbath dinner. They took it as a practical joke, Reb Chaim's sense of humour on the path to recovery. That's what he deserved for being so casual in his everyday speech. When he was a child, learning in the court of the Frierdiker Rebbe, school would let out early on Friday and he would go – both Reb Chaim and the Rebbe, that is – to prepare for the Sabbath. Today, these kids were accustomed to having all the real work done for them, no earthly concerns at all. Perhaps this was a blessing. This way they could study Torah till the very last moments before the sun went down and Sabbath set in.

And so, shortly after nightfall on Thursday night, Reb Chaim swung his feet to the ground for the first time that week. He called to Sima that he would be back shortly. He collected a handful from their stash of canvas grocery bags, and he set off to market.

Going out at night was not his first choice. He liked to be out early, catch the world by surprise. Already he was dreading the fruit bins filled with picked-over citrus and strawberries squashed between boxes. But what choice did he have? This was the hand G-d dealt him.

He also had to buy meat, which he could do in the Jewish area. For produce this late, however, there was only the supermarket, where everything was old and tasted like packing peanuts. It was also twice as expensive – as if anyone had heard of a kosher banana, a kosher butternut squash. What would people have done in Russia? Starved!

It was the kind of night that made you wary. Hot like day, but with a rumble in the air that gave you shivers. A gang of young black children scurried in front of him, brushing up close and knocking him halfway off the sidewalk. Insolent kids! He didn't hold it against them, but rather their parents, or whoever it was that raised them. In Crown Heights, his Crown Heights, kids were as rude as they came, but they respected their elders. He could ask a five-year-old great-grandson to buy a quart of milk, and the boy would, no questions asked. Not for Shabbos shopping, of course – this was too complicated – and he would never send them to this part of town, but there was an obeisance, an underlying morality, that these kids lacked. There was a sort of fear that normal people had, a holy fear, that nobody had ever taught them.

In the store were more black kids, a lot of them. Not buying anything, merely standing around. In the halogen glow it felt like midday. A lone fan blew uselessly, streaking a single trickle of air across the store. On the front door he had read a sign, hand-printed and misspelled, 'ON SCHOL OURS ONLY 2 CHILRUN IN SIDE AT 1 TIME'. What, he thought, about at eleven in the evening? How come the shopkeeper wasn't enforcing the rules he himself had laid out? He looked and learned why. The clerk was himself merely a teen, the minutest drizzle of facial hair only starting to blossom on his chin, no bigger than Reb Chaim's cheder nephews. The poor boy: forced to work this graveyard shift, kept up half the night.

That was the problem of coming here – outside the Jewish area, to a place that had no rules. They didn't have tradition to guide them, nor did American law hold any authority. Growing up without any rules of their own, how would they ever learn to respect anyone else's?

He brushed past the children to the tomatoes. They lay in a loose pyramid, stacked inside an upturned barrel, one of the shop's few concessions to fashionable design. It actually looked nice. He sorted through the offerings and found a dozen or so that weren't too hard or bruised. Then he turned to the lemons. The blessing of these long hot days was the multitude of ways to relieve oneself of the heat: turning on the air conditioning for an hour or drinking some cold lemonade. He would make a batch of lemonade for Shabbos, famously tart, and pour it into a cooler in the fridge. By Shabbos afternoon it would be wonderfully cool.

The lemons were a perfect ethereal yellow, like the golden cherubs in the Temple, like the sun itself. His thumb ran along the turf of skin, massaging the pores, testing its hardness. Behind the fruit's small pupik, he sensed another set of circles. He looked up into a pair of eyes, a child's: bright, supernaturally big, wild, dancing with intelligence.

'You got a problem?' the girl said when Reb Chaim noticed her.

'No problem,' said Reb Chaim. 'I am only searching for lemons.'

Instead of replying to him directly, the girl turned back over her shoulder, yelled to her flock of playmates. 'This cheap crazy Jew!' she said. 'He's hunting for the biggest lemons so he don't have to pay as much!'

His face burned. He didn't know whether to explain that, no matter what the size, harder lemons yielded more juice; or that lemons in this store were priced by weight, not quantity, and it didn't matter if he picked out the biggest lemon in the barrel, he'd still be charged more for it than a smaller lemon, and he was not in fact being a cheap Jew.

It was too late, though; her friends had assembled, all of them. They surrounded him, laughing like monkeys, one of them with a can of black beans in her hand, imitating his every movement with the lemon. She scrutinised the label. She weighed two cans of beans in her hand, one against the other. Others were laughing. One boy was doubled over. Another was bouncing up and down, shrieking out, 'He should shoplift them things in his *beeerd!*' and the rest of them howling in agreement.

A jolt of pain rocked his stomach. It embarrassed him that anyone would think these things, about him or any other Jew. He turned around. He tried to run away, but they were everywhere. He did a full-circle turn. Face-to-face with his original antagonist, he said: 'I would never! Stealing is against the Ten Commandments.' He thought that would help, drawing a bridge between their two religions.

Instead of helping, though, it only fed their spirits. They threw their heads back. Their mouths were wide, white, full of teeth. They rocked with laughter, laughter like an earthquake. 'You,' he growled. 'You paupers.'

Now, in Judaism, being poor is no great tragedy. Certainly it's better to be comfortable, or even rich – there's no commandment against indulging in the permitted luxuries of this world, such as fine food or a trip to Hawaii – but poverty is not a condition that should be disparaged. You can try to make money or you can go with the flow, but ultimately pay and poverty are both up to G-d.

Reb Chaim knew this, and he knew it better than most. At various points in his life, he'd been a successful businessman, investing in a Passover matzo factory that, due to a series of bizarre episodes one year, became unexpectedly the only operation in town whose supplies were unspoiled by a series of freak water leaks. And he'd been basically a pauper himself, after the factory went broke and Reb Chaim was unable to find another job. He was too old to attend a kollel, and too learned in Talmud already. Not to say that he couldn't learn more – you can always learn more – but Reb Chaim was beyond that point in his life. He was too respected to do anything but be a rabbi, but he was too respected to be given anything but the highest rabbinical posts, and they were all filled.

Embarrassing someone was like killing them. Reb Chaim had been alive for 80 years, in Crown Heights for 69 of them – enough time to have been killed several times over – and in Russia before that. Most of his life in Russia, he couldn't remember. But he remembered this. His mother had taken him to the grocery store, unable to hold his hand because she feared dropping her food tickets, and so both her palms were stuffed tight with them. He had held onto the bottom hem of her coat. They stood waiting for hours, long enough for his skin to grow cold and then hot and then numb, a puffy and blustery shade of red. And then men came along. Younger than his mother, older than him. They shouted at them. They started pushing his mother. When little Reb Chaim wouldn't let go, they started on him. Calling him names. Saying things to him. He didn't understand what they were saying, or what these things meant, but he knew he was meant to be hurt.

He cried. The other people in line looked away from the pair, willing them to not exist. His mother picked him up, though he was too old to be carried, and she ran, all the way home, twelve long blocks. Maybe that was the first day he died. Or maybe it was only the first time he remembered. And now he had done the same thing. Half a world away, in another grocery store, he had committed murder.

Then he was falling. He was floating. He was a million miles away. He saw all the esoteric reasons for the irrational commandments they obeyed, listed like graffiti on a wall in front of him. He saw the winter constellations and the summer constellations at the same time, both sides of the sky like a giant sphere observed from the inside.

Now in front of him were Moses, David, the Baal Shem Tov – one a charlatan with a birth defect, born into a princehood he did not earn; one an abused shepherd, forced to run from his murderous brothers; one a teacher to the ignorant masses, who said that singing and dancing was more powerful than prayer, and was attacked by the leaders of the Jewish people, who made their money charging people for prayer. Their faces and bodies danced in the flames. They, too, were dying horrible deaths.

He zoomed back and he saw the whole of Earth, the whole history of humanity. Nations burning. People killing people. And behind it all, so faint that Reb Chaim could barely make them out at all, were the children from the store, the ones he'd so grievously wronged.

He twisted his head. He could barely move – it was like twisting through a block of Silly Putty. From the absolute corner of his eye, he could see the cashier, that boy, floating in the air, hovering above his register, his mouth wide open like he was screaming, no sound at all. Slowly but constantly, he was floating over the counter. Assembled around him in a loose circle were half a dozen tall, thin men. They all wore neat little grey suits. They were all bald.

They had big, prominent buggy eyes that seemed to eat up the whole room, yet saw nothing at all. It wasn't like they couldn't spot Reb Chaim and the children – it was more like, he felt, they just didn't care. Three or four of the men began to guide the cashier along, nudging him in the air like a giant balloon. One of the others tramped ahead. Two more came in their direction, one towards the children, one towards Reb Chaim. The man held up a small grey sphere. It was coated in the same colour as their uniforms. Already Reb Chaim could feel his memories peeling off like paper, flitting away on the night wind. The sickness that he'd let enter his body. His childhood, first in Vilnius, then the boat, then Brooklyn. His home and synagogue address. The first dinner he'd ever cooked his wife. The creature in front of him. The horrible embarrassment of the children and their laughter.

He stopped.

When you get older, your body betrays you. Certain things that used to work perfectly don't work any more. Your memories, which have always been stored in your brain like a well-ordered library are suddenly out of order, dust covers rearranged, pages swapped around, pages ripped out.

But there are certain things, other things, that you discover how to do, like muscles you've just used for the first time. You gain mastery over certain things – the chemicals, in your stomach and over your eyes, that do cleaning and digestion; how the wind smells before spring rain rushes in; the feeling of a lunatic moon; the involuntary spasms and knee-jerk reactions that your body was born with, that you, after 80 or so years, now can override. That was how Reb Chaim learned to make himself sick.

And that was how he grabbed onto his memories now: forced them back into his brain, yanked them with the utter force of his own belief, not because of any particular desire or melancholy but because he needed the embarrassment of being laughed at. It was a sign from G-d, a sign that he wasn't perfect yet. He still had things to work on. No one in Crown Heights – the Jewish Crown Heights, the proper Crown Heights – would ever dare laugh at Reb Chaim. And if he forgot what it was like, if he let the memory expire and float away, then he would have nothing. It would be like he'd never gotten that gift from G-d.

And he couldn't only keep his own memory of it, either. The children had to remember – of that, he was sure. Once the memories rushed back into his head, the creature stumbling toward him reeled back as if slapped, and the other creature, the one working on the children, was similarly shaken.

Reb Chaim used the last of his physical strength to hurl himself at the second creature. The first one was doing a good enough job on his own, shuddering wildly, collapsing against the ice-cream freezer. Both toppled over, and the memory device fell from the creature's hand.

The children shook themselves awake. They stared at each other, into one another's faces, as if relearning forgotten alphabets. Some of them walked over to the fallen creatures, prodded their unmoving bodies, retreating when they felt the soapy consistency of their skin. Then one of the kids looked at Reb Chaim and gave him a squinted-up face, as if trying to remember where she recognized his silvery mane.

Her attention was diverted by a scream from the door.

'They got Jesse!' she cried. 'They floatin' him away in the air!'

That was all the kids needed. They shook themselves into action, dashed through the door, screaming and fiery, in a stampeding pursuit of the creatures and their friend.

Reb Chaim walked to the door and leaned against its mezuzah-less frame. The metal was smooth, but he missed the feel of hard plastic jutting into his back – it had been ages since he'd stood in a doorway with no mezuzah. Out on the street, people were frozen in mid-walk, mid-conversation, mid-fight. The world was peaceful and still. Only the children from the store, the children who'd laughed at him (the children he saved, the thought sprung up in his mind, and was immediately banished) were in motion. They had found the grey men, and were presently engaged in jumping on them, beating them, tearing the creatures away from their friend, the boy at the cashier's booth. Perhaps Reb Chaim should tell them to go lightly. That the One Above punishes evildoers and those who deserve it; that it was not in our province to mete out justice without a fair trial.

But, no. He'd been a distinguished-looking old man for long enough. He knew that some lessons merely had to be learned in the doing.

Reb Chaim turned back to the produce carts. A few had been upended, but most were still in serviceable condition. He did a squat and sorted through a few of the lemons on the floor. A really good one brushed against his fingers, then rolled away into some unreachable crevice. It didn't matter. There were more than enough here.

When he had finished, the children were still not back. The two unconscious creatures who'd been on the floor were also gone – vanished, suddenly yet somehow unremarkably, each into a shimmer of pale blue. He counted out exact change from his wallet and left it on the cash register, obscured from potential thieves by a small bag of potato chips on top. He didn't have exact change: he was half a dollar over, which normally would cause him to stand in a corner of the store and wait, patiently but respectably, for another customer to materialise with sufficient funds for his reimbursement.

Tonight, he decided to leave it and head home.

'Chaim, what took you so long?' said his wife when he crept in. She was already in bed, but not yet asleep – Chaya had a terrible time letting herself go to sleep at night. His absence probably magnified her unease. She had the radio on, tuned to the news channel, which usually she wanted for white noise. Tonight, however, it was buzzing, the announcer talking rapidly and excitedly: strange lights seen over Brooklyn, low-flying planes. Reb Chaim rolled down the volume and, as unobtrusively as he could, switched it to the oldies station.

EXCISION

NAOMI ALDERMAN

Transcript from *In The Spirit*,
a light-hearted weekly vidcast across the five systems on matters of
faith, cultural spiritual practice, ancestor worship and the Quantum
Gods.

Starts at 0012:38:92 of the programme.

...and on that subject, we're joined today from the gas planet Procyon 12 by an entity who's made *quite* the journey in spiritual outlook. N'kk'd>>f – I hope I'm pronouncing that correctly?

Not bad. Human tongues can't really manage the >>.

I'm embarrassed now I hear you pronounce it! Great! So, why don't you tell us what made you decide to convert to the Earth religion of 'Judaism'?

I've always been a searcher, I suppose. The values of Judaism appealed to me: a lot of emphasis is placed on the family. The peoples of Procyon 12 have rather complex families – each grouping contains four genders – so I was pleased to find a system of thought that put the family at the centre. And of course there was a more serious –

Right, right, amazing. Now my notes tell me that the leaders of this religion, the 'rabbis', tried to put you off?

That's right, Dirk. Judaism isn't a proselytising religion. They turned me away three times, according to their custom.

I'd think you might *want* to be put off, given that you have to have... is this right... they cut a bit off your sex organ when you join? That's a bit harsh, isn't it?

Ah, of course, yes, the circumcision process was quite problematic! I am of a gender unknown among humans. I have a protuberance with which I can begin the process of mate-impregnation, but when the act is complete the member breaks off and remains with my partner. A new member then grows within 72 hours. Well, it was faster when I was younger.

A...ha?

Yes, it was quite the conundrum for the rabbis! The sign is of a permanent covenant – but my sexual organs are extremely impermanent!

Sounds like a... puzzler?

Yes indeed. Well put. In the end, after some Talmudic discourse, it was decided that I could cut a permanent notch in my... ah, it is hard to describe in human terms. It is the frilly flesh-part which stands up on the back of my head when I am ready to mate.

Right! And are any of your other partners interested in joining you on your spiritual quest?

Not mine, no. Several friends have expressed an interest, but I believe I'm the first person on my planet to take the plunge, as it were.

To have the snip.

Quite.

Now, fitting a bi-gendered religion to a people with four genders. Tricky at all? I understand that the people of Procyon 12 fall into, basically, for the viewers, two different kinds of bloke and two different kinds of woman.

No, it would not be correct to call them two forms of male and two female, no. It is complex. These terms do not have the meaning for us that they have for you.

What would you call them, then?

The closest form is... you might call them right and left and up and down. And centre.

And centre?

Right and left and up and down and centre, yes.

That's… five.

Yes.

I thought you said there were four.

Yes. There are four.

So what's… centre?

Ah. We hope for their return.

We don't have much time, I'm afraid, N'kk'd>>f, so I'm going to ask you to tell me more – but briefly, if you could?

It is a matter of some shame to my people.

I'm sorry to hear that. But, briefly…

To create new life, four partners are needed. The first impregnates the second. The second hosts the foetus for three months before passing it on to the third, who adds certain DNA modifiers. The third hosts for another 21 days before passing to the fourth, who provides the amniotic sac and swaps in some RNA. After 36 days, the amniotic sac must be passed back to the first impregnator, who hosts the foetus to term – another eight months.

Fascinating. And complicated! Must take a lot of commitment.

This is why we place such emphasis on family.

And the… fifth gender?

We destroyed them.

Right.

They were not necessary to the process.

I see.

The rhetoric was that they were parasites. Their role was only to add certain DNA switching chemicals at the fifth and twenty-sixth week. They never hosted the foetus. It is history for us now. A politico-philosophical movement among my people 300 years ago declared them... lesser beings.

Right.

They contributed nothing, you see.

I'm being told we have to –

They were only a small fraction of us. Fewer than one per cent of births would belong to this fifth gender. We hunted them down. Where they were sheltered, we rooted them out. We knew them by the unusual colour of their eyes. By the lower tone of their voices. It took 100 years. And only then did we know that without their DNA-switching properties there would never be another of them.

And you –

It's not that they had a special power, or some innate ability. But we destroyed part of our own people. The body will never be whole again. There has been a great deal of regret among us for what we have done.

That's fascinating and tragic. Thank you, N'kk'd>>f, for –

This was what I saw among the Jewish people, you understand.

We have to –

I was only a youngster, 300 years ago. I didn't know what I was doing. But I suppose I... I suppose I've been searching for someone to forgive me.

Cut to commercial.

JEWS
VS
ZOMBIES

RISE

RENA ROSSNER

There were once 12 yeshiva students who were graced with long, perfectly curled sidelocks that shone in as many shades as the sample book at the local wig-maker's store. Each one of the boys was an *ilui* – a prodigy of his generation. And they all lived and studied together at the great House of Learning in the mystical city of Safed.

One day, Yossele, the oldest of the 12, was reading an ancient kabbalist tome he'd found discarded in the *genizah*. It was filled with stories about The Ari, Rabbi Isaac Luria, Lion of Safed, and father of modern kabbalah. Yossele read that The Ari once instructed his students to sleep on the graves of *tzaddikim* in the city's holy cemetery, so that even in repose they could learn the words of the greats – wisdom rising up from the hallowed tombs. And so, Yossele read, each of The Ari's illustrious followers would do so every night until the ancient cemetery resembled a campground, and the many-colored sleeping bags that dotted the cemetery began to smell from mildew, caused by the holy mist that blanketed the town each night. Nobody knows what stopped the practice, the ancient book went on to say, but one day The Ari called all his students back to their beds. "There is only so much one can learn from the dead," he said. "Come back to the living, my students, come back." And so they did.

But, the book continued, it is said that those closest to him, the *illuim* of his generation, their souls never left the garden of the dead and sometimes you can see them still, those students he once called his lion cubs, curled up cat-like on the tombstones, sleeping soundly on the graves.

Yossele was charmed by the story. After dinner and night-seder, he told it to Moishe, who told Donniel, and then Yerahmiel, and soon a crowd had gathered in the dormitory room that they all shared. Asher and Bentzion, Efraim and Leibel, Kalonymous and Zevulun, Samuel and the youngest of all of them, Gedaliah.

"We should try that!" Asher was the first to say, his eyes blazing gold like his sidelocks.

"Are you crazy?" said Yerachmiel, twirling his auburn tresses nervously.

"Isn't it cold outside?" offered Donniel, the most fragile and sickly of the bunch, his curly russet *peyot* frizzed and trembling.

"It wouldn't hurt just once to try it," offered Leibel, sleek and dark-haired, always daring, the most athletic of the 12.

"Of course you'd say that," argued Samuel, of the thick chocolate-brown hair. "You could run all night and still show up for morning prayers."

"I say we go for it," said Yossele, his voice loud and smooth like his caramel locks, "but all of us, as a group, nobody stays behind."

"Tonight," chimed in Kalonymous, "at the stroke of midnight." His eyes burnt wild with the same passion as his fiery red hair.

"Midnight?" said Yossele.

"Midnight," said 12 voices in unison.

"Don't forget to dress warm!" advised the youngest of them all, Gedaliah, his face lit up with an inner glow that matched his pale blond hair.

And so to bed they went, each one of them, side by side, in a chamber lit only by moonlight and the white fire of the holy books that lined the room. Though the books threatened to topple in on them at any moment, like most of the crumbling stone buildings in the city, they were held fast by dust and the comfort of the years.

When midnight struck, it was Efraim who whispered first, "Wake up, my brothers! Wake up, the hour calls us!" He hadn't really slept, but counted 24 formations of *gematria* as his clock ticked and every second showed a new prophetic formulation.

He had been trying to decipher if tonight was an auspicious night, but every string of numbers set his mind wandering down different pathways in the number labyrinth of his mind, and he came up with nothing in the end, well, nearly nothing, only 12: "bay" or "yab".

"A number which could mean the abyss," he murmured to himself, "a lost thing or a longing, a desire or a craving, a howl or a silence, a decision or a prayer, rejoicing or trepidation, a lamb, a bear, a fish, the banks of the river or the prince of Magog, a caress or a nail, a babbling, that 'one and the many are one' or it could have meant the *shvatim*, the 12 sheaves in Joseph's dream, or 12 like the number that we are, 12 students, getting up at 12 midnight." He took a deep breath, and then it was time to go.

They rubbed the sleep out of their eyes and fumbled on socks and shoes, *tzitit* and pants, an exaltation of kippot and hats that covered their bare skulls. Lastly went the black jackets over the black sweaters until out of the window they all climbed, whispering softly with the breeze.

They ran down the hill from the yeshiva, down the alleyways and steps, rushing off as if to prayer. If anyone had asked them where they were off to (but no one did), it would have been obvious: to pray *tikkun chatzot*, they would have said, each one of them, for that was what they'd all decided. And indeed, as they made their way down to the graves, one whispered, "At midnight I will rise to give thanks unto thee," and then the next repeated after him, until it was something like a game, of call and answer, or a dirge, that rose from each of their mouths and was borne onto the wind of night.

When they arrived they couldn't see the tombstones despite the light of moon and stars, and while they would have liked to choose the sage whose eternal bed they shared that night, they didn't think it mattered all too much, for every man buried in Safed was a saint, a holy man, a rav of sorts, and it is said that you can learn from every man.

So full of rapture were the boys that they didn't even think to feel the names beneath their fingers. Each one wandered until he found a promising-looking stone. Bentzion sought a comfortable one, and lay down on one rubbed soft by rain and snow, his raven sidelocks falling like silk to grace the marble, having lost their curl in the damp of night.

Carrot-topped Zevulun chose a tombstone that looked ancient, cracking from the weight of years, and thought that certainly his choice was the best one: the older the dead the more he would learn.

And so each boy made his choice and curled up cat-like on a stone, and tossed and turned and shivered until sleep came.

What these bachelors never realized was that each in turn had picked a tomb not of a holy *tzaddik* but of his wife, the holiest of holy women, and when these women, dead so many years, felt the warm blood of a *bochur* sleeping soundly just above them, the ground began to rumble with desire.

Tremors are common in Safed, city of earthquakes. Nobody knows what causes them, for no direct fault-lines ache beneath the city vaults. But that night it was a different kind of trembling, and with a gust of wind came rain. The skies opened up the earth with tender fingers, and as the boys began to wake from cold, 12 sets of bony digits held them fast. Some boys screamed in terror, while others froze in fear, and watched in horror, speechless, as 12 lusty zombie brides rose from the earth.

Leibel thought that he could run for help. He knew he was the strongest and the fastest of the 12, but his bride Miriam, the daughter of the famed Rabbi Nachman, caught his ankle, and try as he might he could not escape the skeletal grip of her fingers. All the other brothers were caught in struggles of their own, until Leibel, swallowing his fear, decided to face her.

He thought perhaps an incantation or a prayer might release him. He started chanting, but as he did he watched her. Her hair was dark as midnight like his own. She wore a tattered dress and had haunted, decayed eyes, but she smiled, he could have sworn she smiled, or maybe all skeletons looked like that. But there was flesh there too, not much around the bone, but enough to soften her in places, and soon from her lips she crooned a melody. It was the softest saddest *niggun* Leibel had ever heard, and she swayed with him, as dancers do, and his heart beat fast, electric in the night, with fear but also awe, and he stood straighter, and relaxed, and took her hand in his and slid an arm around her waist (or where he thought her waist once was) and closed his eyes and danced. It was not the frenzied dance of the Hasidim, but a soft wedding tantz, a waltz. And he felt all the other eyes upon him, eyes and lack of eyes. His brothers and their brides all saw them dancing, and in no time joined them, hand in bony hand and arm around depleted waist.

The women sang songs the boys had never heard, *niggunim*, mouthing melodies like kisses that the boys took from their lips and sang back at them into the sky. And soon words followed songs and they were learning from each other, the boys how to dance, and how to hold a woman, the zombie *rebbetzins* remembering what it was like to be young and to be free.

Yossele danced with Chana, and she told him in her droning voice about her seven sons. As she sang she imparted of their wisdom that she had heard and gathered as she cared for them and heard them pray and learn. His caramel locks twirled in the breeze around her rotting scarf, forming a halo, and if you looked you might have thought that she wore a living crown.

The straw-haired Moishe paired with Raichele, the dreamer, who sang to him of the mountain of straw within her, always burning, but never consumed. They slow-danced as her skeleton crackled, indeed like straw, and moved in tandem above her tombstone that praised her as a modest lady. She told him all the secrets she had heard from Rav Vital, as she eavesdropped at the door to the attic of her home, and of his visions, and of hers, and of her courtyard where all the Kabbalists would gather, and she would serve them tea and read their fortunes in the leaves.

Donniel was whisked into a tango by Donia Reyna, who grew up alongside the great Vital. His twin, she wrote her own grand Book of Visions and she serenaded the russet-haired boy with its words. He was entranced, not just by words, but by her still-red ruby lips, which looked as though they'd been stained with blood.

And so they were all paired, Yerachmiel with Mazal Tov, righteous woman, daughter of the perfect sage, and blessed, blessed, blessed, she hissed through her missing teeth and gums. Asher paired with Mira and she told him all her vivid dreams, and gave him a long list of holy missions, escapades she never got to go on. Bentzion twirled with Frances Sarah, a maggid dervish dressed in furs, and Efraim learned the zohar's secrets to the fox-trot of Fioretta, the wisest woman of her time.

Though Dona Gracia was under the shade of the Nassi in her lifetime, in her death she danced with Leibel and spoke only queenly prose, all about the flowers in her garden, and how each bush grew a thirteen-petalled rose. Kalonymous took the hand of the eldest lady, Safta Yocheved, whose bones knocked with every step, but tap-dancing into the night they went, as she pointed out the path of the Messiah she was certain would still come home to her that day. Zevulun snaked around the cemetery with Sonadora wrapped in his arms, and he could feel the oil of sorcery still on her fingers, as she stroked his face and told him all her divination secrets and her holy lore.

Samuel took the arm of Hannah Rachel, much to his surprise, for he would have sworn he'd heard that she was buried in Jerusalem, yet here she was, the Maiden of Ludmir, in zombie form. Still dressed in *tallit* and *tefillin*, the two locked eyes and hearts and sang in tune. And then Gedaliah, youngest of them all, took the hand of young Anav. Dressed in wedding finery and almost whole, she who'd mastered spirits and possessions, told Gedaliah all the mysteries of souls, how to call them – from *dybbuk* to *ibbur*, and how to send them back to their abodes. With her he danced the longest, a form of wedding *tantz*, until the sun began to rise, and then with all the words she'd taught him, Gedaliah opened up the earth and one by one he and his bride sent them all home.

He was the last one back through the dormitory window, the last to pack the earth of his beloved's tomb, as all the boys fell into bed an hour before sunrise. They shed their shoes, bereft of soles and fell asleep, covered in earth and flesh and shards of bone. And when the rebbes came to wake them from their slumber, they were like the dead under their blankets, comatose and spent. They stumbled out of bed and zombie-like they filed into synagogue, eyes glazed and mouths contorted into constant yawns.

The rabbis knew something had happened. They feared the worst: sexual dreams, they thought, and checked each bed for nocturnal emissions. Yet they found no such evidence, only traces of blood and bone amid the sheets and 12 pairs of shoes, destroyed and caked in muddy soil.

When the boys all took a break for lunch and went to town and all came back with matching shoes, the rabbis only shrugged because their students glowed all morning with new levels of insight, *drash* and *sod*. Let the boys have their eccentricities, the bearded men thought as they took notes. These *illuim* are priceless, minds like these come once a lifetime, what's a pair of shoes destroyed.

And as the day passed the boys grew anxious; they checked their shirts for stains and twirled their curls. Like young girls getting ready for a date they fretted, cleaning under fingernails and checking for blocked pores. They rushed to brush their teeth after the evening meal, and grinned at one another thinking only of what secrets would await them, yet again, in the cemetery down below.

For many nights the yeshivah students woke at the stroke of midnight, then bedded down on their beloveds' graves, and sweet Gedaliah with his newfound words would call them, his voice shrill and melodic, like a flute. And the zombie ladies of the night, the holy *rebbetzin*, would rise and take their places by the sides of boys. They turned them into men at night, and they would talk and waltz and sing and dance and speak of all the mysteries of the world.

Every night they tangoed, rhumbaed, and hip-hopped to beats and jazzy jingles. They danced Israeli folk and then fox-trots, flamenco and ballet, and even tap, and all along they sang and learned Zohar and kabbalah, visions, dreams and conjured souls. And the boys marveled at these women and their knowledge: everything their husbands knew they knew, and so much more, until the boys began to fear that they would never marry, for what earthly woman could ever possibly compare?

That was when the spirits realised their nightly jaunts were coming to an end. Nice as it was to be out dancing, as women priestesses and visionary greats, the place for these boys was with living women, partners who could give them more than ruined shoes. And so it was Anav who told Gedaliah that the night trysts had to end and how, and taught him how to curse them all back into an eternal slumber, and she sealed it with a kiss from her sweet and rotten lips.

And so it was on the last night, after all was said and danced and done, that the lovers laid their ladies down upon each tombstone, and caressed their dead and lovely ones. Tears fell from the eyes of all the holy boys, and wet the eyes of their beloved zombie brides, and while the others listened for the last whispered words of wisdom, the last holy song and fervent prayer, Gedaliah slipped a ring onto the bony finger of his bride and whispered all the words he knew to say. She shrieked out loud as he did so, for he knew not what he'd done, but it was over in an instant and the brides all sank into the earth and all was said and done.

Gone but not forgotten. Never did the boys regret, and sometimes, when they thought no one was looking, one by one they'd wander still. And they'd look and watch and sometimes still they'd see, the holy lions, mist-shaped, curling up onto the graves. And they knew it was the lions who had led them, clothed in mist, each to his beloved's bed. You can still see them sometimes in the morning mist. They answer to the bellow of the largest one of all, The Ari, the great lion king of Safed, whose ghost still haunts the city's cliffs and stones.

And so the boys grew up and nearly all got married, and they loved their wives well and even taught them dance in the privacy of their homes, and the wives all wondered how they learned it, but never questioned, for the fox-trot was a dance they loved to learn. All except Gedaliah, who still waited for his ghostly bride to someday rise again. Celibate, he waited, for he knew no human girl would ever compare. She'd mastered him forever, Anav, she held his soul, and with his gift to her that night he'd made her whole.

THE SCAPEGOAT FACTORY

OFIR TOUCHE GAFLA

After a decade of complete degeneration, even he realized there was no sense in living up to nothing. Solvi Lumsvenson, once a Danish cab driver, presently a member of the formerly dead, couldn't go on doing more of the same, namely sex, drugs and metal-rock. 'Pleasure's a bitch' was the first thought that accompanied his every waking morning during his tenth year of renewed existence. He was craving a change.

The first change took place 15 years ago when Solvi – 30 years old, living in Copenhagen, recently married, about to become a father, relishing the promise of life in all its splendor – came to blows with fate.

It was a sunny day. A group of friends were having a picnic in the woods when a huge oak tree landed on the flabbergasted picnickers like a divine slap in the face. 'Someone forgot to shout "Timber!",' ran the joke among the survivors. 'They died in one fell swoop,' ran another. No one knew what exactly happened until two years later when a teetotal lumberjack came out with it.

On the eve of the tragedy he had been drunk and tired and once he realized he was cutting the wrong tree he stopped mid-cut and went home. 'Couldn't see the forest for the trees,' he tried to excuse himself, but couldn't keep it bottled up any more. He was single-handedly responsible for the deaths of three people and the grave injuries of four more.

Solvi was among the lucky survivors, if brain damage, a vegetative state and a lack of any basic form of communication with the outside world could be considered luck.

'At least he's alive,' some said. 'Of course,' grunted his wife, pulling back the toddler who was climbing all over his statuesque father and pinching his face in a fit of soon-to-be-orphaned laughter. 'My poor alien,' was how she referred to her husband, for she couldn't conceive of a different word. 'Alien, alien,' the kid shouted. 'My dad is an alien.'

A week after the child's second birthday, an errant blood clot brought about the conclusion of the tragedy and Solvi passed away in his sleep. Incidentally, two days later the scrupulous lumberjack stepped into the nearest police station.

The second change was far more shocking. After five years of uneventful death, Solvi woke up one rainy afternoon at the cemetery and instantly began looking for shelter.

While hiding under a big oak tree, he looked up and felt a sudden twinge of regret, soon to be replaced by a terrible sense of panic. Moving away from the tree, he glanced around him and saw another man, and then another, until the whole place was swarming with humanity, cursing the rain. It was a diversion of sorts, for once one of them pointed at a tombstone bearing his name and exclaimed, 'Damn! I think it's happening all over again,' it dawned on Solvi that he was back for more. Life, that is.

That day he spent an exceptionally wet hour in front of his grave, failing to come to terms with the stunning revelation. Then he left the place, took a peek at a newspaper and found out he had been 'away' for five years. He didn't waste another minute and rushed home, only to confront a screaming widow and a belligerent-looking boy who told him to bugger off.

The formerly dead were the subjects of an incredibly expensive experiment whose results have surpassed the wildest expectations of its initiators, a group of neuro-physicists who fell in love with the theory of eternal temporariness, according to which everything under the sun would one day expire. Love, life, misery, sickness – all is temporary. And death. Nothing is permanent for the very nature of existence is steeped in mutability.

When those scientists declared that death is temporary, they were swept by a tsunami of derision. But, true to their beliefs, they knew that derision was not everlasting. They conducted endless experiments at a small cemetery in Copenhagen, away from the public eye, until they witnessed the first sign of life in the maggoty cadaver of a certain 45-year-old woman who had drowned in the bath two years earlier.

They had never revealed their methods and only conceded that since everything is temporary, nothing is irrevocable. Perhaps nothing was irrevocable, but much was certainly irretrievable, as hundreds of the formerly dead found out upon trying to regain their past lives. No one welcomed them with open arms, and petrified hostility was the common reaction of their dearest to that macabre re-emergence. Funnily enough, the only ones who extended a helping hand were members of certain religions and lovers of goth-metal. Solvi opted to take advantage of the latter.

In goth circles, Solvi became a household name. Everybody wanted a piece of him and metal groups dedicated entire albums to the man who was resurrected against all reason. Just like his counterparts, Solvi was invited on innumerable TV shows and interviewed about his posthumous experience. Unlike them, Solvi came up with silly anecdotes and fascinated the masses with his ridiculous fibs. ('We actually keep on living in a world of complete darkness, and after a while we get used to our mole-like existence.')

Soon afterwards, the book deal arrived. The money Solvi got for *Second Notes from the Underground* secured his next five years, although he was constantly sued by other formerly dead who claimed he was nothing but a liar. 'Amnesiacs,' he retorted and resumed whatever he was up to at that moment, which was either sex, drugs, metal rock, or preferably all three at once.

Eight years into his renewed life, Solvi became sick of it all. He wrote another autobiography called *Core*, about his life prior to his death, but no one was interested. The world only wanted the 'husk' version of his life. With the remainder of his money he left Copenhagen and sought retreat in a small village, frittering away his days in his cabin, awaiting death. Solvi was never suicidal; he'd just had enough of it all, but to his dismay he discovered that death was not an option. His attempts at self-annihilation came to nothing.

Still, he kept reminding himself that if everything was temporary, then this loutish resurrection wouldn't last forever. Doing crossword puzzles and watching reality shows only brought about a stronger sense of despair. He was looking for something meaningful to do, some form of occupation that would serve as a blessed distraction. His financial resources were rapidly dwindling, but he just couldn't come up with anything. He even started frequenting forests in the hope that history might repeat itself – alas, to no avail.

On one of his excursions to the woods, he came across a man hanging from a tree. He rushed to help him, but the man called, freeing his neck from the noose, 'Don't bother – it just won't do.'

Solvi realised he'd happened upon another of the formerly dead who, just like him, wanted out. 'Death escapes us,' Solvi told him.

'Well, duh,' the other man said and landed on his feet. He explained that every Monday he came to the forest, picked the same tree and tried to off himself. 'You see, failure will eventually prove to be temporary as well, right?'

Solvi smiled and introduced himself.

'Yehoshua,' said the man, and shook his hand. It turned out that Yehoshua had just come out of prison, where he spent six years for armed robbery. 'You robbed a bank?!' Solvi asked with a slight note of admiration in his voice.

Yehoshua grinned. 'Sorry to disappoint you. I never robbed a bank. It's just that I was so bored and saw no meaning to my renewed life and, as you can imagine, couldn't put an end to the whole travesty until I heard about the factory.'

'The factory?'

'The Scapegoat Factory. They are always looking for new employees, for lack of a better word. Preferably Jews.'

Solvi pondered what he'd just heard. He knew about Jews but, as far as he could tell, he'd never met one. Bible. Jesus. Circumcision. Holocaust. Israel. Pork. This was the extent of his knowledge as far as Jews were concerned. The first time he heard someone mention them was when a high school friend was singing 'Hey, Jews' and another friend told him to shut the fuck up. Ever since, he had associated Jews with songs by the Beatles, although he knew the connection had been totally misconceived. *Yellow Submarine* started playing in his mind when he asked, somewhat cautiously, 'But... isn't it a bit discriminatory, you know, to hire employees based on...?'

Yehoshua shook his head. 'I said they prefer Jews. It doesn't mean they're the only ones they hire for the job.'

'And when you say "they"...'

'The people who run the factory. Or should I say the man behind it all: a certain Felix Cohen. You see, this guy came up with an interesting premise. Looking around, he realised the easiest way to make money these days is to present a new application to the world. The future's in application or, as my nephew likes to say, "The only way is app." So he came up with the guilt application, where people take the blame for other people's crimes.

162

Well, not really crimes, but rather slight misdemeanors, petty insults, you know, the daily manure of human relationships.'

'But why would anyone take the blame for another's…?'

'Money, peacock-brain. Money!'

'I have to say, I'm not very impressed.'

'Well, perhaps this is going to impress you. What started as a strange idea became something totally different when Felix realised the amazing potential at hand. You see, Felix got his brother, a retired police superintendent, involved and he suggested an upgrade.'

'An upgrade?'

'There are so many unsolved crimes, cases that will forever remain open for lack of material evidence or will be shut because the police have reached an impasse. Well, Felix and his brother weren't really thinking about the perpetrators but rather about the families of the victims. Nothing is worse than a feeling of injustice. As far as those families are concerned, someone has to take the blame, right? When you point an accusing finger there must be someone to point that finger at. So why not provide a scapegoat, someone who'll take the blame and rid the families, the police and the masses of that terrible sense of injustice?'

'But then the perpetrators walk away scot-free.'

'Well, under the circumstances they do anyway, don't they? And trust me, the families are so grateful once the factory supplies a criminal that soon enough they forget that he or she isn't the genuine scum who's put them through hell.'

Solvi was speechless. They were already out of the woods.

Yehoshua scratched his neck absentmindedly. 'And you know what's the best thing about it? It gives us, the formerly dead, a true sense of purpose.'   Solvi smiled weakly.

'Are you by any chance a Jew?' Yehoshua asked him Solvi was thinking of a celestial lapidary named Lucy and shook his head.

'A shame, but you can still take the blame.'

'Why do they prefer to employ Jews?'

Yehoshua patted his shoulder and wore a condescending expression. 'Read a little history, my friend.'

Which he did. Right after reading about the factory. Right after coming to terms with his decision to find some meaning for his vacuous existence.

A week after he met Yehoshua at the forest, Solvi arrived at The Factory. He found himself in a corridor teeming with dozens of bearded men. To his surprise, each time one of them was ushered into the office for an interview, he was instantly asked to leave.

'Vot more do you vont? Not only am I a Jew, but I'm a dead one! Even now you refuse to let me be a part of your vorld?!' complained a gaunt creature of unimpressive height, overlooking the strange dance of his lopsided beard with his twisting yarmulke.

'I came back to claim the blame, I came back to name my shame,' shouted another.

The loudest of them all climbed a bench, a minute after he was kicked out of the office, and cried aloud, 'You have no idea! We are to blame for everything! Cancer! Earthquakes! Nine Eleven! Aids! Global Warming! Triglycerides! Famine! Hell, if not for us, who will the world come after?'

When Solvi entered the office, a middle-aged man greeted him with a smile and said, 'How refreshing.'

Solvi sat and cleared his throat before speaking. 'I'm with the formerly dead.'

The man said, 'Yes, I guessed so. So, what are you after? Robbery? Tax evasion? Drug dealing? Rape? Murder? Or perhaps some exquisite monstrosity of the highest degree?'

'Before I say anything, I'd like to point out I'm not a Jew.'

The man exclaimed, 'No!' and giggled. 'Didn't take you for one. Let's make one thing clear: you don't have to be a Jew to work for us, but you have to understand what's expected of you. Once you assume the blame for a certain criminal act, there's no turning back. You will be held accountable for it ad infinitum. You have to believe it. Just like those morons who believe the Jews killed Jesus, even after the Pope himself has absolved them of that imaginary crime.'

'But it's not the same, is it?'

'It is, for you have to believe you are to blame to the same extent that those who shout "J'accuse!" believe it. That's the only way to be a convincing scapegoat.'

'But isn't my taking the blame proof enough of my...?'

'Not at all. Once again, it is only convincing if both condemner and condemnee believe in it. Credibility's the name of the game.'

'And the fact that you're seeking dead Jews for this job?'

'It's quite obvious, isn't it? If you're to be blamed just because of who you are, at least try and get something out of it, right?'

'And what about me?'

'You seem like a very conscientious piece of work. Why don't you go and mull things over?'

'No need for that.' Solvi leaned over the desk and extended his hand. 'I need meaning.'

Three years later, prisoner Solvi Lumsvenson, serving time for manslaughter (a hit-and-run accident) was once again running out of patience. Having undergone a self-inflicted brainwash, Solvi came to believe he had been the man behind the wheel responsible for the tragic death of Marketa Gloon, an 86-year-old woman who was crossing the street, pushing a trolley full of groceries back from her weekly visit to the supermarket. But the principle of eternal temporariness suddenly applied to his sense of guilt. Three years were price enough, as far as he was concerned, to pay for a mistake, as serious as it might be.

Unfortunately, he had another year before the authorities would let him go. Now, more than ever, he wanted out. Out of this prison cell, out of this city, out of this world. He tried escaping for the umpteenth time and was shot in the back. How he hated that moment when the guard gave him a hand and helped him up, muttering, 'Still no luck.'

But on his fourth return to his cell from solitary confinement (rules are rules, weird circumstances notwithstanding), a surprise awaited him in the form of a visitor: a 50-year-old woman who looked like a whore turned librarian.

'My name is Rosa. Rosa Gloon,' she said.

His heart skipped a beat. 'Are you related to…?'

'I'm her daughter.'

'Why has it taken you so long to come and see me?'

'I have been living in Paris for 20 years now. I had no idea. I got here two days ago and went to pay my mother's grave a visit, when… I saw that her tombstone was sprayed in some phosphorescent green. I didn't know what it meant until a certain lady explained to me that my mother's stone is marked since she was of the formerly dead.'

Solvi bit his tongue. 'Your mother has just returned? Was there another second coming?'

'No. I don't know how I've never heard of what happened a little bit over a decade ago, you know, when the dead were resurrected by those crazy scientists. As far as I know, it only happened once. Anyway, my mother was one of them, which means that the woman you killed had already been dead when you hit her.'

Solvi didn't correct her. Evidently she hadn't heard of the factory. He didn't even mention the bizarre realisation that both he and his 'victim' had returned to this world at the same time. But, despite his sudden surge of happiness, there was something wrong with her story. 'But if your mother had already been dead...?'

'She forgot.'

'Excuse me?'

'My mother was an extremely senile woman. It turns out that when she came back from the dead, she didn't give it much thought. She just wandered the streets looking for her home until she found it. Luckily for her I hadn't managed to sell it because it's a tiny place in the middle of nowhere. Anyway, she did remember she used to keep the key under the rug and got in as if she hadn't just returned from the dead.'

'You're telling me your mother forgot she was dead?'

'Yes. And so, when she was run over several years later by you, she actually died I came here to let you know that –'

'Hang on a minute. Didn't anyone contact you after she was run over?'

'They weren't able to track me down. I got married and changed my name. Now I'm divorced and – anyway, that's beside the point. I came here to tell you that since, according to the law of the living, one can't be held guilty for a crime committed against a dead person, you are to be released effective immediately.'

Solvi stared at her in disbelief. 'But there's one thing I don't understand. If your mother had already been dead when she was run over, then how was anyone held responsible for the accident? I mean, there was no body to begin with. She probably got up and went back home, slightly shaken up but still alive. So to speak.'

Now it was Rosa's turn to stare at him in disbelief. 'Oh, but she didn't. She died. And she was buried again, although at a different spot, which means she has two tombstones. Funnily enough, no one bothered to check.'

'She died?'

'Yes.'

'For good?'

'For good.'

Solvi didn't look back. Upon leaving prison he realized that Marketa had probably been the first among the formerly dead to regain death once again, yet her second demise had been a secret of sorts since no one but her daughter had known about her first death.

He went to the cemetery and looked for Marketa's stone. He wanted to address it but felt like a fool, contemplating his life ever since he arose. He spent ten minutes in front of the silent grave and wondered about Marketa's first death. Then he went back home. The following Monday he wandered to the forest and saw Yehoshua pouring gasoline all over himself.

Yehoshua called, 'Well, if it isn't…'

Solvi wanted to let him know about the new promise when Yehoshua opened his eyes in shock and pointed behind Solvi, shouting, 'Watch out!'

Solvi looked around hopefully and heard Yehoshua's laughter.

'Just kidding,' he said.

'You stupid arsehole!' Solvi roared at the laughing man. He grabbed the matchbox from his hand, struck a match and threw it at him.

The burning man screamed like there was no tomorrow, and Solvi retorted, 'Just kidding,' before leaving the forest.

It was only a week later, during one of his gloomy constitutionals, that he happened upon the human lump of coal that used to be Yehoshua. He bent over the burnt corpse and called, 'Yehoshua! Yehoshua! Stop playing this silly game!' but it was evident no life remained in the formerly dead man, who'd resumed his old status courtesy of Solvi's momentary fit of rage.

Solvi was thinking about the second dead person who managed to prove the theory of eternal temporariness and tried to banish from his mind the other thought, about himself being the culprit, since he'd killed another man, albeit a once dead one. And then it hit him, like nothing before – not even the tree that had changed the course of his lives. Perhaps the only way to help a formerly dead person fulfill their death wish was to have another formerly dead person do the deed.

The excited pounding of his heart reminded him of his not-so-long-ago metal days, and by the time he got back home, he knew he was right. That was the secret. Marketa died because she was run over by a formerly dead driver. Different rules applied to the dead, and one just had to follow them.

Another month went by. Solvi was waiting beside the familiar prison gates for another member of the scapegoat factory to emerge. After talking to Felix and finding out about the next formerly dead person to be released, he contacted the woman in question and told her about his secret plan, assuming she was seeking death as well.

When she stepped out of the gates, he smiled at her. Her name was Diana Bloomberg, and she'd served four years for fraud on a national scale.

At first she said she wouldn't want to waste another minute, but then she changed her mind and said she wouldn't mind having one last cup of coffee before they annihilated each other. They had that coffee and forgot themselves a little, talking about this and that, when they noticed the sky was darkening. Then they had a quick bite and headed for the forest.

Solvi, who'd got hold of two pistols, gave her one and asked her to pull the trigger at the exact moment he would.

Diana smiled bashfully. 'How about one last kiss.'

Solvi sighed and humoured her. Then they made love. Twice – once for each life. Eventually, when all was said and done, they stood facing each other and, on a count of three, fired the pistols.

And this is the end of Solvi's story.

For now.

LIKE A COIN
ENTRUSTED IN FAITH

SHIMON ADAF

1

They wake up Sultana the midwife at the dead of night. Poundings on the door, which she disguises in her sleep. Hides them within the symbolism of the dreams. But her consciousness arises at last. She identifies the knocking, the intervals between knockings. And she is alarmed. The alarm is not shaped yet. She covers herself quickly. Out of habit. Ties her headdress and goes out. In spite of the urgency of the knocks, the man is standing with his back to her hut. Almost indifferent, his small cart, tied to a grey ass, in the starlight of the beginning of autumn in Morocco, is also cut from the landscape.

Afterwards she remembers the light gallop of the ass and the cart on the slope, the rustle of the world she senses whenever she leaves the hamlet, out of the protective imagination of its inhabitants. The wind is warm still, unexpected warmness, and the lucidity of the air. She smells the sea in it, Essaouira's daily commotion caught in it even at midnight. But they circumvent the city. She already recognised the driver, Shlomo Benbenishti. It's been years since she's last seen him. He hurries the ass. He tells it, run like the storm, my beauty, and laughs. She does not understand the laughter. A shred of shyness is apparent in it. Maybe nervousness.

The road becomes steep. The ass brays, even neighs. Shlomo turns to her. He says, do not eat or drink anything in the house at which we are about to arrive. Had dar hadi fiah Jnoon[1]. The Moroccan is light on his tongue, and his Hebrew heavier, the heritage of the synagogue. He knows that she understands Hebrew, though she's a woman. She nods. Now she grasps the nature of her alarm. The moon is a thin etch in the thickening darkness, thickening more and more as they near their destination. The moon still breathes his first breaths of the month. That is the alarm. Why was she summoned now? The time is the ten days of repentance.

2

The mother died with a scream. Her face was veiled and the scream was almost silenced. Sometimes they are marked; the demon leaves his marks

---

1   There are demons in this house (Jewish Moroccan)

on their cheeks. A scar of a bite. Every now and then, when Sultana hands them their baby, they remove the veil and she sees. But the woman died while delivering. She twisted and turned with spasms when Sultana came in. Sultana imagined her nails burrowing into the flesh of the hand. A small lamp threw light on her round belly, about to burst. Shlomo stayed outside. Inside, close to one of the dark hut's clay walls stood a man she couldn't make out clearly. She said she didn't want to deliver the baby, that they shouldn't have called her during the ten days of repentance, between Rosh Hashanah and Yom Kippur. The man insisted. He switched to Hebrew, he said, what is forbidden within the boundaries of the land of Israel, isn't forbidden in foreign lands. Is he Jewish, she thought to herself, the accent was strange, but his voice, she knew the voice, where from?

The mother shuddered at her touch. Her cries begun. The newborn fought, Sultana could tell. She lifted the woman's dress. She saw the little egg-shaped skull, through the widened lips of the vagina, smeared with blood and liquids of the womb. She pressed on the belly. He was blue, the baby, his skin, his hair, his eyes when opened shortly. The irises filled the sockets. She couldn't figure out if he was blind. A spark of intelligence burned in his eyes, curiosity almost. She shook. When she severed the umbilical cord the newborn shook too and went still.

The man told her to put the dead baby alongside his mother's corpse. I told you, she said. Her voice broke a little. He didn't react. Shlomo's head peered from the entrance and he called her name delicately. She followed him. Anger grew in her during the journey back. When he stopped near her hut, she said, why are you working for them, why? He asked her, with his former softness, why they sent for you, you tell me.

3

From: Tiberia Assido
To: Doron Aflalo
RE: Rose of Judea

Say, what is this nonsense you've been sending me? You promised to report what you've been discovering about Rabbi SBRJ. Instead you're telling me some made-up tale about the days Rabbi Shlomo was young? I realize that stories about demon births were widespread in the villages in Morocco. My mother told Akko and me a similar tale once. Akko couldn't sleep that night. But what has that to do with the Rose of Judea? If I recall, you claimed that evil spirits are nothing but a story intended to cover up the involvement of Externals in Jewish history. You also claimed that they aren't born, but are some kind of Jews who've been mutated in a distant future, didn't you?

Akko is advancing with the development of "Solium Salomonis", at least with parts I'm exposed to. He makes me talk daily with the software. A little scary. When we started the output was confused (look at me, writing as if I had the first clue about computing), without any relevance to the sentences I typed. Now, half of the time she answers my questions.

BTW, it's beautiful here in Massachusetts. Thanks for asking. And I enjoy being around Akko, even though he kept all his annoying habits from when we were children. He still won't talk to me about his sexuality. It's beneath him to show any interest in such an inferior human activity. He also forgets to eat. Anyway, he needs as detailed information as possible, not stories.

What about you? Haven't gone crazy yet from staying at your parents' place in Mevoe-Yam?

T.

4

But certain stories are sometimes the only way to give someone a key. The stories of my father were left hidden. My mother forgot. Only Miriam, once, told me a real horror story. The birds' song, she said, is full of razors. When she's passing by, they sing about it to her. Not the content of the song, but the song itself, the way it slashes through the air and reaches her ears. That's the razor. It cuts reality. In the following days I ceased listening. Like I turned towards other voices. The world called my name.

Years went by before I figured out that it's not what we fear that frightens us. What frightens us lurks at the edges, behind the gates of cognition. The fear we know is nothing but a defense mechanism against this, the thing. How to explain? Maybe that I understood that Tel Aviv fell on New Year's Eve of the year 5767 to creation. Suddenly I saw only parts of the reality of the city. On the stairs leading to the university, on Jaffa pier, on Allenby. They peered through the shroud of the city. What is reality if not the memory of others leaping from you when you look? Their life, their bodies that created in their movement the space you occupy, gave it meaning. Yet, woven in this weave of remembrance, you are left to your own devices; you have a resting place, a place of becoming. And the city was lost, as Miriam was lost, washed into the abyss from which only a choked, undecipherable sound, is coming back. And the stupid dreams of the Tel Aviv dwellers preserved the city, a dull copy under the sun of Israel.

5

Sultana remembered Shlomo. She remembered him when she lay awake on her bed, and she remembered him afterwards, when she slouched to the cave at the break of dawn. He was a Yeshiva student, who came from a community in Istanbul with a recommendation letter from the community's rabbi. She was about to get married and didn't pay him much attention, even though her father, the rabbi of the newly formed community in Essaouira, whose members retired from one of the communities in Fez, took him in.

For a while he was her father's protégé. He was rumored to be extremely gifted. He knew many tractates from the Babylonian and the Jerusalem Talmud by heart, and was versed in the writings of the Geniuses and Maimonides; he even read the prohibited book. He was exchanging epistles with an Israeli sage, Rabbi Yosef Karo, and her father let his pride be known at Sabbath meals, when she and her husband came to visit, and she was carrying a child in her womb. But something changed. She was only able to get some parts of the story. The young lad Benbenishti and her father were becoming estranged. She couldn't attend to it; her husband fell ill and she was about to give birth. When she returned to her parents' home, after her husband's death, her father wouldn't hear about Shlomo Benbenishti. He wasn't welcomed anymore.

6

Her mother told her, when Shlomo appeared one day famished at the kitchen entrance of their house. Her mother fed him somewhat fearfully, as if he were a leper, and made Sultana stand watch at the doorway to the house, to warn her if her father or one of her younger brothers was approaching. Shlomo couldn't make a living. No member of the community would hire him. Occasionally he would work for Arabs, to drive a cart, to run errands, to sell in the market, to whitewash houses.

Shlomo would pursue issues best left alone. He asked about corpses coming back to life: are they still infused with the profanity of the dead, can they be cleansed by bathing in a mikveh? Is the tent in which a body is vitalized clear of its impurity, the tent and every object within its space? What was the status of the children revived by Elijah and Elisha? Were they still in need of red-cow ashes? What was the meaning of the Jerusalem Talmud argument that the dead live among the dew? And so on, and so forth. Her father, who detested any discussion of the sort, was convinced he was possessed, god forbid, La Yister[2].

The memory flooded her – no, slashed her. That day, when the males of the family went to pray mincha, the afternoon prayer, and the soft light anticipated the coming of the evening. Shlomo sat in front of her mother and her in the kitchen, munching leftovers of couscous and meat, and his eyes darkly sleep-deprived, haunted.

7

From: Tiberia Assido
To: Doron Aflalo
RE: Rose of Judea

Doron,
I'm a murderess, murderess. I know the term is a bit melodramatic, but it describes well my shock. I've killed Akko's software. I've already named it in my mind: Malka. You know how you'll ascribe human features to everything that shows a will or imitates life, like pets or toys, when you're child? When I was eight, one of the girls in the neighborhood got a talking doll. Akko coveted it so much that I helped him steal it. It made me feel sick when he took it apart to see its inner workings. I heard her crying in my head, begging me to stop the torture. Now, thinking back, I think the doll's owner was Malka. Or maybe I'm rewriting the recollection to make it meaningful.

---

2   May God protect us (Jewish Moroccan)

I wasn't doing it on purpose. I just held my daily conversation with her. And I couldn't resist. I quoted, half joking, the dubious exegesismy father taught Akko, about king Solomon's throne (solium salomonis) and the kings of Edom and the Externals fighting over it, and I asked Malka her thoughts on the matter (I was tired, and bored). She crashed. Akko claims that restarting her won't do us any good, that the backups won't help, because she'll only crash again. He says I need to start training a blank module anew, and that he hasn't much time to deal with it at the moment.

Poor Malka, I've destroyed her. How can I raise another module, to see it grow, develop a consciousness?

And Akko won't tell me why he's so adamant about me being the one who raises it. True, it's crucial to him that the software language be Hebrew. He has this hypothesis that Hebrew is prevalent all over the Worlds, that it's the Ur-language. No, that in each and every one of the Worlds, a version of Hebrew came to be out of a family of languages similar to it. That's why Hebrew is the closest to the Ursprechen. But why the hell me? He can hire an Israeli student. They are fucking everywhere nowadays.

So you have time to get serious with your investigation. Yet, why is your story so indirect? Why do you suspend the information? What's your point, really?

T.

8

Sultana remembered. She stood in the cave, in whose depths her son was kept, and he failed to appear, even when she called out his name. Hosea.

9

When your son shows signs of a mysterious illness, which brought down his father, an illness gnawing his organs while the spirit stays sane, trapped in the cage of flesh, it is easy to prevent his death. All you need is a device to stop time.

But there's a setback; there's always a setback. Time-halting objects aren't as widespread as they used to be. Let's say Moses' wand. Or Joshua's Shofar.

10

And there's always a price, evidently.

11

She'd been told there was an Arab who lived on a mountain. He was a master of the dying. She walked many miles. Wore out two pairs of shows. Her son was with her, riding a donkey, his life force leaking.

The Arab gave her a ring made of a bone of the upupa epops that was passed down from King Solomon's hand to the hands of the Kahlif Harun El Rashid, and lastly came to his possession. The ring radiated decay and corruption and gangrene. He commanded her to change her name, to leave her parents' house without speaking to them. He told her to dwell in a certain hamlet, outside of Essaouira, and study how to serve as a midwife. He said that she would be called for, that he for long has waited for a Jewish woman to come his way.

12

1. All conscious creatures are sentenced to die.

    1.1 But not all of them are sentenced to perish.

        1.1.1 The consciousness may linger after the death of the body; parts of it may. A knot of memories and sentiments. The ghost is best suited to depict this sort of lingering.

        1.1.2 The body, a complex system of appetites and cravings, may survive alone, without the bridles of consciousness. The vampire, one can argue, is the representation of this sort of lingering.

        1.1.3 What is the third variation of outliving death that's illustrated by the zombie? In contrast to the other two, the zombie is devoid of memory, identity, passion. The living entity was erased. Only a blind instinct is left, the will of another that possesses it whole. It has been devoured.

      1.2 The livings are constantly thrown into mourning.

          1.2.1 Which means the complete collapse of the means of expression.

          1.2.2 Nevertheless, every culture aspires to endow loss with meaning, to tame it through rituals.

          1.2.3 All of human experience is characterized by the tension between the urgent need to be expressed and the failure of language to fully express it.

          1.2.4 The greatest and most unbearable tension is to be found in grief. And in the mystical experience. That's why those two are the ones driving humans to the highest degree of creativity, to a multitude of forms of expression.

          1.2.5 For a while, therefore, there's an identity between the two.

2. A categorical border divides the living from the dead.

      2.1 The ability to experience the border from both sides is the mystical ability in itself.

13.

From: Tiberia Assido
To: Doron Aflalo
RE: Rose of Judea

    You ask what I did with Malka before I quoted her the exegesis. (Malka! Suddenly I get that Malka, queen, is the Hebrew word Sultana. What was her name before she changed it? Please don't tell me it was Malka. What is it, one of your exaggerated poetical devices? But you couldn't have known it's the name I choose for the module. Are all coincidences this dreary?)
    Akko has also asked me.
    I quoted her some of my poems. Not *The Artificial Child* that refers to Akko and solium salomonis. It was the first time Malka was exposed to the term. Do you think the system in the whole became intelligent enough that, through the quote, she realised she was made-up, might

have understood her raison d'etre: to uncover the Ursprechen in which the Name-givers hold the Worlds? That she understood it is the task of Rose of Judea? It seems far-fetched.

I told Akko my suspicions. I don't know how the other modules of the project function. He said he couldn't be bothered. An Israeli writer wrote him to inquire about the part of exegesis I mention in *The Artificial Child*. It's funny someone still reads that magazine we published.

(Do you still write poetry? I have to ask, even if you'd give the same answer all over again, that poetry per se isn't enough for you.)

Anyhow, Akko did say he was bothered by the timing. Do you get it? He is bothered by the timing and not by months of work gone down the drain for no apparent reason. I never am going to get this kid.

I know he's already a man, but for me he's the kid with the grumpy manners, who closed himself in the garage with his computers. The same kid who became hard all of a sudden, distant. The kid I'm the only human he can show emotions towards.

My heart goes out to him, as if he were twelve.

It's stupid.

But maybe I'm overflowed with feelings because I haven't yet overcome Malka's passing. Parts of me were imbedded in her. Is this clinging narcissistic? Because in every loss we lose the parts of us that were immersed in others who left us? Do we mourn ourselves really?

I refuse to believe that.

Write me back soon,

T.

14.

I refuse to believe it either. If love may save us for a moment from our perpetual egoism, than losing it is losing a possibility of salvation. Another way out that has been blocked for us, that keeps us so much in here.

15.

Sultana was very stingy with the time left for her son. The ring suspended his life. She put him in the cave, near the hamlet she was told to live in, and she waited. They called for her. Always around midnight. She watched demon offspring, with crooked organs and features, being delivered from human females wombs, and every time refused the food and drinks she was offered. And there was always someone who came and took the hybrids. She didn't see the takers' faces, didn't recognized them. And every morning following the birth, she went to the cave, where she undid the time paralysis she had casted upon her son, and he was beautiful and spoke to her. And she remembered why she was willing to assist the strange births. Why she continued to live in the shadow of the Sitra Ahara.

But this morning Hosea wasn't there. And she thought, Shlomo, for no reason she could fathom, just out of basic fright. It's Shlomo's doing.

16.

*Externals: in Jewish folklore the expression serves as a substitute term for the Sitra Ahara, the more common Aramaic name for the powers of evil, whose meaning is literally 'The Other Side'.

The disciples of the order of the Rose of Judea believe that the Externals are a group of shape-shifting entities whose influence can be traced throughout Jewish history, and that they are the servants of the Kings of Edom, a nation whose home world was destroyed and who now roam the other worlds in order to find the keys to the destruction of the Chain of Worlds. These keys, as the Rosaic tradition goes, are implanted in the Name-givers' consciousness.

Their belief is based on the interpretation of a series of Jewish exegesis from the second half of the third millennium to creation, and is related to the sage Ben-Zoma and his acolytes. These exegeses are not part of the holy canon of mainstream Judaism today.

One of the important exegeses is as follow:

The Rabbi's mind was not set as to Solomon's throne till Ben-Zoma explained –

it's written, It is an abomination to kings to commit wickedness, for the throne is established by righteousness, for the descendants of heavens and the offspring of Edom were fighting over its construction, this one says it is my craft and the other says it is my hand making, and it stood between the sky and the earth until the sun retreated.

An extreme interpretation, which isn't considered valid, claims that the Externals are not connected to the kings of Edom, but are mutant Jews from the future who travel in time and memory and whose goal is to collect every piece of information relevant to the Rose of Judea and manipulate it for their own ends.

17.

Shlomo looks at her bewildered. He doesn't understand what she's talking about. He repeats her words, a cave, a ring, a son. Sultana stops midway through the blame and starts anew. Slowly she realizes that he doesn't have a clue. That's the first time he's been hired for a job like this. That he was paid handsomely for it. He's able to deduce much from what she's been saying. He is sharp. He has an ear for nuances. The story is clear to him in its fullest extent. Until now he stood in front of her; she sat at the table in the centre of her hut. He sits down heavily. His eyes are ablaze with thoughts. A pretty man, she notices, a soft darkness floats in the irises, and the cloud of thoughts enhances his beauty. Suddenly she's aware of herappearance. She tightens the cover over her hair, glides a hand down her face, as if she could smooth the skin. She's four or five years older than he is, but he seems younger to her, a lad.

Shlomo asks if she knows why this village, outside the borders of Essaouira, if demonic forces are more active there. She says she doesn't know, that she delivers a hybrid once a month at least. But never during the ten days of repentance.

The holiness of the days, Shlomo says, and nods. He asks about Hosea, how the black ring is able to time-freeze him. She looks at the ring for the first time since she left the cave earlier that morning. Shlomo is right. The green and ivory shades faded. It's totally black.

He inquires about her recollection of the Arab warlock. She says she doesn't remember a thing. Did he wear the ring? She says that he didn't. He pronounced few words and then some windows were torn in the air. They moved very slowly, the windows. The Arab reached into one of them and pulled out the ring.

Windows, Shlomo muses: a similar account is to be found in the stories of Raba bar bar Hana in Baba Batra.

In the Talmud? she asks.

Yes, Shlomo says and adds that bar bar Hana tells about a meeting with an Arab who showed him windows in heaven, where the sky and the earth kiss, and the sky turns as a wheel. The stories were always dismissed as fiction, but he believes they have some kernel of truth in them.

And the home owner, he asks, did she know him?

She says his voice was familiar, but she couldn't exactly tell where from.

Shlomo suggests they return to that hut: maybe they'll find a lead.

On the way there he turns his head. The small ass is walking at a moderate pace. He says it amuses him that the daughter of Rabbi Aflalo found a way to cheat death. She asks for the reason. He says Rabbi Aflalo expelled him from the yeshiva because he argued that underneath the Talmud sages' discussions about necromancy and seers lurks a knowledge they wished to discard. Rabbi Aflalo accused him of idolatry.

18.

From: Tiberia Assido
To: Doron Aflalo
RE: Rose of Judea

You're right. I wasn't very sensitive in my last mail. I didn't take into account what you're going through. But you are also to blame. Whenever we talked about Miriam and what she'd done, you insisted you moved on, that you can't dwell in sorrow, in guilt. Tell me more about the book you're writing. In what way does it deal with the impossible language of loss? Once you wrote in a poem, "There comes a moment / you know / your hymn from down under / no soul could speak." What happened to that moment? Why does it flicker?

Yesterday we held a ceremony. Akko said it would help me let go of Malka. He didn't say, "Help you let go of Malka." He said, "Maybe you'd stop nagging." Midway he cried. Of course it wasn't Malka he was missing. He has several servers he calls the Cemetery Cloud. He stores his dead software there. The little conniving bastard. Not once did he mention that it wasn't the first time a module of solium salomonis has crashed beyond repair. He doesn't say "store", btw. He says "lay to rest".

T.

19.

From: Tiberia Assido
To: Doron Aflalo
RE: Rose of Judea

I almost forgot. You ask what I mean by "died"?
You push the module icon and the software doesn't run. Akko said he ran Malka's code through a debugger (tell you anything?) and he ran diagnostics on the databases built by her. Everything seems to be fine. No reason why she wouldn't work. Yet she doesn't, like a body whose life spark's been extinguished.
    T.

20.

Out of the urban mischief, out of the wreckage, my sister Miriam rose. Still 17 and not ceasing to rise. And Tel Aviv already fell. In aimless roaming I was nearly run down by bike riders. Sons of bitches. Lately they multiply. The year 5767 and the city is lost. Their eyes hollow, the mouth gaping with a groan. Among the dust-ridden trees, in the delayed autumn. New Year's Eve at my back, and they're around me, circling, copies of what they were once, blind urges in flesh golems of streets and traffic lights. Trampling. I have to get out of here. I have to go back to Mevo-Yam.

21.

The recently deceased mother's hut is empty. It's almost evening. Sultana and Shlomo stand inside and inspect it for traces. The ring on Sultana's finger is black as a scorched bone. There's no cradle. No bed for a child. The kitchen is infested with shadows.

Shlomo asks her what else she knows. All of a sudden she's indignant. It's not his business. It's not your business, she says. He lifts the lamp he brought with him and lights it. It's requied. The night fell quickly, unnoticeable. His expression is a mix of curiosity and alarm. A rage builds inside Sultana. She says, Hosea, and begins singing, a song her mother sung, when she cradled her son who wasn't named yet, in his firsts days on this land –

Stahit ana me'a momo lilah fi lilah
Wal'am he'tata yiduz geer fehal ha lilah
Lochan ma tenzar shams, ma tedwi gemara
Geer didlma fi kulal rachan
Wunbit ana wu-momo, geer sehara fi laman...[3]

She sings, hums to herself. Shlomo lowers his head. In the lamp light his hair is anointed with glamour. Someone is knocking on the door, beating with urgency.

22.

From: Tiberia Assido
To: Doron Aflalo
RE: Rose of Judea

We're having a little crisis here. It has nothing to do with the Israeli writer inquest. Akko resolved that matter. Something else. I started working with the new linguistic module yesterday. This time I was cautious about getting attached. I typed simple indicative sentences. Something happened at night. It's not clear what. In the morning I sat in front of the screen. Ozymandias (yeah, maybe such a ridiculous name will prevent me from developing feelings) didn't react at first to the sentences I fed it. After several minutes words appeared on the screen: ARRGGG, GRRRR, ARRGGGG...
Funny, right?
But then the computer started emitting sounds. The other computers in the lab present similar symptoms. Akko lost his temper. At last he was

---

3   I wished to spend with the baby night after night
      To be with him a full 12 months like this night
      And the sun might not rise, the moon won't shine
      Only darkness all around
      And the baby and I would sleep like a coin entrusted in faith. (Jewish
Moroccan)

able to show rage. There's a good side to it, to see him in a human moment.

I'm scared.

T.

23.

The door fell.

In spite of the lamp in Shlomo's hand, the outside seemed more lit.

The glee of autumn stars in Morocco's sky, apparently.

The shining heaven above Essaouira.

Against the glare of the busted door a small figure shows.

Its stride slow.

The organs rigid, mechanical.

And still its face is unseen yet.

Shlomo takes out a small chain from his galabia's pocket.

It shimmers. It has a certain glow.

He throws it. It wraps around the figure's neck.

Shlomo cries: Shma De-Marach Alech![4] Shma De-Marach Alech!

The figure continues to advance, oblivious to Shlomo's cries.

Shlomo retreats.

He puts the lamp on the floor and takes a stool from next to the wall.

He raises it.

His silence releases Sultana from her short paralysis.

She bends to have a better look.

Now she screams.

24.

From: Tiberia Assido
To: Doron Aflalo
RE: Rose of Judea

I left Akko alone with his codes in the lab for several days and went on walks in the institute's grounds. Akko suggested I take the laptop

---

4   The name of your master binds you (Aramaic)

he prepared for me, with all the insane amount of security he put on it. Before I left he asked if the laptop was connected to the lab's intranet. I haven't turned it on since he gave it to me. There was enough computing for me with the computer that ran Malka's module, may she rest in peace, and Ozymandias's module, curse it.

Akko also said, strangely, that the programs' codes in the cemetery cloud were corrupted. That they're full of inexplicable characters. He said, "As if they've rotted somehow."

I was hoping to have my spirit lifted by the gnaw marks autumn left on the trees, the seasonal decline in temperature, the pressure of coolness against the skin, and the architecture, by which I was enthralled when I first got here. Instead, I think of Israel, on my tongue the syllables of the month Tishrey are rolling. Before Rosh Hashanah we called our mother to congratulate her for the New Year. Akko was choked with excitement. He was stricken by longing. Then we called our father. I mean, I called. Akko still refuses to speak with him. Who would have thought we'll all be here, in 2011, some years after the fall of Tel Aviv.

Well, the architecture is still lovely. The state centre's game of perspectives are wonderful, I'll give you that. The placement of futuristic buildings in the gloomy surroundings of New England as well.

I wonder if they burned witches here.

I think about your Sultana.

Where is the story going? I wait for the part in which young Shlomo is entering the Pardes and gets the knowledge of the Chain of Worlds, and becomes Rabbi SBRJ. That's your intention, right? To illustrate the revelation of the Rose of Judea.

But why tell the story from Sultana's point of view? Shlomo is the interesting character.

I don't want to push you. I know you too well for that. But what happens here seems to stem from our efforts to find the Ursprechen of the Worlds. It seems we reached some forbidden zone. Years ago Akko told me that this knowledge has the price tag of loss, of guilt, and you said – bad luck.

Well, Doron, bad luck has caught up with us. And I'm scared.

I sit at a café in Cambridge, MA, and I write to you.

I need desperately to understand something. But what is it? This is the awful thing here, isn't it? That we can't identify the real mystery. Help me, Doron.

25

*Pardes (Orchard). Entering the Pardes: more than a few visitations of humans to the realms of angles in heaven are accounted for in the Jewish esoteric literature from the second half of the third millennium to creation. The literature of Hechalot (Palaces), for instance, is a detailed one. Yet the term Entering the Pardes is ascribed to one mystical experience only, the experience of four sages of the Mishna around the year 3890. The chronicles of the Entering are mainly reported in the tractate Hagiga in the Babylonian and Jerusalem versions of the Talmud.

No doubt an elementary form of experience is outlined in the exegeses. It's possible that the four sages represent four different attitudes toward the place of mysticism in Jewish life: Akiva ben Yosef, who goes through the experience unharmed, is its exemplar. According to his method, Judaism is hiding the magical thinking at its base and sanctifies practices of study and memorizing instead. Shimon ben Azay died while entering the Pardes and left no evidence for his method. Elisha ben Avoya turned to heresy, id est, cancelled the validity of Judaism as a worthy practice for gaining wisdom. Of Shimon ben Zoma, it was said that he peered and was harmed or, in the common interpretation, lost his sanity. His experience is the most curious, for what is insanity in the context of mysticism?

The devotees of the Rose of Judea believe that the knowledge ben Zoma unveiled contains a different description of the structure of reality.

26.

When the features of the small figure are clear to Sultana, her scream dwindles and she gazes. Parts of the child's body — it's a child after all — are blue. An arm and half of the face. The expression is empty. The skin at the other part is sallow, pale, oozes viscous miasma. The right eye is buried in its socket, and worms twist in it. The bare teeth are spreading a sickly glow. And he, the child, doesn't smile, but his lips are stretched in spasm.

He advances slowly, jerking. His arms are reaching for her. She's unable to move. Even the stench and the whiteness of the worms turning in the right eye can't force her nerves to shock her into motion. The child emits guttural syllables, indecipherable. He's almost upon her; his nails are ready to cut her flesh.

And Shlomo pushes her aside and hits the creature with the stool. The blow is muted, not even the sound of a crushing bone, just a heavy note, the note of an object sinking in soft mud, in clay. The neck is crooked, the head lies on the left shoulder. His stretched lips stay the same and he keeps on moving forward in a rigid, stubborn walk.

Shlomo stands between her and the creature, blocks her view, but she knows nothing will stop it, that what drives it is beyond the decaying flesh, that the flesh is but a realization of a will. She knows that as well as she knows the origin of the organs that have been made into this shape, Hosea, and the baby she helped deliver just a while ago. Shlomo hits it again. Something like a fart escapes its body. The stench grows. The child-thing starts to shrill, a high pitched, ear-shattering shrill, like the cry of a prisoner being tortured in a concealed, underground cell. And Shlomo hits it again and calls to her. He says, get out of here Sultana, run.

27.

From: Tiberia Assido
To: Doron Aflalo
RE: Rose of Judea

It's awful, Doron. I'm here, in the storage room of the lab, with all the pieces of useless equipment.

I've just arrived at the lab. Akko was crouched over his keyboard, motionless. I didn't understand what he was waiting for. I haven't seen him for a couple of days and he didn't even turn his head to look at me. Then I realized the screens were all displaying the same words ARRGG, GRRR, ARRGGG, GRRRR, GRRR and some animation of a viscous liquid, a green-yellow jelly, shaking, oozing down the screen, the inside of the screen.

I approached Akko and touched his shoulder. His small body was rigid. His head moved, turned, like it was revolving on the spine. His eyes were opaque, and the skin bloodless, the face without expression. The smile, it had nothing to with the facial muscles. It terrified me. He didn't say anything.

I retreated, stupid me, to the first door in my sight. The storage room.

It's terrible. But the panic I felt before, when I walked around the institute, weakened. I've already dreamed this scene. I've seen it to its last detail, and I know the blows on the door are coming next.

In spite of Akko's warnings, I connected ARRGGG the laptop to the lab's intranet. So my GRRRR time is short. The ruined computers here start to hum*%*$#_)++

I'm thinking hard – Rose of Judea, the revelation of Ben-Zoma, the retrieval of the knowledge in Rabbi Shlomo Benbenishi's era, in the 16th century. I've always been bad at pattern&$&$*%(recognition. There must be something ARGGRRR you can tell, some detail you observed, in the story GRRRRG that escaped me.

&what is in our investigation that raise the dead&
&and how to put them back to the dust&
&even the digital ones&
He###########lp me, Do***************ron.

Don't leave me ARRGGG alone again, in half-light, as you did ARGGGRRR years ago.

Please, DoARRGGG GRRR ARRRRG ARRRG
GRRRRRRRRRRRRRRRRRRRRRRRRRRRRRRRR

28.

[Clear sky, in which huge stars are buried. The moon is like a Chinese brush stroke. Dark trees. A wind is passing through them. Light rustle, like a buzz. Sultana is running out of a hut. She's terrified. She stops. A Man comes out from the shadow of trees.]

Sultana: Halt, you stranger, tell me who you are.
A Man: I am who I am. Though not whom you assume.
Sultana: And yet, someone you are, whoever that be.
     Tell me who.
A Man: The shape, the speech
     Are nothing but skin.
Sultana: Now I know, now
     Sevenfold my fear grows. You are deceased.

A Man: I told you, body, looks, are but a skin

      Which entities would wear to come here.

Sultana: Here. Where is here?

A Man: The Humilitas.

Sultana: My beloved's flesh you wear, and he is not you.

      Who you are, you stranger, tell me.

A Man: Centuries will pass before I'm born and for millennia

      I've lived, I walked this world, the Humilitas.

      Its paths of time are clear to me, I am at home

      But this is not my home. The chains of human voices

      Of human cries, I left behind, and even then

      I'm force to cloak myself with them

If my will is to find my kind's place within the Worlds.

Sultana: Your kind? Who are they? Who are you? The man

      Who spoke from shadows, in this house. What

      Was the faith of the dead infant?

      Why was my boy snatched from me, and you show

      Yourself in semblance of his dead dad?

A Man: Faith,

      Conspiracy, simple and transparent, but as for you

Sultana: It's wrapped in mystery. I do not wish to hear.

      What do you strive for, devil?

A Man (laughs):   devil I'm not.

Sultana (aside): Nor man he is. Oh Lord

      Who torture us, who draw a line

      Between the living and the dead which we

      Crave to transgress.

A Man: Hush. Soon you'll see.

Sultana: But Hosea, my son, and the unnamed child

      You control them, the boy whose organs

      You assembled and your will drives.

      For what end?

A Man: I roamed Humilitas

      In the third millennium I wore the body of

      A Jewish sage, Rabba bar bar Hanna, I

      Spoke through his lips, I thought warlocks

And magicians, I weaved my nets in silence
Now comes an hour I put to test
Will he transfer the knowledge destined
To give us life, if we chose wisely –
A child who was prevented from
The realms of death and a child dead
From womb.

Sultana: not a child was he
But demon.

A Man: There are no demons. Just folktales
Claiming them to be. No plan is fertile
Without misguiding and mischiefs, tricks
As old as humanity.

Sultana: Nonsense. Insanity.

A Man: My part I've done, woman, and so did you
It is my time to go back to my shelter in the shadows.

[Man exits. Sultana falls to her knees with a howl.]

29.

Sultana's face is streaked with dust when she looks up. Shlomo is coming towards her. His face bears an expression of elation. His arms are stretched and the sleeves of his galabia are torn. The arms are covered in bite marks, small circles, tiny imprints of teeth, and shiny beads of blood. His hands are cupped, as if he is carrying a precious gem, but to Sultana the hands look empty. He gazes from the invisible content of his hands to Sultana and back. His features are washed with glamour. He says, Rose of Judea. He repeats the enigmatic phrase, Rose of Judea, Rose of Judea, till Sultana is back on her feet and puts her hand on his mouth.

30.

I would have helped you, Tiberia. I would have left everything and rushed to you. But Miriam is filling my dreams, and my mother walks the house. I'm sure she put a tap on my heart beats.

But what it is I wish to say and can't convey any other way, is that the words in Hebrew, they had been through fire and water, they were killed by the sword and by strangulation. And we salvaged them from their grave.

They carry knowledge from beyond death, Tiberia, maybe the knowledge we need to retrieve Ben-Zoma's method. But in what form they are coming back and what they ask of the living, this we will have to find out the hard way.

TEN FOR SODOM

DANIEL POLANSKY

They had reached Classon, and Ben was thinking about G-d.

Ben was a Jew to the extent that at one point he would have been put in an oven. He was cut but never bar Mitzvahed. He had not recited the prayer over the wine since he had been old enough to legally drink it. The point being there was not much there to work with, in his efforts considering the Almighty, little grist for the mill. But still he was trying; he was doing his best. This was the time to be thinking about G-d; if ever there was a time, this was it. And in fact he was surprised to discover that there was one portion of the Torah which he could suddenly recall with perfect clarity, as if printed on the back of his eyelids, and this was the wording of the covenant that Noah, socks still wet, had wrung from his Creator, after he had laid waste to everything that he had thus far created. "Never again will all life be destroyed by the waters of a flood; never again will there be a flood to destroy the earth."

The Lord was a righteous god, the Lord was an honest god, the Lord had stayed true to his words. Though standing on the roof of his building, watching them shamble eastward, the breeze carrying with it odors which were indescribably fetid, Ben could not bring himself to feel grateful. Noah's world had been destroyed by a rising tide of water; his would be a consumed in an infinite deluge of flesh.

Ben was not sure why he was the only one on the roof – he had expected there would be others. It seemed like the obvious choice, under the circumstances. If he'd had a gun or enough of the right sort of narcotics to make sure of the matter he would have used those, but all he'd had was some hash and a kitchen knife. The kitchen knife could barely cut a tomato and anyway the thought of all that sawing made him sick. He'd rolled the rest of the hash into a joint and grabbed his emergency stash of gin from behind the cereal, thinking that this most certainly qualified as that. Then he had climbed out of the window and up the fire escape.

G-d have not provided 40 days to prepare for the end this time, not even 40 hours. The night before there had been some strange reports on the news from Central Asia, but Ben hadn't been paying attention: he had a date to prepare for and what he was hearing was obviously too crazy to be believed. When he had woken up late the next morning the power was off, and there was chaos in the streets, and people were trying to leave the city.

But now it was early evening, and things were very quiet, and no one was trying to go anywhere.

They were at Franklin now, and after Franklin was Bedford, and after Bedford was Rodgers, and Rodgers was Ben's intersection. The best West Indian restaurant in the neighborhood had been on Franklin, they had done this conch roti that was out of this world, and the owners were always friendly. Ben would never eat West Indian food again, or sushi, or pizza, or bread and tepid water, and no one would ever be friendly to him again either, and those people who had been, friends and family and lovers, they were all dead or wishing that they were. It was enough to make a man want to take another swallow of gin.

Which he did, though after some consideration he decided not to light the joint. It would have been the James Dean thing to do, but Benjamin was not feeling very James Dean at the moment, just terrified near to madness and unspeakably sad.

And also, he didn't think the hash would help when it was time to make the jump.

Because the roof meant that he couldn't punk out at the last moment, needed to make sure he went clear over with enough force to do the job proper. At a party some months earlier a doctor had told him that a fall from the fourth floor of a building would kill 50 per cent of the people that tried it. The roof of Benjamin's building was five floors up, so it was a little better than even odds, but far from a sure thing. And if he stumbled, if he landed upright, maybe only breaking his legs or severing his spine, he'd be down there amongst the sea of them, amongst their teeth that bit and their fingers that pulled...

So he had better not flinch, Ben told himself. They were at Bedford.

It wasn't like the movies. They didn't wail or moan, there had been plenty of screaming that day but not from any of them. Still they had their own sound, one that arose from sheer mass, a river of tissue oozing through the streets of Brooklyn, bottlenecking thicker and thicker, submerging the buildings like ants on carrion. He had seen quickly that escape was more than impossible, was incomprehensible – like trying to run away from a sudden change of weather, sprinting from a rain cloud across an open field.

He remembered now that the Hasids had been acting crazy these last few weeks, though he hadn't paid them any attention. So far as Ben was concerned, the Hasids were always acting crazy, to each their own but still Benjamin was glad theirs wasn't his. At least you didn't need to worry about them mugging you, which was more than he could have said for some of the residents of his neighborhood, back when he had lived in a neighborhood and not an abattoir. But anyway, they'd been posting themselves in packets all up and down Eastern Parkway – the men of course, even the coming of the apocalypse wasn't enough to break their sexual segregation – and they'd been flagging down Jewish-looking passersby, like he'd seen them do in the past during the High Holidays. But this time they didn't look happy, and they weren't trying to blow the shofar for him.

Benjamin didn't really believe in G-d – or at least he hadn't last week – but still he felt it incumbent on himself to at least deal with their beliefs honestly. "I am not a Jew by the standards you use," he would tell them, politely but briskly, "and thus it would be a waste of your time to continue. But I wish you a pleasant evening all the same."

In the past that had been enough to gain release, but not this time. They insisted that it didn't matter anymore, that he needed to throw himself on the mercy of G-d, to beg for it, that it was too late but he needed to beg anyway. Benjamin had found the whole thing unseemly. They might as well be Jehova's Witnesses, he had thought to himself, with that vague sense of contempt that the assimilated has for the sore thumb, the city mouse for the country. One of them, a boy really, probably not 16 though it was hard to tell with their dress, began to cry uncontrollably, and had to be hustled away by the elders – though even the graybeards, solemn-eyed men no strangers to misfortune, seemed to be close to breaking as well.

By the time Benjamin snapped out of his reverie they were at Rogers, and he figured he had about five minutes to live. He swigged heavy from the bottle of gin, felt it do the things that liquor does. How many righteous had the Lord demanded of Sodom? It had been 10 at the end, hadn't it? New York was bigger than Sodom had ever been; only reasonable that He would want more. A hundred? A thousand? Whatever it was, Ben supposed they had not made it.

Ben leaned out over the side, felt his head wobble from the drink. What was it that let them know to stop eating, that the thing they were chewing on had become one of them? It didn't seem to be uniform. Amongst the legion below there were specimens that had gotten it very bad; a businessman with rich red raw flesh, a boy in girl's jeans whose forehead was open to his brain, an indecipherable mass of meat devoured nearly from head to waist, the spine and the skull sticking out of a limping bag of pulp.

Stop looking, Ben told himself, taking another swallow of gin. Don't look at them. Look at the sky, look at the bricks, look anywhere but don't look down at them. He only had to be brave for a few minutes longer, he told himself. Anyone could be brave for a few minutes.

He heard them break into the front of the building. He did not think they had any exact notion of where he was, or even that they were coming after him exactly, so much as simply spreading themselves across everything, like the swell of evening. No, it wasn't like the movies at all, really. They did not make noise, and they had come quicker than anyone had imagined, could possibly have imagined – but mostly what Hollywood had got wrong was that the movies were about survivors, or people trying to survive, and there would be no survivors, and indeed there was no point even making the attempt. G-d had decided to overturn the board, and you were not going to escape his wrath by holing up in some rural compound with an assault rifle and a few thousand cans of spam, no sir you were not.

The bottle of gin had done its work. He thanked G-d – for the first time in his life he really did, truly and with all of his heart – that he had kept enough of it around to make this last leap a little easier. They were coming up through the building now, the Indian couple on the first floor who never ever smiled at him, the Trinidadian Rasta who was always smoking grass on the stoop, the various hipsters who had constituted the borough's second-most recent invasion.

Without giving himself time to think, Benjamin broke the bottle against the edge of the roof and brought the shard swiftly across his chest, shredding the logo on his T-shirt and cutting through the baseball sleeves. A sharp spike of adrenaline came through the pain, one he would ride to a reasonably painless death, G-d willing, all glory to G-d, no that wasn't Judaism at all, was it? He was getting his children of Abraham confused. Benjamin laughed and discovered that he had broken what was left of the bottle in his hand, the glass cutting through his fingers and his palm. He rubbed his face and his hands with it, painting himself, working his mind into madness.

"One good leap, you motherfucker!" Benjamin screamed, unsure if doing so would draw their attention but knowing it did not matter. "One good leap!"

The blood was flowing fast and free now, and it wasn't as bad as he had imagined. Maybe the last snap wouldn't be so bad either. Don't lie, the last snap would be bad, the last snap would be the worst pain he had ever experienced, but the last snap would be nothing compared to what happened if he stumbled.

The door to the roof groaned open, and he was off like a shot.

THE FRIDAY PEOPLE

SARAH LOTZ

It was Jimmy Lowenstein who first started calling our motley group of middle-aged men and women the 'Friday People'. We'd gotten to know each other over the years, nodding in recognition as we met in the lobby or the lifts, trading 'what can you do?' eye-rolls and small talk. We weren't close friends or anything like that. Like soldiers thrust together on the front lines, it was a camaraderie born out of shared misery: the fact that our respective relatives had guilt-tripped us into spending every Shabbat at the Benchley Heights apartment block. It became tradition to meet beforehand and huddle outside the building's lobby, trading quips with the homeless who lived on the beach, bouncing cigarettes like teenagers and popping breath mints.

Like its residents – most of whom had lived in the building for decades – Benchley Heights resisted change. A curiously unappealing art deco building overlooking the Sea Point promenade in Cape Town, it lurked between a row of brand new chrome condominium developments like a fusty octogenarian surrounded by flashy teenagers. Most of the Friday People's relatives – my mother, Jimmy's uncle, Rachel White's aunt, Tony Apteker's parents and so on – lived on the top three floors, where the corridors always reeked of soup, slow-roasted chicken and stale cigarette smoke.

My mother had spent the last two decades obsessing about the minutiae of my personal life and phoning me several times a day: 'I had to phone, Nathan, because I was hungry. How could I eat? You might call and then I would have food in my mouth.' She'd worked tirelessly to hone herself into a stereotype in every way except the pleasant ones. She wouldn't spend days preparing some lavish Shabbat feast – she'd throw a cabbage in a pot on Friday morning like she was living in the ghetto she never knew. No, Friday nights were reserved for bringing me up to speed in excruciating detail on the comings and goings of her neighbours. I knew more about Sarah White's bursitis and Zachary Lowenstein's insomnia than was probably healthy.

One Friday night, I'd barely walked through the door when she grabbed my sleeve and pulled me into the lounge. 'Nathan, now sit, because you won't want to hear this news while standing. You know Estelle Apteker in number seventeen? Well, she was feeling sick last week and her daughter-in-law took her to the GP. Indigestion, she thought. But you'll never guess what – it's cancer of the liver. They think it might have spread. It won't be long.' She loved the drama of it. They all did. It had been years since there had been a death in the building.

Jimmy clapped me on the back and greeted me cheerfully when we met in the lift after I'd escaped my mother's clutches that evening. He was a phlegmatic man whose large, drooping face had the look of a melting candle. I'd rarely seen Jimmy smile, and there was something disturbing about seeing him brimming with so much bonhomie. 'Hey, Nate,' he said. 'Did you hear about Tony Apteker's mother?' I told him I had. 'It'll be like dominoes, you watch. I know how these things go. One will go, and the rest will follow.' He paused. 'Hey. Do you know how much the apartments in the block next door are going for?'

I did. 'Three million plus.'

'The penthouse went for six. And listen, I heard through the grapevine that Melvin & Sons are looking to expand. Might be interested in developing Benchley Heights. We could all be sitting on a goldmine.'

I gave him a non-committal nod. We both knew that it would be a cold day in hell before my mother and his uncle considered leaving the building.

Like Jimmy and most of the Friday People, I saw myself as a piece of life's flotsam, bobbing along with the tide like the rest of the rubbish. Middle-aged, slightly overweight, an ex-wife who'd scalped me out of my share of our Tamboerskloof duplex. Single, and no hope of being otherwise. Childless, which was naturally an endless source of worry for my mother: 'Nathan, it is never too late for you men, look at that Charlie Chaplin. Find a nice girl who wants babies already.' I'd been working for the same firm as a recruitment agent since my twenties, watching younger, brighter people scurry past me up the ladder. It wasn't that I wished my mother dead so that I could live large on the proceeds of the sale of her flat. I'm not a monster.

I don't think any of the Friday People were actively wishing for their relatives to die. Well, with the possible exception of Rachel White, who bought her emphysemic aunt Sarah a fresh carton of Rothmans every week. The truth was that the building wasn't suitable for them. Most were in their eighties, and if the lifts were out of order, they'd never manage the stairs. Sure, okay, it was true that the block was becoming 'highly desirable' and almost daily 'We Have a Buyer!' fliers were pushed under my mother's door.

(Which of course necessitated a phone call: 'Another one! Why would I leave my home?')

A couple of days later, I was in the midst of the day from hell – one of my temps had been caught dipping into the petty cash and I hadn't bothered to do a thorough background check on her – when the phone rang. 'Mom. This isn't a good time.'

'Nathan. You won't believe what has happened.' For once, she sounded genuinely distressed; this wasn't one of her usual daytime calls to discuss my nutrition or gripe about what was happening in Downton Abbey. 'It's Zackary. Zachary Lowenstein. You know, from number twenty-two.'

Jimmy's uncle. 'What about him?'

'I'm trying to tell you. You can't listen to your mother? So he was on his way to the Checkers store, catching the bus, like he does every day ...'

'And what? He was robbed? Mugged?'

'Don't hurry me! Why do you have to use that hard tone of voice? He was hit by one of those tourist buses. You know the ones. The ones that creep along, blocking the traffic.'

'Is he okay?'

'Okay? What a thing to say! Did I raise an idiot? You think you would be okay if you were hit by a great big bus? Lily from number fifteen was on her way back from the chiropractor – you know the trouble she has with her back, bad posture, I've told her a thousand times, but what can you do when people won't listen? – well she saw him being put into the ambulance, and his pelvis, it's not even the right way on his body.'

'That's awful.'

'And that's not all...'

Naveed, my prepubescent supervisor, was making 'hurry the fuck up' gestures at me. 'Mom, I got to go. Important work stuff.'

'What could be more important than life and death?'

'I know, I know. Can I call you back? There are people listening in.'

'What do I care about people listening in? You must come and take me to the Groote Schuur. I must see that Zackary is being looked after. That hospital... I've heard stories about it. You go in fine and you come out in a body bag, or worse.'

'Ma – I can't. I have a meeting –'

'You want me to take the bus? You want me to get run over like poor old Zachary Lowenstein?'

Somehow – don't ask me how – I managed to convince Naveed that I had a genuine family emergency and an hour later I pulled up outside Benchley Heights. Mom wasn't alone. She was flanked by Sarah White and Estelle, both of whom were busily confounding medical science by not dying.

'What took you so long? What, did you come here via Johannesburg?' my mother greeted me, ushering her neighbours into my car.

'He was usually so careful,' my mother began, the second I streamed into the traffic.

'You think he did it on purpose?' Estelle chimed in on cue.

'He always said he was tired.'

'But tiredness, that's a reason to die? He would never do such a thing.'

On and on it went.

'Nate!' Jimmy hurried up to me when we bustled into the accident and emergency waiting room. 'Thank you for coming.'

'How is he?'

'Hanging in there.' He sighed exaggeratedly, but his eyes were gleaming. 'We all have to be prepared though. Consensus is that he won't last the night.'

While my mother and her coterie moved to the coffee shop to harass the waiting staff, I followed Jimmy to Intensive Care. Zackary did not look like a man destined to live much longer – his skeletal frame seemed twisted, wrong somehow, as if Death had already started dismantling him without waiting His turn.

But he made it through the night. And through the following week. For the next month, until he was discharged, my evenings were a misery of taxiing my mother and various Benchley Heights residents to visit him. As his uncle continued to cling to life, Jimmy seemed to age. He put on weight, his skin took on a yellowish tinge. He looked like a man who thought he'd won the lottery, only to discover that he'd lost the ticket.

Jimmy called me up a few weeks after Zackary was discharged. 'He's not dying.'

'Oh. That's great news. Isn't it?' What else was there to say?

'You don't understand. He's not getting better, but nor is he getting worse. Man, it's a fuck-up. I've had to hire a nurse to come in and look after him – it's draining my savings.'

'Can't you put him in a home?'

'You know how much those places cost?' For my sins, I did. I'd done my research. 'And he's still refusing to sell up.' A bitter laugh. 'There's nothing wrong with his mind.'

'He's speaking?'

'Oh, ja,' Jimmy said. 'He's speaking all right.'

'Is he in pain?'

'No. The doctors are baffled. And get this... he no longer even goes to the lavatory. He eats, but where does the food go? All day he sits, watching the television. God help me, but I keep hoping that he'll just wake up one morning, stone cold dead.' He caught himself. 'It would be a merciful release.'

Ja, I thought. But for who? I mumbled something about it being 'just a matter of time'.

'But how much more time?' Jimmy's voice dropped to a whisper. 'He's eighty-fucking-seven. Nate, this property boom, it's not going to last much longer. You know how these things go. It'll just take another recession, Obama coming out as gay or something, and property prices will crash. Knock-on effect. You know.'

Summer slid into winter. I missed out on another promotion. The Friday People still congregated outside the building every week, but the mood was more subdued than it used to be; Jimmy became a silent, lurking presence. Still Zackary clung to life, my mother generously sending me almost hourly updates on his condition. 'He ate almost a whole bowl of my soup, and a slice of bread. It's a miracle!'

It's been five years since Zackary Lowenstein's miraculous recovery. He's still going strong, as are Estelle and the rest of the old people. Jimmy's not doing so well. He turned to the bottle, his wife left him, and he was retrenched from his job. He's been forced to move into Benchley Heights, and some days you can see him, a stooped greyish figure, wheeling his uncle along the beachfront.

More than once, Jimmy has cornered me in the lobby. 'Figured it out, Nate,' he slurs, his breath laced with Bells, forgetting that he's said it all before. 'Rachel's aunt's emphysema should have killed her years ago. Then there's Uncle Zack and Estelle with her liver cancer. Not to mention the others... They're all so fucking old, Nate. I'm beginning to think... Nate, they're not going to die. They're never going to die. It's a punishment. A punishment from God. We're being punished, Nate. You, me, all of us.'

'That's ridiculous.'

'Is it?' His bloodshot eyes filled with tears, and I had to look away. 'Is it, Nate?'

The building itself remains much as it ever was. We Friday People still slog our way through the rush-hour traffic to Sea Point every week, although we rarely meet for a sneaky cigarette these days. We're all older, greyer, more worn down. I'm still clinging to my job by my fingernails, and my mother still calls, daily. 'Ninety-one, my boy, but I feel like I could go on forever.'

TACTRATE METIM 28A

BENJAMIN ROSENBAUM

MISHNAH

CONCERNING THAT WHICH ARISES FROM THE GROUND OUT OF ITS PROPER TIME, IF IT FACES TO THE EAST, IT IS SAID OF IT, 'THEIR LEAVES NEVER WITHER'[1], BUT IF IT FACES TO THE WEST, IT IS SAID OF IT, 'THEY BEAR THEIR FRUIT IN SEASON'[2].

GEMARA

TO THE EAST. Raba asked, why is the east preferred? Because it exemplifies gratitude, for they[3] greet the sun. R. Abye objected, but is not he who accompanies a guest when he departs greater than he who greets him on his arrival? For on arrival, one may be seeking something.[4]

THEY BEAR THEIR FRUIT IN SEASON. Raba said, it is a rebuke, because they have arisen out of season: therefore 'you shall not eat any abominable thing'[5]. R. Abye objected and said, if it is unwholesome, you shall say 'it faces to the west', but if it is a gift from heaven in time of need, then you shall say, 'it faces to the east'.

It has been taught: after R. Shimon bar Yochai had left his confinement[6], he disputed with R. Shimon ben Gamliel concerning cucumbers[7]. He [bar Yochai] said: if they are caused to appear [by magic], they will face to the east. But the other [ben Gamliel] said: to the west; but, [he said,] the law [of

---

1   Psalm 1:3.

2   Psalm 1:4.

3   The crops arising out of season.

4   But on his departure, surely all business has been completed. The crops facing west accompany the setting sun's departure, while those facing east greet the rising sun. It is no longer clear how the Talmudic sages determined which way crops were facing. Rashi regards the direction in which most of the grain's tassels were pointing as determinative, while Rambam interprets the phrase to allude to the orientation of the leaves.

5   Deut. 14:3.

6   In a cave, by reason of Roman persecution. cf. Shabbat 33b.

7   The cucumbers that R. Eliezar ben Hyrcanus was able to summon by invoking the Divine will, cf. Sanhedrin 68a.

causing cucumbers to appear] is no longer known, because R. Meir did not get it [from his master, R. Akiba].

Then R. Shimon bar Yochai said, let us ask R. Eliezar ben Hyrcanus. He [ben Gamliel] asked, how can this be? [For R. Eliezar was deceased]. R. Shimon bar Yochai said: come and see. They went to the grave of R. Eliezar, and R. Shimon bar Yochai said, 'Arise, my darling, my beautiful one'[8]. Then R. Eliezar arose from the grave, although his condition was poor. R. Shimon [ben Gamliel] was afraid, because of the condition and because of his father[9], but R. Shimon [bar Yochai] consoled him, saying 'be of good courage'[10].

They sought to learn from R. Eliezar the laws of cucumbers, but R. Eliezar was compromised in his faculties[11] and pursued them to do them harm.

They sought the counsel of R. Meir, but he was not at home. They did not reveal their errand to Bruria. She served them food, and when they had eaten, she rebuked them, saying: did you not decree that no ruling shall be recorded in the name of my husband?[12] How can it be that you come to us? It is written, 'They close up their callous hearts, and their mouths speak with arrogance.[13] 'Then they confessed [the reason for their visit].

When R. Meir arrived, Bruria went to meet him before the house, and asked him: did not our teacher Moses rise up to meet [his enemies] Dathan and Abiram?[14] Then R. Meir knew who was in the house. He said, but

---

8   Song of Solomon 2:10.

9   R. Eliezar ben Hyrcanus had caused the death of R. Shimon ben Gamaliel's father, after the dispute over the Aknai oven, cf. Baba Mezia 59b.

10   Psalm 27:14.

11   Lit. 'his thoughts were eaten'

12   Because of the dispute over honours due to the various offices of heads of the Academy, R. Shimon ben Gamliel had decreed this punishment for R. Meir, cf. Horayot 13b.

13   Psalm 17:10.

14   Numbers 26:25, cf. Sanhedrin 110. Moses approached the supporters of Korah, about which the Talmud observes, 'This teaches that one must not be obdurate in a quarrel.' Bruria thus urges R. Meir to emulate Moses in pursuing

did our teacher [Moses] greet [their leader] Korah? Bruria replied, are you Moses, that you speak of Korah? It is written, 'Every wise woman builds her house, but the foolish plucks it down with her hands'[15] And if 'her house', how much more so the house of Israel?[16] Then R. Meir entered the house.

He greeted R. Shimon bar Yochai heartily, but he stood four cubits from R. Shimon ben Gamliel.[17] R. Shimon bar Yochai said: regarding the disposition of cucumbers, we sought the opinion of R. Eliezar ben Hyrcanus, but his faculties are compromised.[18]

R. Meir rebuked them, saying, it is forbidden [to resurrect the dead by means of necromancy]! But R. Shimon ben Gamliel said, I did it in order to teach. In this he cited the opinion of our sages, that 'IF HE ACTUALLY PERFORMS MAGIC, HE IS LIABLE'[19] refers to [the practice of magic for] its effects, not [to the practice of magic in order] to understand.[20]

R. Meir said, if [you had done so] in order to teach, [he would have arisen with] his good inclination and his evil inclination, but [as you did it] for honour[21], [he has arisen with] the evil inclination only.

R. Meir went to discover what had arisen in relation to R. Eliezar, and he met Acher[22] on the way. Acher came with great haste and R. Meir asked

---

reconciliation.

15   Proverbs 14:1.

16   According to Rambam, 'the house of Israel' was threatened because of R. Eliezar ben Hyrcanus having arisen, and it was with this argument that Bruria sought to persuade her husband to put aside private enmity. The Wilna Gaon observed in response: every feud between scholars is a danger to the house of Israel.

17   As if the latter had been excommunicated.

18   Lit. 'his thoughts have been eaten'.

19   cf. the Mishnah cited in Sanhedrin 67a.

20   cf. Sanhedrin 68a, regarding the permissibility of the magical production of cucumbers solely for the purpose of research.

21   i.e., to impress R. Shimon ben Gamaliel with your learning.

22   R. Elisha ben Abuya, R. Meir's former teacher, who had been excommunicated as a heretic, cf. Hagigah 15b.

him, are you well? Acher said, 'When the wicked, even mine enemies and my foes, came upon me to eat up my flesh, they stumbled and fell.'[23] Then R. Meir knew that R. Eliezer was pursuing the living, as he had been deprived of his good inclination.

Raba said in the name of R. Huna, in the name of Rav, in the name of Rabbi[24], regarding this tradition, that, when the Holy One revives the dead through justice and mercy at His will, they are to be regarded as alive, as it is written, 'THEIR LEAVES NEVER WITHER', but if they arise through other means, they are not to be regarded as alive, as it is written, 'THEY BEAR THEIR FRUIT IN SEASON'. R. Abye objected and said, what then is the law concerning them? If a priest or Nazirite comes into contact with them, shall he be regarded as unclean and obliged to bring a guilt-offering? Yes. But R. Abye further objected, we have received in the name of Eleazar Ben Arach[25], if one revives the dead to teach, he arises with both the good inclination and the evil inclination.[26] If he [the person arisen from the dead] is a priest, will he make himself unclean? And if so, what will a guilt-offering avail him?[27] The question stands.

Rava then asked Raba: how is it with R. Zeira? Must your house guest observe a period of mourning for himself? Raba had once invited R. Zeira

---

23   Psalm 27:2.

24   Rabbi (R. Yehuda ha-Nasi), the son of R. Shimon ben Gamliel, was thus the teacher of Raba's teacher's teacher.

25   This may be a pseudonym or cognomen of R. Meir, used by later sages to attribute teachings to him indirectly, in deference to the decree of R. Shimon ben Gamliel forbidding rulings to be recorded in his name, cf. Erubin 13b.

26   Because he is arisen through magic, and not through the Divine will.

27   If the person is himself regarded as technically dead, but is still in possession of his faculties, he will be unable to cleanse himself of the impurity arising from contact with the dead. This presents a legal puzzle. Various Gaonim argued that if he returns to life through no fault of his own, he cannot be held liable for the impurity, but if he asks a friend to resurrect him, he is liable. Rambam regards the resurrection of R. Eliezar as metaphorical, representing the resumption of the debate over the aknai oven (cf. Baba Mezi'a 59a) at a time when it was no longer appropriate, that is, after the majority had already decided, likening stubborn debate without legal justification unto a reanimated corpse deprived of the good inclination.

to a Purim feast, and, becoming drunk, had risen up and slaughtered him. The next morning, he prayed for mercy and R. Zeira was restored to life.[28] Raba said: in the case of R. Zeira, [he has arisen with only] the good inclination! R. Abye however said: was it not [through] the Divine will [that R. Zeira returned to life]? Raba said: I have taught my nephew [R. Abye] to eat bread, but he will not eat cake.[29]

A heretic came to R. Meir and said: a plague has come upon the Romans in Caesarea. One bites the other to feast on his flesh, and each one who is devoured and dies, then rises up again and pursues the next, as a wild animal. Meir said: has something then changed?[30] Upon returning home however, he said to Bruria, this is related to the matter of R. Eliezar.

R. Shimon ben Gamaliel called together the men of the Academy. R. Phineas said, 'The kings of the earth set themselves against the LORD[31]'. R. Shimon ben Gamaliel however responded, 'Let all who take refuge in you rejoice'[32] – all who take refuge in you, not all who honour you. From this we learn that also the wicked must be protected in time of general calamity. Others say, not until they repent, as it is written, 'for you are my refuge; into your hand I commit my spirit'[33]; that is, only when they are sufficiently contrite.

---

28   cf. Megilla 7b.

29   R. Abye, taking Raba literally, objects that since Zeira's resurrection was accomplished through prayer rather than magic, the problems discussed earlier do not apply. Raba responds by saying that Abye has only learned to eat bread, and not cake. According to Rashi, bread here represents serious study, while cake represents light-heartedness. According to the Tosafot, bread represents literal meanings, while cake represents the deeper metaphorical level. R. Abye has failed to apprehend that Rabba's compliment to Zeira is figurative rather than literal. Rabba was known for employing humor as a pedagogical tool, cf. Shabbat 30b.

30   That is, this predatory behavior is typical of the Romans.

31   Psalm 2:2. In other words, we have no obligation to assist the Romans, our occupiers.

32   Psalm 5:11.

33   Psalm 31:4-5.

While they were thus engaged, a great number of those [of whom it was said, it arises from the ground] 'OUT OF ITS PROPER TIME', approached the Academy to pursue [the people there]. R. Jose said, 'if your enemy is hungry, give him bread to eat'[34], and cast loaves before them, but they did not eat. R. Judah then said, 'at twilight you shall eat meat'[35], and he cast a hen before them. The pursuers devoured the hen. Then R. Nehemiah cast two ducks before them, and they devoured the ducks. Then R. Phineas cast three ewes before them, and they devoured the ewes. Then R. Nathan cast four goats before them, and they devoured the goats. Then R. Yochanan cast five calves before them, and they devoured the calves. He said, 'They slice meat on the right, but are still hungry, and they devour on the left, but are not satisfied.'[36]

Then R. Shimon ben Gamaliel cast six bulls before them, and they devoured the bulls. R. Phineas said, 'When they had eaten them, no one would have known that they had eaten them, for they were still as ugly as at the beginning.'[37] R. Judah said: May we also awaken![38] Then R. Judah cast seven oxen before them, and they devoured the oxen. Then R. Meir cast eight elephants before them, and they devoured the elephants. Then R. Shimon bar Yochai brought a Leviathan from the sea, and they devoured the Leviathan. At once they became so rotund that their bellies were like the wheels of a chariot, and the men of the Academy rolled them into the sea.

R. Eliezar ben Hyrcanus meanwhile entered the house of Acher to pursue him. Because Acher was unable to escape, he said: my master, I have a question about the [ritual purity of] ovens. Although R. Eliezar was compromised in his faculties, the matter interested him greatly, and so he ceased [to pursue].

---

34   Proverbs 25:21.

35   Exodus 16:12.

36   Isaiah 18:20.

37   Genesis 41:21.

38   The passage which R. Phineas cites, in which Pharaoh recounts his dream to Joseph, is followed by, 'Then I awoke.'

Acher said: consider an oven like that of Aknai[39] which, in the year of the Destruction of the Temple, was used on the first day of Passover to store unleavened bread that had previously been wrapped in a cloth that was stained with the menstrual blood of the oven's owner[40], and the owner then purified only the parts that had been touched by the unleavened bread.

Now, consider that the mother of the owner was a proselyte; however, the rabbinical court which converted her had said: we will allow you to convert only under the condition that your parentage is pure.[41] But the proselyte's father had been a Jew who was conceived after his own father had given his mother a bill of divorce about which he said: this paper belongs to me, except under the condition that the Temple will be destroyed, God forbid, and that on the first day of the festival of Passover of that year, we will have a great-granddaughter who, G-d forbid, will own an impure oven, in which case this paper belongs to you.[42] In such a case, is the oven pure or impure?

R. Eliezar said: it is pure! And with that he returned to dust.

Rava asked Raba: who is more to be praised, R. Meir, because he warned the Academy, or R. Shimon bar Yochai, because he brought the Leviathan? R. Abye objected: but perhaps Acher is to be praised, for his task was the greater?[43] Raba answered: R. Eliezar ben Hyrcanus is to be praised. At his second death, he remembered the Temple and turned towards Jerusalem, as we learned: IF IT FACES TO THE EAST.

---

39   An oven composed of many parts; the debate about whether the whole, or only the parts, must be purified, led to R. Eliezar's excommunication, cf. Baba Mezia 59b.

40   Which would render the cloth, and thus the matzah, and thus the oven impure, presuming the owner of the oven is Jewish.

41   In other words, only if her immediate ancestry is free of illegitimate births; in this case, the legitimacy of her father is in question.

42   The divorce is valid only if the bill of divorce, including the paper it is written on, is given entirely to the wife. If the husband retains ownership, the divorce would be invalid, and thus the woman would be the legitimate offspring of the couple, and hence her daughter, the oven's owner, would be Jewish. cf. Gittin 84a.

43   Because R. Eliezar was a more formidable threat than the others.

WISEMAN'S
TERROR TALES

ANNA TAMBOUR

Irving Wiseman's uncle Leo dropped some magazines on Irving's bed. 'Enough dreaming,' he said, pulling the book from his nephew's hands and placing it on the bureau. He would have liked to toss it, but it was a book, and even more than that, a library book.

'You gotta make a living,' he said.

Irving sighed, but rolled over and laid the magazines out before him on his bedspread like cards in a game.

'You got talent,' said Leo. 'You must have. So they're showing it, no?' He pointed like some professor in the movies at the middle magazine.

The right breast of the woman in the underwired but otherwise unstructured pink brassiere stared at the 17-year-old. It wasn't just the woman's youth that perked those breasts, Irving knew. His uncle had told him that 64% of women, once they hit the age of 20, already have bosoms that not only fail the pencil-test, but are as perky as easy-over-light fried eggs. This woman's bazoongas were held up in their most flattering form, high as they could go. Irving didn't know but guessed that the reason was those arms pulled up by wrists clamped into cuffs on that chain pulled over the swing-bar by the scientist's assistant.

Leo stabbed that cover – *Marvel Tales*, May 1940 – with his pipe. Ashes fell on the assistant's manic frown. 'What have you to tell me?'

Irving opened his mouth, looking ready to recite, or yawn.

'No, that's too easy,' said Leo. 'What does that remind you of? And this is no bordello. What you lying down for?'

Irving sat up and ran his hand through his thick curls. 'The other pink job.'

'And when are they not pink?'

'When they're red or chartreuse or – '

'If you can't piece these together, just how you think – '

The boy took off his glasses and pinched his nose, an odd gesture considering that without his horn-rims, he looked like Michelangelo's son of stone. 'Long blade of paper-guillotine in action of cutting a brunette in half. All right already. False underwire of round cotton-waste piping, non-adjustable rayon-satin ribbon straps, one-inch separator of same connecting bandeaux-style shallow unshaped cups. Suitable for women with no body who think they don't need fill. A Twenties look.'

'Better.' Leo produced yet another magazine from inside his fitted suit. 'This? I just picked it up.'

Irving pulled the magazine close to his face. Its ink was still loud, crude. Only out for a few months, this February 1941 *Spicy-Adventure Stories,* 'Space Burial', featured a screaming redhead slipping off the back of some flying bird – the important thing being that apricot sateen number with the shaped straps and wholly improbable way that the breasts could be supported. He snorted. 'Artistic license. No can do. Not with that fabric and no seams.'

'Now we're getting somewhere.' Leo pointed to the bed. 'What do you think of that one in the line-up?'

'"The Soul Scorcher's Lair"?'

The middle-aged man with no paunch waited. After all, he had once had dreams, too. But 15 seconds was enough.

'If you think I'll let a fantazyor eat your mother's kreplach. And she a widow working her fingers off… '

'Hot-formed lace, steel underwire, flare-banded from armpit to breast differentiators, elasticised arm straps, presumably three-hook back, D cup, black, suitable for full but firm breasts because there is still no adequate support for the average woman.'

'Excellent, my boy.' Leo smiled broadly, the picture of the proud uncle, even possibly, though he'd never seen it, the university professor gratified that his student had actually listened to all his lectures. Leo was proud of himself, too, for he had successfully hidden the hurt that the boy, through the callousness of youth, had dealt him. For Irving was right. That bra had been a great seller in '37 – but its success had rested on the racy lace and daring black. Women don't know how to fit a bra, and this one, for all its advertised appeal, was two flimsy colanders, so the average woman's breasts were sadly earthbound or showing their inadequacy of build with an embarrassment of collapsed cups when what they needed was adequate shaping, filling, engineering, uplift.

As Irving civilised his hair and washed his face and hands, he heard his mother setting the freshly scrubbed table in the kitchen – laying it with three places for the three people who lived in that little flat in the Bronx.

He was pleased in one way that he'd made Uncle Leo happy. Of course he didn't want to hurt the man – and besides, he felt sorry for him.

But he also felt a simmering anger that he could hardly admit to himself. To sign his life away. Yes, so Mama had started in the sweatshops at the age of nine. But still. Irving put that out of his mind while he dried his face, and dreamed for another snatched moment of designing rockets.

What he knew of the breasts of the average woman, of any woman for that matter, was the sum of what he'd seen of Egyptian, Greek and Roman statuary in the Metropolitan Museum, all those magazines his uncle brought home for him to study, and Leo's own blueprints and lectures about the real things.

Irving wondered if the man, that lifelong bachelor, had ever touched the real things. He'd gone from being a tailor of men's suits, an unenviable specialty in New York in the 1930s, to a brassier designer, only because of a friendship made by Irving's mother, who when her husband dropped dead of a heart attack when Irving was only 13, went into business on her own, sewing foundation garments to fit particular women, especially those with a breast or two cut off, and opera singers.

Her constructions, all made of pink canvas, could have held cement. Their fillings felt rather like it, and never shifted. Sometimes she made shapes that looked quite beautiful to Irving, but that she inevitably had to modify for her conservative clients, who seemed to prefer what Irving thought of as the 'squashed look'. Maybe they were ashamed. He didn't know but felt frustrated for his mother, who couldn't afford that luxury.

It was she who had talked to her brother about setting Irving up. She not only didn't have the money but there was also that limit of 'Hebrew' students already reached in all the top schools. So he had to take that job Uncle Leo wangled for him, opening in January. Until then, after graduation from high school in a week (what a waste of science classes!) he was to learn the trade – designing for three dimensions with two-dimensional materials, under her. Not that this training came, of course, with an opportunity to look at or touch the goods inside these constructions.

The first day on the job he successfully ran a Singer needle through his forefinger. It was a good lesson in driving speed on the newly electrified machine. After that, he surprised himself on the thing, finding that the more difficult the curves, the more fun he had making the turns, and he grew so skilled that his mother started trusting him with ever more mountainous jobs.

The fittings were all done in her bedroom, and the clients looked nothing like, say, that blonde with manacled hands and the rayon full-torso breast-delineating underpiping but otherwise purely unsupportive cups fronting *Terror Tales*, September 1934. Most of her clients were, frankly, variations on the potato or a cubist painting, even with her expert foundations giving them shape. 'Today's woman,' he said to her one day, 'should thrust out rockets, not your matzo balls.'

'So, Irving. This today's woman? She tells you this?'

Her son blushed reassuringly.

'You fantazyor,' she said, patting his cheek. 'Your today's woman is in the future, and she's made of steel.'

But to make him happy, she let him create two designs that were quite astoundingly shaped, giving body where needed he said, but always 'up and outlift'. She hated wasting the canvas and thread, but kept that thought to herself. After he had constructed both models – impeccably cut and sewn, she was pleased to note – she offered them to her two youngest clients, having quickly to explain that it was just an idea. She almost lost both women.

So instead, she asked Irving to tell her of his dreams while he sewed.

It helped him to hear her sigh.

The months passed more quickly than he imagined they would, and he was doubly sorry to see them go. His mother had always been a heroine to his way of thinking. One day he would find a woman like that, he thought when he forgot that he'd be a brassiere designer, something to laugh at. So embarrassed did he feel that he refused all comers, and with looks like his and his shy, thinker's manner, he could have explored all he wanted, even the nice girls.

December came, and with it, the Day of Reprieve.

He was told that there was no way he could get into the Air Corps, so he went to the Army office across the street, but after interviewing him the guy there after interviewing him, wrote something on a piece of paper and sent him back across the street. And he walked out of that office signed up for a course, launching him into the Air Corps.

With his new skills in map-making, he flew over Germany and then was stationed to Burma, where he learned to hate the English for their filled storehouses, meant not for the people who needed them, but for export; visited temples that he laughed to think about gracing towns in the US of A – the horror! And in this alien land he felt for the first time, the real things, if only stone; and after much encouragement and teasing, the real things with a real-life woman, who said she 'love' him, but she kicked his pet mongoose.

He hadn't been surprised that the stone women on the temples had matzo-ball breasts. After all, they were ancient, weren't they? But this woman in the flesh – hers were something he had only imagined. She was soft and warm, but they could have been made of tin, they were so conical. They only confirmed, however, his thoughts that the woman of today would love to look like that if she could. Of course, she must have been a freak, a beautiful one but nevertheless a fantasy come to life in flesh. Breasts like these didn't grow on women, or he would have seen them on statues. They needed guidance.

Not that he planned to give it to them. No siree. Now that he'd escaped, he saw – through the squalor of death and fear, the confusion of cruelties intended and unthinkingly dealt out, this war that he helped to serve – not only the opportunity but the responsibility to engineer a shining, uplifting future.

He was just having what isn't supposed to be but what many have experienced: a great war – when in a nightmare, a blonde turned up, 'Dead Man's Bride' from *Terror Tales*.

One pitiless noon he was sitting outside his tent, a wet kerchief over his head. He had been dreaming – but only daydreaming, and sketching rockets.

'Wise guy,' she cracked, as if that nut were fresh. She had a hand on her hip and one of those so-sure-of-herself voices that fit her cover-girl looks, on that cover. But she mustn't have travelled with a compact. Her peach-gold skin was pitted with oozing sores, one eye filled with dirt, and her skull poked out like the Andaman Islands, from a blue-tinged scalp.

Yes, Irv had been around. He noticed not only that, but that her breasts were like two flops of camp stew. Man, did she need engineering, and uplift.

She sidled around behind him and hung her head over his shoulder. 'That's what I want,' she said. 'We all want it.'

'This?' He drew the nose cone, then another one beside it, and drew straps.

'Exactly.' She snatched up the paper as something precious, and held it to her ravaged chest. He was almost charmed. And she didn't smell half as bad as other unexpecteds he'd come across, unreported 'casualties', the still oozing dead.

He wondered if someone had put her up to this. 'Do you know the woman in that black lace number in *Eerie* – '

'Corinne? She prayed for you! Thank her for your luck changing.'

He repressed a smile. He'd always reckoned this blonde for a tale-spinner, but it was flattering nonetheless.

'Can she come here?'

The earth moved, and up from it crawled Corinne. That bra had not lasted half as well as it should have. It was even less recognizable than Corinne.

But she retained some of her strawberry-blonde set hair. It had looked to be so shellacked that its preserved curves looked set for her to be displayed in a museum.

'Dis war will end,' she said through her lipless mouth. 'And you will become the greatest brassiere designer there ever was.'

He jumped up. They could have tossed a grenade in his lap, his heart pounded that bad. He wanted to flee into the jungle, but knew they'd follow. What did they have to lose? He couldn't lose them, so he said simply, like some dumb grunt, 'I'm sorry but I'm a rocket man.'

'Not on your life, you're not,' said the *Dime Mystery* Maid, now to his left. He looked her over, and was unsurprised to note that her flimsy slip of a bra, which couldn't hold two flies, had slipped to her waist. What with her ribs sticking out, and her breastbone and all, he had to remember what her problem was. Ah yes, no breasts to speak of.

Before the rest of his troop came back from manoeuvres, he was surrounded by a bevy of former cover girls, all insisting that he heed their call. Their story was that it was too late for them, but they still had their duty, which they would carry out no matter what.

'Not,' chuckled the siren named Mitzi ('of "Crisis in Utopia" ', she reminded him) 'that "no matter what" means anything to us. We have forever. And a purpose in death.'

'But why should you care?'

'Haven't you noticed that we're all young dead?' said Mitzi. 'Models don't last long. But that doesn't mean we don't feel solidarity with the girls still walking the streets in flesh and bras. They don't want old-fashioned bodies. They don't want straps that fall down. They need up and outlift! And you're gonna give it to 'em, Captain.'

The girls, as they called themselves, gave her the best they could with a Bronx cheer.

They were more persistent than gunfire in an assault. And they didn't let up for sleep or regrouping. He'd seen so much already in this war that he didn't think them any more strange than some of the orders he'd been given by Command. Nor the sights that he came upon and helped to make, because of the orders from people whose war experience was intensely spent on maps only pocked by pins.

He argued with the girls. Then he tried to reason, telling them what a waste a creative brain like his would be – to engineer brassieres – when space (and the needs of war of the future) cried out for a genius with solutions.

'But you're such a genius in this,' said Corinne, giving her lacquered hair a flick, which exposed her shapely bones. 'Besides, you can't deny your heritage.'

'What's that s'posed to mean,' Mitzi shot.

'He's a Hebe, that's all. No offense, Mitzi, but you know.'

Mitzi would have flashed her eyes, but she couldn't even blink them. Instead, she said, 'Captain Wiseman. Irving. Be a doctor.'

'Or better yet,' piped up the woman who still had chunks of her zaftig build, dug into her terrible torture marks. 'A psychiatrist.'

So suddenly he had two allies, sort of.

And there was war amongst the girls till finally, he was shipped home, a month after the war officially ended.

The ship was crammed full of men, but that didn't stop the girls boarding too. They weren't alone. There was a whole contingent of dead with missions, attached to both troops and officers. Irving sensed this, though they were better at hiding than any soldier he'd ever known. He never talked about them to anyone, and no one told him of the dead who stalked them. Does it take war to bring them out, he wondered. And if so, could at least there be the retribution of having them pester just as much the idiots in Command, the civvies who made money from the war, or glorified all the wrong things about it. But he'd been around enough by now to figure that only soldiers were delivered these particular rations – these dead, all on missions.

So while the living had to come to terms with peace, war raged amongst the girls and at him – a constant ack-ack about his future, all the way to New York Harbour. But not one of them advocated rockets. Even to reminisce about riding them on covers, as (formerly) big-chested Bertha L'Amour had in 'Payload: Vavoom', rockets were a no-go zone. If he brought them up, the girls would sing Big Band hits – and with their torn-out and rotted voice boxes, now *that* was the stuff of nightmares.

So when he walked down the plank and saw his mother, shorter than he remembered, he strode up to her and hugged her long and hard, with a grip less manly than his looks. Then his uncle shyly shook his hand. Leo looked at him with awe, his mother with simple pride. Nothing more had reached them but the briefest 'I'm doing well. This land is beautiful' for years.

Two hours later, over the gefilte fish, he said to his uncle, 'There still a job working with you?'

'Irving.' His uncle placed his fork on the plate and wiped his mouth. 'Don't you dream any more?' He looked intensely at his fish. 'I'm sorry. I can only imagine what you've seen.'

'Leo,' Irving said. 'You've seen it too.'

Leo reached out and took his hand. 'You can come to work tomorrow. I'll make sure they take you. A veteran with skills.'

'Over my dead body,' said Bessie Wiseman, splashing the chicken soup. 'You must go back to school. That's an order, Rocket Man.'

And somehow, in that little apartment in the Bronx, the wind howled outside and the lift creaked with arthritis, but the girls couldn't get in. Out on the pavement this chorus of sirens pitched everything they had up at that window – wheedles, soft-soap, promises, demands – in brassy blare to rot-muffled croak, they threw their voices up at Irving, safe inside.

But they knew they'd been defeated.

And Irving Wiseman did become a rocket designer, a military scientist on typically low pay and sworn to secrecy about his achievements, but happy as clams are supposed to be, and they don't complain. A clam who didn't even notice, and was never told by his uncle, that while he was gone, the Conical Bra had come out, a great success, and from a competitor. It was engineered with military precision, even had maximum reinforcement.

When the girls found out, they felt so stupid about having missed it all, having gone on a mission to the other side of the world (that failed anyway) when all the action was happening at home, that they slunk back to their holes and never regrouped.

ZAYINIM

ADAM ROBERTS

1

Jonie stole one of Daniel's books. 'Borrowed', we might say; but she knew what stealing was, and she knew what she was doing. On the other hand, her mother was always pressing her to read books, and – to be truthful – there was little else to do. Jacob and the others were away, so the rest were supposed to lie low, which was the mostest BORINGness, and Jonie had read all her other books. So she snuck into Daniel's room. It was actually the cab of one of the trucks, but he'd hung up drapes and set up a bookcase and made it quite homely. She picked a likely looking codex, and danced back to her den.

The book was called *Beyond Good and Evil* by a guy called Nate Char – an American, presumably, by the name. The title promised a crime-and-punishment story, or (more exciting) a crime-but-no-punishment story. But actually it was all dense prose like this:

> *Assuming truth is a Jew – what then? Is there not reason to suspect that all philosophers, in so far as they were dogmatists, have known very little about Jews? That the terrible seriousness and clumsy importunity with which they have usually paid their addresses to the Truth, have been unskilled and unseemly methods for impressing the Jews? Certainly Truth has never allowed herself to be won; and at present every kind of dogma stands with sad and discouraged mien – IF, indeed, it stands at all!*

That was the point at which Jonie bailed. She threw the book on the floor and lay on her bed for a while, chewing her fingernails. She spent five minutes trying to nibble her two pinkie nails into talons, and then gave up on that and bit them both close to the finger. Then she leapt up. Ran, with the uncoiled sudden energy of bored youth, out of her room, past the fence and to where her mother was working.

'What's a philosopher?'

'Somebody who tries to fathom the universe,' her mother replied, without looking up.

Jonie waited. After a while she cracked. 'Don't you want to know why I asked?'

Her eyes still on what she was doing, her mother returned, 'Why did you ask?' in a level voice.

'I borrowed one of Daniel's books. It says that philosophers are in love with the Jews. So are they *not* Jews, these philosophers?'

'There have been many Jewish philosophers,' said her mother, with that particular tone in her voice that was the closest she ever came to laughter. 'But there have also been philosophers amongst the Goyim.'

'Zombies? *Zombies* want to fathom the whys of the universe?'

Her mother looked up, and angled her head. 'I didn't say there were any zombie philosophers'

'Isn't Goy another word for zombie?'

'No,' she replied, returning her attention to whatever she was writing.

Jonie waited an age in the ensuing silence – whole minutes – before the energy danced out of her. She pirouetted from one end of her mother's desk to the other, and back again. Her mother continued plugging away at whatever she was doing, undistracted. 'Is Daniel on the prim?' Jonie asked.

'Your uncle is on perimeter duty, I believe,' mother replied. 'Perhaps you wish to apologise for taking one of his books without asking his permission?'

'Later!' Jonie cried, and raced out of her mother's room.

Elisheva was on the main door, but she'd always had a soft spot for Jonie and didn't need much persuading. 'Take one,' she insisted, pressing a loaded bolt-gun into her hands. 'Remember: aim at the bluest eye.'

'Sure, yes, OK, of course, I *know*,' Jonie told her, in an ecstasy of impatience. Then the heavy triple-shield iron door grated noisily open and Jonie ran out into the sunshine. She didn't so much as look back at the compound; she just ran. Lay-low week take that!

The long grass hissed like snakes as she sprinted through it. She came out at the rise, and the lake was spread out all before her in the afternoon sunshine, each of the myriad wavelet inset with a pip of bright sunlight. To the left was a bole of willows, like a knot of giant green jellyfish trailing their tentacles in the water. Everything was pale green and dark green, and the water was blue-green, and Jonie ran in the sunlight direction: widdershins around the island. Down into a declivity, and up onto a small hill, and then she saw Daniel – dressed in bright red, standing like a flame in the field.

The red was on purpose, of course. The Zayinim were attracted to the bright colour, and would strut and stumble in Dan's direction, rather than bothering the compound. Of course, that put the pressure on Dan's marksmanship. But his marksmanship was fabled. Zayin was the Hebrew Z, Z-for-zombies, although it also meant *dick*, and lezayen meant *to insert the dick*, which Jonie thought was pretty funny, actually. Not that she had a whole lot of experience of dick, and still less of insertion. She hooted Daniel's name, and galloped so hard down the slope to him that she was out of breath by the time she arrived and it took her ages to get her breath back, and she had to lean her hands on her knees and face the ground like she was about to spew.

Daniel's creased face was trying to do stern. 'Shouldn't cry *out* like that, little one,' he told her. 'Shrieking. They're not deaf, you know.'

'To what do you owe the pleasure?' Jonie said. 'I'll tell you, Daniel. I read one of your books.'

'But I haven't written any books, Jonie,' said Daniel, genuinely puzzled.

'It was called *Better than Good and Worse than Evil*,' Jonie pressed. 'It's by an American, and it's about philosophers. It said philosophers were in love with truth, and also in love with Jews, and I figured that meant they *weren't* Jews. But who isn't a Jew? Apart,' she added, sweeping her right arm in a broadcast indicative gesture.

Daniel looked nervously around, in case one of them was slouching towards them. But the view was clear. 'Slow down,' he begged.

'A Zayin can hardly talk, and surely a Zayin can't write, so I'm thinking a Zayin can't be a philosopher. Thus and *therefore* I was wondering – since it's your book, you explain.'

When old Daniel frowned the three horizontal lines on his brow went, as it were, from normal to bold font; but more than that, two angled lines converging on the bridge of his nose sprang into visibility, like a giant V.

He holstered his gun, and pulled a long, sharp-ended stick from a loop on the other side of his belt. Jonie couldn't imagine what he was going to do with it, until he jabbed it hard into the soil, and then unfolded a sort of hinged canvas seat, no bigger than two cupped hands. He sat on this and took a breath. 'You're going too fast for me, child,' he said, and began extricating materials for smoking: a white tube the length of a live round; a lighter as red as his clothes. 'But the book is called Beyond Good and Evil, and it's not by an American. It's by a German, and it was very popular with the people who – ' And he nodded in the direction of the lake, to indicate all the Zayinim in their terrible masses, somewhere over there.

'No,' said Jonie, delightedly, 'kidding.' She flopped into the grass at her uncle's feet, and clutched her own knees to her chest. 'So it is a zombie philosophy!'

'No,' said Daniel, sounding now like a ventriloquist talking whilst simultaneously holding his cigarette between his lips. A click and the end became an ember. He breathed the smoke in deep. It made a loud, sibilant sound going in, like silk on silk. Then he let it out very slowly. 'It was written before that. But it inspired the people who made themselves into – that.'

'Wolf Hitler!' exclaimed Jonie, excitedly.

'He was one of them, one of the worst. But not the only one.'

'Tell me the story again,' insisted Jonie.

Daniel drew hard on his cigarette again, and breathed out a spear of smoke into the mild afternoon air. 'Well the Wolf hated Jews. And he was a ruler of Europe, and he made allies with others who hated Jews. And there was a big war; the whole world fought it. But the Wolves and the Bears banded together, and won that war.'

'If they hated the Jews, why didn't they kill them?' Jonie asked.

'They did. They killed the Jews in Europe, and Russia, and north Africa. There were other Jews in America, and although America lost that war and signed away reparations and agreed to,' Daniel coughed sharply, 'dis-ad-van*ta*geous trade agreements and so on, they at least kept their Jews.'

'What happened next?' Jonie pressed. She knew what happened next; but it was good to hear the story told.

'Well, the Wolf had a dream. He wanted to make a race of supermen, and this was because of books like the one you *stole* from my room, you know.' Jonie made a shocked face, but her uncle was smiling. 'The archetypal warriors, new warriors of a new war, were the überboatmensch, and they were the prototype. That's what the writer of your book talked about,' (Jonie began to suspect he couldn't remember the guy's name) 'how to become more like the überboatmensch, solitary hunters, utilising new technologies to destroy and inhabit new worlds and so on. Anyway. Anyway, the Wolf had the resources of the world at his disposal, so he made it come true. Through –' Daniel drew a curlicue of smoke in the air with his cigarette, gesturing at the vagueness of the next word '– science. Invincible warriors. Regenerating flesh, self-repairing gene-loads, immortality. *Beyond* mortality. And from a simple dose of a serum! So he dosed up an army and invaded China, and destroyed it. But it wasn't enough to give it to the army only – the people wanted it too. Everybody wanted it!

'The Wolf's allies begged for the serum, and he used it to force them to submit further to him. But eventually everybody got it. Everybody except the Jews. He agreed a treaty with America, and part of the agreement was: not the Jews. He thought – the Aryan Americans and the Spanish Americans and the Noble Native Americans will live forever in a warrior world, but the Jews will be mortal, and die out.' He was down to the stump of his cigarette now, and Jonie was impressed at the way he held the last bit of it with his nails, so it didn't scorch his skin.

'But we're still here.'

'Immortality is a bad idea. The body keeps going, but eventually the mind fall apart. The human mind isn't built to last forever, and eventually it curls up on itself and shrivels down. That's why the Zayinim are so... thoughtless.'

'That's because we shoot for their brains. We shoot their brains and they can't think. They don't die, but can't think,' said Jonie.

'Every human on earth was made a zombie, except the Jews!' said Daniel. 'You think that we shot every one of them in the head?'

'I can't believe everyone in the world was made a zombie,' challenged Jonie. 'There must have been thousands and thousands.' She remembered reading something about the pre-Zayin world. 'Millions!'

'Indeed. And a lot died in fighting over the serum. But a lot more got it – just not *us*, though. Then the new supermen and superwomen discovered that they couldn't carry children to term any more. The supermen could *plant* the seed like ever they did before, but the superwombs couldn't hold on to the babies. But they figured: I'm upset by this? Me? I'm immortal! And they lived to a hundred, and were still as young as when they took the serum. And then they lived to a hundred and twenty, and they were young. And then, at a hundred and fifty – don't ask me why, am I a scientist? –

their minds started folding in on themselves, like a spider sprayed with water in the washtub. You've seen the way they're all legs and motion, and a quick slurp from the tap and they curl into a full stop?'

'Yes, yes,' said Jonie, impatiently. 'And?'

'And they all went the same way. Immortal, but thought-impaired. Stumbling about. Too stupid and disoriented to avoid banging into things. Like leprosy, they began to knock bits off. Even serum-repair don't cover everything – fingers regrow like courgettes; eyeballs grow back white as gobstoppers. And the Zayinim were too slow-witted to help themselves, stumbling about. The only thing they knew was: war. They'd been made as warriors. So they stumble about, and when they meet another of God's creatures they tear it to pieces! Which is why we have to keep them at bay. That's the definition of a warrior. A warrior is someone whose whole thought is: war.'

'Other people, apart from the Jews, must have resisted the temptation of the serum,' mused Jonie.

'You think we Jews *resisted* the temptation? We're such expert temptation-resisters? Don't be pumpkinny. If they'd've offered us immortality, wouldn't we have taken it? Only they didn't offer it. That was the deal. Because the Wolf hated us.'

For a while they sat in silence, looking at the lake. The little slurpy waves kept kissing away at the reed-bank, over and over. The sun was lower. Daniel pinched out the last quarter-centimetre of his cigarette, and brought up his tin. Then he placed the demi-stub on the metal, and lit it again with his lighter, bringing his face close to it to suck up the very last wisps of smoke. His cigarette tin was brushed with a score of black marks where he had done this before. But what can you do? Tobacco is precious.

'When did all this happen?' Jonie asked. 'I mean – I know it was a long time ago. I know it wasn't *living* memory.'

'My grandfather remembered those times,' Daniel said, musingly. 'He used to tell me about it.'

'He died. So that,' said Jonie, with the pedantry of youth, 'is not living memory.'

'He died, thank God!' agreed Daniel. 'There were a lot more of us, back then. Whole villages-full. Not like now. Ah well. Onward I suppose.

Until we find the island and build the New City.' And he heaved himself off his stick-seat and folded it away.

2

That night Jonie had another go at reading the book; but it was indigestible stuff, and Daniel's handwriting didn't make it any easier – assuming it had been copied out by Daniel, and not some other scribe. His spelling was idiosyncratic even by Jonie's teenage standards, and sometimes his vocabulary was simply baffling.

> *Physiologists should think twice before positioning the drive for self-preservation as the cardinal drive of an organic being. Above all, a living thing wants to discharge its strength, to roll it forcefully from birth to death: life itself being fundamentally a Wheel to Power. Self-preservation is the oblique perversion of this wheel, the most frequent consequences of zombie life.*

Physical-what-nows? And then there was a series of weird proverbs, almost none of which made sense.

> *Anyone who despises himself will still respect himself as a despiser.*
> *It is the desire, not the desired, that we fall in love with.*
> *The consequences of our actions take us by the scruff of the neck, altogether indifferent to the fact that we have 'improved' in the meantime.*
> *We are punished most for our virtues.*

Vices, she presumed he meant to write there. And –

> *He who fights with monsters might take care lest he thereby becomes a monster. And when you gaze long into zombies the zombies also gaze into you.*

Cold blue eyes. But, though young, Jonie had enough experience of the Zayinim to know that when they looked at you, there was nothing *behind* the look. They could not gaze. Most were repulsive-looking, but even the

237

good-looking ones were no better than beasts: naked, filthy, dangerous. At breakfast the next day, she challenged Daniel: 'Do you write it out, Uncy? Is this book I *borrow-éd* in your handwriting?'

Daniel glowered at her. They were expecting Jacob back soon: later that day maybe, or maybe tomorrow, or the day after; and until he came back Daniel had to conserve his tobacco. Accordingly he was grumpy. 'You've a problem with my handy writing, maybe? Stealers can't be choosers, my girl.'

'It's hard going, and your spelling is a shocker, and I don't know,' Jonie said, haughtily enough. 'Tell you what the problem is? The problem is the book has no story.'

'No story,' snorted Daniel, rubbing the palm of his hand over his tall, lined brow. 'Stories you want, eh? But we're beyond stories now. The world has ended, and we're living in the afterwards, and there are no stories any more.'

Her mother nodded sagely at this, sipping her tea.

This was hardly a very satisfying answer, and Jonie vowed to give Daniel the book straight back – or burn it, or throw it in the lake, just to annoy him. But she didn't. She kept reading. There was something weirdly compelling in the mumbo-jumbo of it. And that night, as she drifted off to sleep, it occurred to her with a force like revelation – maybe this was a holy book. Maybe it contained the answer to the problems of the Jews and the Zombies.

She was jolted awake by raised voices. She knew immediately what the shouting meant. Sat straight up in bed. Slapped herself on the face. But she knocked her lighter on the floor when she reached for it, and wasting time scrabbling around before she could get a candle lit. Then she put shoes on, and put on her leather coat and gloves, the material stiff as thick cardboard in the cold. Cradling the candle she came out and along the corridor, and clanging up the metal steps to the top of the tower. Even before she reached the top she heard the *snap, snap* of rifle fire.

Everybody was there: her mother, Daniel, Elisheva, Esther, K. and Ash. K. swivelled the spotlight, and the others took turns at shooting at the indistinctness below. Ash handed Jonie a pistol (all the other rifles were away with father), but the moon was no bigger than a toenail clipping and some mocking clouds were playing peekaboo with even this small light.

The Zayinim could be heard rather than seen, rattling the wire fence, making their distinctive 'ch' hissing noise, occasionally letting out dog-like high-pitched whimpers.

'It's not good, them being out at night,' Jonie gasped, excited despite herself. K. moved the spotlight, and three of them were visible in the circle. They turned their eyes up at the sudden Illumination, and mother shot the one on the left – drove a groove right down the crown of its head, like parting its hair. It danced backwards as a spray of black fluid appeared above its head like a rooster's comb. Then it fell out of the light.

Abruptly, the Zayinim started shambling away. They were dumb, 'severely mentally impaired' as mother put it, but they were not wholly brainless. The fence was not giving way, and they weren't getting through. 'It's not good, that they're out at night,' Jonie repeated.

'Indeed not,' said Elisheva. Zombies usually got active in the warmth of the day. Unless they got food, that was the only way they *could* get active. Shambling around in the small hours must have meant they'd been feeding. And feeding carried with it the inevitable correlative: *feeding on whom?*

'I'm going to start one of the trucks,' said Daniel, heading down the stairs. 'We need more light.'

'Don't waste the petrol,' said mother. 'They're going anyway.'

'You sure?'

As if in answer to his question, clouds parted and enough pearl-coloured moonlight fell on the field in front of the camp to show it deserted.

'They're gone,' mother pronounced.

Jonie was sent back to bed, but of course she was too wired-up to sleep now. She read some more of the Char book, though reading by candlelight always made her eyes tired. Was Char really his name? Or was it a pseudonym. The only sure way to destroy one of the Zayinim was to burn it to ash; and in the latter days, when there had been end-times attempts to stem the tide of the zombermen, much of civilisation had gone up in smoke. Several times, when the camp had moved, Jonie had seen the scorched remains of cities, squares of slag where even weeds would not grow, black earth. It was why there were so few books. So little of everything. *The philosopher of the charred.* He had the answers! If only she could interpret the book aright.

239

*The Jews – a people 'born for zlavery' as Tictacus and the whole
ancient world says, 'the chosen people' as they themselves say and
believe – the Jews achieved that miracle of revaluation of values
thanks to which life on earth has for a couple of millennia acquired
a new and dangerous fascination – their prophets fused 'rich',
'godless', 'evil', 'violent', 'sensual' into one and were the first to coin
the word 'world' as a term of infamy. It is in this inversion of values
... that the significance of the Jewish people resides: with them there
begins the slave revolt in morals.*

'Zlavery'? Was the word an artefact of Daniel's orthography? It wasn't in
her Websters – she got out of bed and checked. So was it a slip of the pen?
Or actually intended as a portmanteau of *zayin* and *slavery*? How were the
Jews born for that?

She snuffed her candle and lay down again, until she felt sleep
creep over her, like sinking into a hot bath. Then it suddenly shot through
her mind, a fiery spear in her thoughts. They *were* slaves – slaves to the
persistency and hostility of the Zayinim! A hundred disparate things fell into
a gorgeous and meaningful pattern for the first time – with what splendour it
all made sense. The Egyptian pharaoh undead mumzombie people keeping
the Jews in bondage until the red sea of blood opened its doors across
charred black sands and they fled along the Mobius-strip pathway of DNA.
The struggle between Jews and Zombies would drag on, itself zombie-like,
unless they found a way to pass beyond Jews and Zombies. The future. She
was the future. New blood, and a new beginning. Breaking the old wheel of
tradition. Helix and double-helix, and the doubling was a necessary part
of the helix.

She debated with herself whether to get up, relight her candle, seek
out her mother and explain things – but she could anticipate the cross
temper of waking her at this hour. She'd explain it all in the morning. And,
giving herself permission, she fell into sleep.

3

In the morning she woke with a fizzing in her stomach. But when she got up, and as she was rinsing her face in the basin outside, it dawned on her that she had *forgotten* the whole glorious unified vision she had had in the night. She sat on the end of her bed and waited for the inspiration to return to her, but it didn't. Then she grew angry with herself for slothfully falling asleep instead of getting up and doing something. Anything! Writing it down, shouting it in Daniel's ear. She propped her pillow against the end of the bed and punched it for a while. But that didn't do any good. Oh, she was in a foul temper went she went through to see what there was for breakfast.

Everybody was there, and they were right in the middle of a discussion about moving the camp. 'Include me out of this discussion, why don't you,' she wailed.

'We didn't want to wake you, princess,' said Ash, separating his beard into two forks that he plaited round one another, undoing the plait and smoothing the beard into one again – a nervous tick of his.

'We can't move until Jacob gets back,' said Daniel.

Jonie scowled at him. 'Of course we can't,' she said, sarcastically. 'We need the extra hands to help us load the trucks.'

'I didn't mean that,' said Daniel.

'He didn't mean that,' mother echoed.

'Then what did he mean?' snapped Jonie. And as she asked the question she saw, with a horrible internal clatter, what he meant. He meant: what if the others *don't* come back? What if they can't? She saw it. Those Zayinim from the night before had been eating something.

Her thought processes must have been obvious, because A. said, 'I'm sure they chanced upon a deer, or a sheep, or something.'

Jonie announced: 'Father is fine. And I've been reading Daniel's book, and I have had a vision. A vision! I suddenly saw how we could escape the predation of the Zayinim!'

Everybody was looking at her now. 'All right,' prompted her mother. 'How?'

'Actually I can't remember now,' she said, trying to look dignified. 'But I'm sure it'll come back to me.' She took a mug of porridge from the breakfast pan and retreated to her room to read more of the Char. But her attention jittered over the words, and she kept trying to cast herself back into the middle of the previous night.

...be assigned to pretence, to the will to delusion, to selfishness, and cupidity. It might even be possible that WHAT constitutes the value of those good and respected things, consists precisely in their being insidiously related, knotted, and crocheted to these evil and apparently opposed things – perhaps even in being essentially identical with them. Perhaps! But who wishes to concern himself with such dangerous 'Perhapses'! For that investigation one must await the advent of a new order of philosophers, such as will have other tastes and inclinations, the reverse of those hitherto prevalent – philosophers of the dangerous...

It was no good. She couldn't concentrate. There was some commotion outside, so she gave up on her reading. She put on her jacket and gloves and hat and went to the main gate.

'There's one left over from last night,' said Esther, excitedly. 'They're all out there now sorting it out.'

'Let me through,' Jonie demanded.

'Your father wouldn't want me to.'

Esther was, like, a hundred years old. 'Don't be a shrivelled old *stupid* person, Esther, and let me *out*.'

'I'll tell him it wasn't my idea,' Esther grumbled. 'Take a gun, at least.'

'Yes yes yes,' said Jonie, snatching the weapon and squeezing through the door before it was even a quarter open.

It always felt good to be outside. Spring was everywhere now, which was good in one sense – no more sleeping in all her clothes wrapped in two blankets and still shivering with the cold – and very bad in another. The Zayinim became much more active in the warm months of the year. Not just in terms of moving more rapidly and with more purpose – although until you'd seen a zombie immediately after a feed you had no idea just how quickly they could go – but in terms of aggregating into larger and therefore more dangerous packs. Nonetheless, it was good to breathe the fragrant air.

Someday, she mused, she would escape it all. Start her own life. Have kids, maybe. Except that having kids would not be to escape.

They were all standing, a circle of folk in the long grass. It was indeed one of the Zayinim from the previous night – the one mother had shot across the top of its skull. It was lying on its back in the grass. Jonie came up behind Daniel, and then peered past him.

It was naked, as all the Zayinim were. Their bodies long outlasted whatever clothes they had once worn. This one was nude, but not all of them were – some were covered in hair, like beasts of the field. The thing was the serum, or whatever it was, that made them immortal. It prompted regeneration of the flesh, with almost miraculous speed and accuracy. But the accuracy was not perfect, and over long enough stretches of time weird glitches worked their way into the operation. This could take any number of forms, but a common one was that hair follicles grew thicker and thicker hair. Not this guy, though: he was bald, eyebrowless, pubic-nude and stark as a skeleton. But there were other oddities. At some point in its long life the zombie had been split open across the side. This wound had, of course, healed; but teeth had grown in an irregular pattern along the scar. It had only a finger and a thumb on its right hand, but its left hand was a root-tangle of extra fingers all clutched together. She couldn't help looking at its genitals: a smaller penis grew from the end of its actual penis, the way potato-buds sometimes sprouted from whole potatoes. The gouge carved by mother's bullet, an inch deep at its deepest point, divided its cranium along a black crease. But it still had both its eyes, and its mouth was working. 'Ch-ch-ch.'

'Burn it,' said K. 'The grass is spring grass, the fire won't spread.'

'Waste the petrol?' returned Ash.

'Jacob will be back soon,' said K. 'The others will be back soon. They'll bring more.'

'And if they don't?' Ash replied, adding hastily, lest he be misunderstood, 'Don't bring more *petrol*?' In case anybody thought he meant *don't come back*.

'We can't just leave it here,' said Daniel. 'I'll get an axe, take its head off.'

'There's another!' called Elisheva, pointing. Everybody looked. Not one but two Zayinim were shuffling round the margin of the lake. Further off were half a dozen more, also approaching. With a nice sense of the incipiency of the drama, the breeze suddenly woke up. It began shaking the willows, which moved their branches sluggishly as if waving the people away. There were, of course, no birds.

'Back inside,' said Daniel, aiming his bolt-gun downwards. 'I'll try and take out the rest of this one's brains.'

The others started back towards the camp. Ash started off first, and straightaway, with a booming yell, he fell. The long grass swallowed him. 'There's one here!' he hollered.

Daniel reacted quickest, leaping nimbly over the supine zombie at his feet and hurrying to Ash. There was a jarring bang as he discharged his weapon, and the next thing Jonie saw was Ash being helped back to his feet, blood all over his old head.

'They're in the grass,' mother cried. 'Scores of them! They've been creeping up!'

'Back to the compound,' bawled Daniel. He turned, and shot again at the ground. 'They're everywhere.'

Jonie felt her heart go dabbity-dabbity in her chest. She set off running for the compound, but at once the whole world swung about the axis of her right ankle, and the earth smacked her hard in the face. It took a moment to comprehend what had happened. Grabbed. Its undead hand around her ankle. She twisted in its grasp, aimed her weapon and fired it – missed. Its ghastly bifurcated head turned to her, and its mouth opened. She saw then that its teeth were not teeth at all, but fingernails.

'It returns,' the creatures hissed at her, in weirdly accented English. 'Eternally it returns. And –'

Her second shot did not miss.

The zombie flopped back, its whole face horrible compressed and distorted where the bolt had punched its way in, at the mid-point of its nose. But it did not let go its grip. She put the gun down to free both hands, and tried to prise the fingers off. The creature was still moaning, or trying to make words, or something – but its fingers were set like a stone bracelet around her leg. It twitched and tried to rise again, and Jonie felt a nauseous sense of panic coil in her stomach. The creature's free hand grabbed her left wrist. With her right hand she scrabbled behind her for the bolt gun – but with only one hand she could hardly reload it. Shuffling her position, she tried to bring her feet to bear. To kick out. The thing's mouth was still going. 'It,' it hissed. 'Always,' it hissed. 'Returns,' it hissed.

Drums sounded, or maybe it was an earthquake. Sunlight flashed, as if her soul were leaving her body. But she was free, and she hauled herself backwards. The light flashed again. The drums were the hoof beats of a horse, and her father was on the horse. The flash was his sabre, cutting through the two arms of the Zayin.

'Go,' he bellowed.

She got up and began running, still wearing the clamped hands of the creature, one on her wrist, one by her elbow. The only thought in her head now was to get back to the gateway. When the force caught her and lifted her from behind she did cry out, terrified that another one of the beasts had her. But it was her father, hoisting her up into the saddle behind him, as they galloped over the undulating ground.

4

For several hours they were all too busy in defence for thought. Jacob's party had not found any petrol, but the assault was on such a scale as to necessitate using their flame-throwers anyway. Ash cut away the two still twitching hands from Jonie, and burnt them in the fireplace. Then she went and took her place in the tower with most of the others, and picked her shots, and tried not to think about how horrible her experience had been.

By dusk the assault had been beaten back. The scale of it was alarmingly unprecedented: dozens of zombies, coordinating their attack. 'Not so stupid,' said Esther. 'I've always said so.'

'One spoke to me,' Jonie said, but nobody seemed to hear, and she didn't press the point. Because, once she'd said it, it sounded stupid. How could they *speak*?

'They followed us back,' said Jacob. 'They tracked us. We rode day and night, and day again, and they followed the whole way.' How tired he looked! 'And more will be along soon. We have to pack up. We must go.'

He had departed with three men and three women. The women were all right, but only two of the men returned. This fact only occurred to Jonie after sunset, when everybody gathered in the yard to wash and snatch food under the spotlight. 'Where's Beuys?' she asked.

Nobody answered this question. A particular answer would have been worse than no answer. It wasn't as if they needed to ask, actually.

Daniel was sitting on his strange shooting stick, smoking. So clearly Jacob had found some supplies, including tobacco. But no petrol. 'It's getting harder and harder to forage round here,' said Charley, one of the women in the party. 'We're going to have to move.'

Feeling bitter and angry and weary and depressed Jonie went back to her room. As if calling the back of a truck with tarpaulin for a ceiling a 'room' made it one! Her mouth was full of ashes. It was pointless. They should give up. What was the point in going on?

She slept for a while, and woke up from a nightmare, and slept again. In her dream she heard hoof beats again, but it was not her father's horses; the horses themselves were undead, chasing her down. She was running through long grass, and the undead horses were just behind her. She had time to think: they must have tried out the serum on animals as well, there must be zombie animals as well, when she woke sharply.

'Jonie?'

It was her father's voice. The hoof beats were him knocking on the slats at the end of the truck. He always knocked, politely, before disturbing her in her room.

She put her head out. The sky directly above was pre-dawn pale, mother-of-pearl, and a broccoli-bunch of rainclouds was squatting by the horizons. 'Dad,' she said, and jumped down.

Jacob was not a great one for hugs, but he clapped hands to her shoulders and kissed her quickly on her forehead. 'I'm sorry,' he said. 'It was such chaos yesterday, I did not have the chance properly to greet you.'

She looked around: everybody was busy. They were packing up. 'Do we have somewhere *actually* to go?' she asked. Her voice was still croaky with sleep.

'We cannot stay here,' replied Jacob, nodding slowly. 'Come. We foraged some coffee.'

'What a treat!' she said; and then felt immediately sorry for looking forward to the coffee when Beuys was dead.

'I will take a cup with you, my daughter,' said Jacob, with characteristic pompousness, 'and then we must both help with loading the trucks.' He was looking old, Jonie thought. Everyone around her was old. Except Beuys, and he wouldn't get any older..

Somebody had already folded away the tables, and stacked them ready for loading. But between them, Jonie and her father pulled out the legs and set one up again. Jacob poured two cups of coffee, and stirred in sugar, and they sat at the table opposite one another and drank.

Behind her father, away to the east, the rim of the world was starting to glow red. The sun returning. The sun always returned. But then, so did the night. That was the nature of *return*.

'I've been reading one of Daniel's books,' she told him, unsure what else to say. Obviously it was impossible to talk about Beuys.

'Oh yes?'

'I think it has the answer,' she told him, and as soon as the words came out she felt their infinite foolishness.

'The answer to what?' her father asked, with ingenuous seriousness.

She couldn't back away now. 'To all this. To us, and to – them.'

Jacob raised one of his impressively horticultural eyebrows. 'There's an answer?'

'We have to go beyond us and them,' she said, uncertain where the words were coming from, or where they were going. 'It's always the same thing, and that's a kind of slavery. The struggle to turn the wheel is a kind of slavery. We have to break the wheel. Or – no, wait. Unpack it, unroll it. Squirl it out into a moebius strip. Or ...' She took refuge in the mug, and drained the last of the coffee. Some of the sugar had formed a crusty sludge at the bottom, and she dipped her pinkie finger into this. 'When we fight the Zayinim, we become Zayinim. The difference between us and them is that we can choose *not* to be Zayinim. But that means going beyond the fight. Making peace of some kind.'

The eyebrow was still up. Behind Jacob the sky was starting to acquire the same golden-brown sweetness as she knew the sugar possessed. The storm clouds were away to the north, and – who knows? Maybe they would stay there. The light that suffused the heavens was also in her bloodstream now.

'We can't go on like this,' she said.

The eyebrow came down. She had said something to which her father could relate. 'We cannot,' he agreed.

247

They were silent for a while, and the sky grew more gloriously honeyed in its clarity.

'Daughter,' said Jacob, putting the cup down. 'I have rebuked Esther.'

'It wasn't her fault,' Jonie said, automatically.

'She should not have let you out. I have rebuked her, and she assures me she will not be similarly delinquent in the future.'

'Dad!' Jonie squealed. The sunlight had vanished from inside her. Now she felt only resentment and a kind of dull panic. Stuck inside! Stuck inside for ever.

He held up his hand. 'We cannot afford to take risks with you, daughter. You are the future. The only future.' He meant babies, of course. She hated when he referred to this, although he was never very explicit. She hated the sense of responsibility, not just for her, but for the whole of humanity. 'Which brings me to my news: we met another tribe.'

This was huge news. 'You did?' A whole new group of people? Some handsome young guy her own age?

'Not a large tribe, and with no... no young people, I'm afraid.'

This was a disappointment. 'None at all?'

'I'm sorry. But they said they had heard tell of a larger community, away to the north on the coast. My worry is that we lack the petrol to move the whole camp there. But we must try. The island...'

The island was Jacob's long-term plan: to move onto an island large enough to support them, cleanse it of any Zayinim that might be there, and build a New Jerusalem. But there was no point in doing that with only 13-year-old Jonie old enough to bear children, and the only men around capable of impregnating her close family. The goal was to gather together a viable number of different families, including youngsters. That had been the goal for as long as Jonie could remember. With the certainty granted only to the very young, she was convinced it would never come to anything.

'We must look to the future,' he said.

Jonie wanted to reply: yet we spend all our time looking to the past! But the sun had risen now, and he was standing up, so she stood up too. They washed the cups together, and folded the table away. 'The youngest,' Jacob said, 'was fifty-nine.'

'The youngest?'

'Of the tribe we met. Seven people – not a viable number. Two women in their seventies, the rest old men. My age, or older. The youngest was a man called Ephraim, and he was fifty-nine.'

With that he went off to help Daniel and mother with the crane on the back of the biggest truck, to move the fence portions. Jonie went off to help the others, packing trunks, checking the horses were all right. It only occurred to her much later that Jacob might have given her that information because some manner or type or kind of discussion had taken place about wives and husbands. Who else but her as the wife? But the very idea was so ghastly she put it away, behind her, and refused to think of it. There was a needle voice, inside her head, and it went: *what's the alternative, ducky? What's the alternative, my little brood mare?*

What's the beyond? Good question.

They were halfway through packing the fence portions onto the big truck, and had folded down the tower into its lorry-back, when Ash called out that he could see Zayinim in the field.

It was a horribly vulnerable time for them to attack, but sometimes it happened that way. Daniel, father, mother and K. mounted their horses and rode off as the others doubled their efforts. The sky brightened with early morning, and then darkened again as the rainclouds rolled over. Half an hour after setting off, the rider returned.

'Something off,' mother told the group. 'We put a few down, but they're not attacking.'

'Why not?' K asked.

'Never mind why not,' Daniel called. 'Let's just get packed up and head out before they change their minds.'

They finished up the fence sections just as the first rain began to fall. They air chilled and went bluer than before, and big nut-sized raindrops splattered onto the dusty windscreens and dry tarps. Within moments it was a heavy downpour, lines sketching the air all around, hissing hard into the long grass with the sound of somebody frying up food.

They tied down the last of the cargo, hitched the cart to the back of the smallest lorry, tethered the horses behind the medium truck and set off. Jonie rode in the big truck; mother driving, with Daniel and Esther. They had to wait a minute because the steaming bodies of the passengers misted up the windshield, and they had to run the air-blowers to clear their view. But eventually they were off, driving in first-gear (as always), moving forward at a horse's walking pace.

The drove through the grass easily enough, and had an alarming moment going up the slope when the wheels slid intermittently on the new mud. But they crested the top, and if the big truck could do that, the rest would manage.

It was true, though: the field was full of Zayinim. It was the weirdest thing. Indeed, in all her short life Jonie had never seen anything like it. Two rows of zombies formed a kind of blank-eyed honour guard as they drove down the middle. They made no attempt to attack. They did not move at all, in fact. At one point Daniel climbed into the roof of his cab and put a few down with his rifle, but mother called to him to stop – why antagonise them? And they didn't seem bothered.

The clocklike tick and tock of the windscreen wipers.

Jonie watched. This one tall, hirsute, with too many ears and the arms hanging at his sides so long they reached almost to his ankles. This one had been a woman once, naked, with her skin covered either in scales or perhaps boils, Jonie couldn't see very clearly. This one stocky, muscles, with fangs like a tiger poking through the skin of his lips. This one black, this one white, this one with a third arm sprouting from a cankerous looking mass on its shoulder, this other long and smooth and genital-less as a doll. All standing, and just watching them as they rolled by.

'Spooky,' opined Esther.

The rain stopped. Soon enough the clouds moved away, and the sun came out.

'I'm always struck,' said mother, as the steering wheel, 'that the earth must be heavier after a rainfall than it was before. Isn't that a striking thought?'

Finally they reached the end of the Zayinim row and passed it, and left the whole grisly crew of them far behind. But the very last individual was the most unsettling of all, for he was dressed in clothes. They cannot have been the clothes in which he had dressed before; for those threads must have long since crumbled to powder. He must have dressed himself – or been dressed. Of all the zombies she had seen, he was the least deformed (unless the deformities were hidden beneath the clothes) – a stack of white hair on his head, and an ageless face. In the sunlight his eyes glinted a clear blue, and he looked straight through the window at Jonie with what seemed like intention. But it can't have been – of course. He almost looked handsome. If he hadn't been a zayin, he would have been handsome: with his strong nose, and white-blond hair, and primrose eyes. His head turning slowly, so that his gaze could follow her. A *dressed* zombie? Wearing his smart suit, and gazing forlornly as the squire's own daughter passed by. I mean, obviously not that. *Obviously* not. But it was weird.

'Have you ever seen them act like that before?' Jonie asked Daniel.

'They act weirdly,' was Daniel's opinion. 'Weird is the height and breadth and depth of them.' To celebrate the fact that they'd gotten away without further mishap he took out a cigarette and lit it. His sigh of contentment was not the sort of noise a human usually made.

It was hard for her to put the intensity of the creature's blue gaze out of her head. So she took out the book, the Beyond book, from the inside of her leather jacket, and tried to settle to reading it again. There was an answer in there somewhere, she knew.

CONTRIBUTORS

ANDREA PHILLIPS is an award-winning writer and game designer who has worked on projects such as *The Walk, Zombies, Run!*, and *The Daring Adventures of Captain Lucy Smokeheart*. Her debut novel, *Revision*, was published in 2015.

One of ROSANNE RABINOWITZ's first stories appeared in *The Slow Mirror: New Fiction by Jewish Writers*, but no extraterrestrials were involved. Her fiction has since found its way to places like *Postscripts, Midnight Street and Black Static*, and she completed a writing MA at Sheffield Hallam University. Her novella *Helen's Story* was shortlisted for the 2013 Shirley Jackson Award. She has also contributed to anthologies such as *Rustblind and Silverbright, Never Again: Weird Fiction Against Racism and Fascism, Extended Play: the Elastic Book of Music, Mind Seed* and *Horror Uncut*. Her reviews and articles have appeared in *Interzone* and *Paradox*, and she contributes non-fiction to union, community and activist websites.

ERIC KAPLAN is a television writer and philosopher. He has worked for *Futurama, Flight of the Conchords, The Simpsons* and *The Big Bang Theory* where he is currently a co-executive producer. His book *Does Santa Exist: A Philosophical Investigation* was published by Dutton in 2014. His work is available at ericlinuskaplan.wordpress.com.

RACHEL SWIRSKY holds an MFA in fiction from the Iowa Writers Workshop where she wrote a bunch and learned about how to be very cold. She is now back in California where she lives in a desert and is learning about how to be quite hot. Her short fiction has appeared in numerous magazines and anthologies including Tor.com, *Subterranean Magazine*, and *Clarkesworld*, been nominated for several of the major science fiction awards, and won the Nebula Award twice. Her second collection, *How The World Became Quiet: Myths Of The Past, Present And Future*, came out from Subterranean Press in 2013.

JAY CASELBERG is an Australian author based in Europe, His work has appeared in many venues worldwide and his most recent novel, *Empties*, is available now. He can be found at http://www.jaycaselberg.com

ELANA GOMEL is an Associate Professor at the Department of English and American Studies at Tel-Aviv University. She is the author of six non-fiction books and numerous articles on subjects such as postmodernism, narrative theory, science fiction, Dickens, and Victorian culture. Her latest books are *Narrative Space and Time: Representing Impossible Topologies in Literature* and *Science Fiction, Alien Encounters, and the Ethics of Posthumanism: Beyond the Golden Rule*. Her fantasy stories appeared in *New Horizons, Aoife's Kiss, Bewildering Stories, Timeless Tales* and the anthologies *People of the Book* and *Dogstar and Other Science Fiction Storie*s. She is also the author of a fantasy novel *A Tale of Three Cities*.

GON BEN ARI is a writer, screenwriter and musician currently living in Brooklyn, NY. His feature film, *Yiddish Speaking Western Der Mensch*, is now in pre-production with director Vania Heymann.

LOIS H. GRESH is the New York Times Best-Selling Author (6 times), Publishers Weekly Best-Selling Paperback Author, Publishers Weekly Best-Selling Paperback Children's Author, and USA Today Best-Selling Author of 27 books and 55 short stories. Current books are *Dark Fusions: Where Monsters Lurk!*, story collection *Eldritch Evolutions,* and *The Divergent Companion*. Anthology *Innsmouth Nightmares* is forthcoming. Lois has received Bram Stoker Award, Nebula Award, Theodore Sturgeon Award, and International Horror Guild Award nominations for her work.

MATTHUE ROTH is the author of *The Gobblings*, a children's book about a boy who saves a space station overrun by monsters, and the picture-book adaptation *My First Kafka*, and some other books that aren't for children. He lives in Brooklyn and keeps a secret diary at matthue.com.

NAOMI ALDERMAN is a novelist, broadcaster and games designer. She's won numerous awards for her literary novels which include *Disobedience* and *The Liars' Gospel*. She broadcasts regularly on BBC Radio 3 and Radio 4, and has a regular monthly column in the *Observer*. She is the co-creator of the hit smartphone fitness game *Zombies, Run!* In 2012 she was selected by *Granta* as one of their once-a-decade list of Best of Young British

Novelists, and in 2013 she was picked for the Rolex Arts Initiative as the mentee of Margaret Atwood.

RENA ROSSNER is a graduate of the Writing Seminars program at The Johns Hopkins University, Trinity College Dublin and McGill University. She works as a foreign rights and literary agent at the Deborah Harris Agency in Jerusalem. Her poetry and short fiction has been published in a variety of online and print magazines and journals. Her cookbook, *Eating the Bible*, was recently published by Skyhorse Publishing.

OFIR TOUCHE GAFLA was born in 1968 in Israel. He has written five novels *(The World of the End, The Cataract in the Mind's Eye, Behind the Fog, The Day the Music Died* and *The Book of Disorder)* that garnered great acclaim. He won the Geffen and Kugel awards for his first novel and in 2014 won the Creation award for Writers. He has also written numerous short stories which featured in different anthologies and magazines. He teaches creative writing at Sam Spiegel School of Film in Jerusalem, and is currently a visiting professor at the University of Texas in Austin.

SHIMON ADAF was born in Sderot, Israel, in 1972 to parents of Moroccan origin. He began publishing poetry during his military service. Later, he moved to Tel Aviv and joined a rock band as songwriter and acoustic guitar player. He published three poetry collections and six novels so far. His third collection of poetry *Aviva-No* won the Yehuda Amichai Poetry Award in 2010. between 2010-2012 he published the Rose of Judea trilogy, which deals with the issue of Jewish identity in different realities and with the role of poetry in initiation to adult life. The second volume of the thematic trilogy, Mox Nox, won the Sapir Prize (the Israeli equivalent of the Booker Prize) in 2011. The novel *Sunburnt Faces* came out in English in 2013 (PS Publishing). He resides in Tel Aviv and teaches Creative Writing and Literature in Ben Gurion University.

DANIEL POLANSKY is the author of the Low Town fantasy noir trilogy. His new series, beginning with, *Those Above*, is out now from Hodder & Stoughton. He is sometimes in Brooklyn.

BENJAMIN ROSENBAUM's stories have appeared in F&SF, Strange Horizons, Harper's, and Nature, nominated for the Hugo, Nebula, Sturgeon, BSFA and Locus Awards, and been translated into more than 20 languages. He has been a party clown, rugby flanker, synagogue president, and programmer for the Swiss banks. He currently works in Washington, DC with his wife Esther and his kids, Aviva (author of the blues song "Homework") and Noah (author of the RPG "Galaxy World"). He is writing a roleplaying game about the fantastic shtetl, called *Dream Apart*.

SARAH LOTZ is a screenwriter and novelist with a fondness for the macabre and fake names. Among other things, she writes horror/thriller novels under the name S.L. Grey with author Louis Greenberg, a YA pulp-fiction zombie series with her daughter, Savannah, under the pseudonym Lily Herne, and quirky erotica novels with authors Helen Moffett and Paige Nick under the name Helena S. Paige. Her latest solo novel, *Day Four*, was published in 2015.

ANNA TAMBOUR's fiction is always 110+% true tales, minus the names. Tambour's last novel, *Crandolin*, was shortlisted for the World Fantasy Award. Her latest collection, *The Finest Ass in the Universe*, was published July 2015 from Twelfth Planet Press.

ADAM ROBERTS has published fifteen science fiction novels and many short stories, some of them collected in *Adam Robots*. He is a university academic as well as a writer, and lives a little outside London.

LAVIE TIDHAR is the author of *A Man Lies Dreaming*, *The Violent Century* and the World Fantasy Award winning *Osama*. His other works include the Bookman Histories trilogy, several novellas, two collections and a forthcoming comics mini-series, *Adler*. He currently lives in London.
REBECCA LEVENE has been a writer and editor for twenty years, working in the games, publishing, TV and magazine industries. Her new four-part epic fantasy series, The Hollow Gods, launched with *Smiler's Fair* and continued with *The Hunter's Kind*.

SARAH ANNE LANGTON has worked as an illustrator for Hodder & Stoughton, Forbidden Planet, EA Games, *The Cartoon Network*, Sony, Marvel Comics and a wide variety of music events. She has written and illustrated for Jurassic London, Fox Spirit, NewCon Press, Anachron Press and The Fizzy Pop Vampire series of children's books. Her work has featured on *io9, Clutter Magazine, Laughing Squid* and *Creative Review*.

Mosac (Charity No: 1139077) provides practical and emotional support to non-abusing parents, carers and families of children who have been sexually abused.

The charity was formed in 1992 when four mothers whose children were abused came together and drew strength from each other's shared experience and realised the need for a similar service for others.

Based in Greenwich in south London, Mosac offers a national helpline, as well as counselling, advocacy, support groups and play therapy, and aims to break the silence surrounding child sexual abuse by raising awareness through training and consultancy.

All proceeds from the sale of this book will be donated to Mosac.

Made in the USA
Lexington, KY
14 October 2016